MAR

MW00981719

The Secret Feast of
Father Christmas

The Secret Feast of Father Christmas

DARRYL PICKETT

iUniverse, Inc.
Bloomington

The Secret Feast of Father Christmas

Copyright © 2012 by Darryl Pickett.

All rights reserved. No part of this book may be used or reproduced by any means, graphic, electronic, or mechanical, including photocopying, recording, taping or by any information storage retrieval system without the written permission of the publisher except in the case of brief quotations embodied in critical articles and reviews.

This is a work of fiction. All of the characters, names, incidents, organizations, and dialogue in this novel are either the products of the author's imagination or are used fictitiously.

iUniverse books may be ordered through booksellers or by contacting:

iUniverse
1663 Liberty Drive
Bloomington, IN 47403
www.iuniverse.com
1-800-Authors (1-800-288-4677)

Because of the dynamic nature of the Internet, any web addresses or links contained in this book may have changed since publication and may no longer be valid. The views expressed in this work are solely those of the author and do not necessarily reflect the views of the publisher, and the publisher hereby disclaims any responsibility for them.

Any people depicted in stock imagery provided by Thinkstock are models, and such images are being used for illustrative purposes only.
Certain stock imagery © Thinkstock.

ISBN: 978-1-4759-5517-0 (sc)
ISBN: 978-1-4759-5519-4 (hc)
ISBN: 978-1-4759-5518-7 (ebk)

Printed in the United States of America

iUniverse rev. date: 10/15/2012

For Mae Louise,
who still conspires to make
every Christmas joyful

Also For Sharon,
In Loving Memory

Chapter One
Heaven Song and Angel Sound

December 19th, 1937
Christchurch Cathedral
Christchurch, New Zealand

"You can't kiss the Virgin Mary," said young Clive, in a commanding tone.

"What's that?" I replied, though I had heard him. Clive Murney smirked at me, and folded his arms imperiously over his chest.

"I know it's what you're thinking of doing, but you can't."

And he was right. Mary was standing beneath the mistletoe, and kissing her was all I could think about. Of course, she wasn't really Mary. She was Olivia, Clive's older sister, and she was only dressed as Mary for the pageant. She was standing on a chair, waiting patiently for her mother to adjust her gown. Olivia was smiling, talking to her father, and barely keeping the pasteboard halo, attached by wire, from falling off her head.

A sprig of mistletoe hung just above her, one of dozens rolled up in twine, hanging every several feet along the rectory hall. The place was in chaos. Junior cherubs and flannel-covered shepherds were running riot around the folding tables. Harried stage mothers were smearing glittery face paint on their children's impatient faces, or trying to patch the rips and tears in the long, flowing costumes. On her chair, Olivia stood above it all, literally. I waved to get her attention, to no avail.

"I'm pretty sure you're committing a mortal sin even thinking about it," Clive continued. I decided to visit the refreshment table.

Clive followed me. "I hate to think of you falling into mortal sin, Candlewax."

"I hate to think of you falling headfirst into a rubbish dump, Clive," I countered.

He gave an overdramatic gasp. "I'm writing that down," he said. He began to fetch his notebook out of his knapsack, then he spied the servings of raspberry trifle on a silver tray just within arm's reach. "Brazen saints! Look at that!" He soon had one in his greedy possession. "I'd lay off if I was you, Candlewax," he said. "Time to think about your figure, old man."

Clive spooned the sweet stuff into his mouth, with speed but not precision.

"You're smearing your face," I said.

"You do know that 'Livia's got a boyfriend, don't you?" he countered.

"What do you mean?"

"I mean you haven't got a prayer. She's practically engaged to Nate Garrick. He's sixteen, you know. Real man of the world. You can't miss him. He's playing Joseph."

I had never seen anyone relish the delivery of unwelcome gossip as much as Clive clearly did.

"So, what of it? I don't care," I said.

"Like Hades you don't. Your face is going crimson right now. You're an open book, Candlewax."

"And you're an unholy turd, Clive."

"Strong words. I'm going to write them down." This time, the notebook came out. It was tattered and faded from constant use. Clive wrote things down. He started the practice out of frustration with adults dodging his questions by saying 'I'll tell you when you're older.' Clive decided to keep track. Now he jotted notes on anything he thought might make good ammunition in the future.

"Unholy . . . turd," he said, as he recorded my slur with a stub of pencil before shoving it back in his pocket. "That one's going to come back on you, Candlewax." He scrunched his face as he looked at the page in front of him. "Gosh, I could extort money with the silly things people say around me. Look here, if you dare. 'Livia tried to tell me she met Santa Claus. She didn't blush or anything! I ask you!"

"I suppose she could be right," I said.

"You would say that," he answered.

Now Olivia was stepping down from the chair, and an entourage fluttered around her. She smiled as her father, Cyrus, snapped a picture, and the burst of flash made her flinch. I couldn't help gazing at her every expression. At fifteen, she had grown out of her gawkish years, and now she moved with elegance and self-assurance. She still had a slight overbite, a feature that Clive enjoyed mocking. It was no flaw. It was fully part of her inarguable charm.

I hadn't seen Olivia since June. In summer, our families stayed together at a cabin in the Southern Alps during an ecumenical retreat. I had a memento, a photograph of Olivia and myself, wobbling on skis and laughing. She had sent it to me in late October. It was tucked into a pastel yellow envelope, decorated with rubber-stamp kiwis and flowers. Along with the picture, she included a brief note.

Mannie,

I can't wait to see you at Christmas. There's something I'm dying to tell you.

Love,
Olivia

No message could be better calculated to send a daydreamer like me into romantic reveries. I knew she wasn't likely waiting to declare undying love for me, but that didn't prevent a hundred imaginary conversations, every one of which ended with a kiss. I was thirteen, so I hadn't told a soul about this crush of crushes. And yet, everyone seemed to know.

A high-pitched voice called out.

"Mannie! Mannie Candler!"

It was Olivia's older sister Annabella. Always easy to spot, Annabella was taller than anyone else in her family. She hurried my direction but soon noticed Clive, now adorned with sloppily eaten trifle.

"Oh, Clive! You beastly brother." She reached into her pocketbook and produced a green-colored wipe. She licked it and began rubbing it on Clive's face. "You're about to enter the house of God. I'd like to think you had a little more reverence."

"I didn't want anyone else to eat it first," Clive said, then added an *Ow!* of protest to Annabella's relentless scrubbing.

"I want you to go and change into your robes now. And put your notebook away, please. I won't have you carrying it around the church."

"Bossy, that's all I'm saying," Clive whispered in an aside as he stepped away. "They're all like this, Candlewax. You might as well know."

"Mannie Candler, you've grown seven inches since summer!" Annabella sounded dismayed that I was so inconsiderate as to keep growing. She knelt down and inspected my face. She licked the green handkerchief again and rubbed at my left cheek. I winced, as I should think any rational person would. "You should try to aim for your mouth when you eat," she said, though I hadn't actually eaten anything since arriving at the cathedral.

"Nice to see you, Annabella," I said.

"Did you take the train to get here?"

"Yes. Dad drove over yesterday, but Mum and I took the train from Springfield this afternoon. It was nice."

"You're lucky. We came in Dad's car, and it was beastly hot with all six of us."

"Six?"

"We brought Nate Garrick along. That's him over there," she added, waving the handkerchief above my head.

I turned around and spotted a handsome young man, blond hair, well-defined chin, bright blue eyes. Just as I saw him, he was taking Olivia's hand and all but dragging her out of the room.

"Is that who Clive was talking about?"

"Yes. He's become a family friend. Crazy about Olivia."

"They're not really engaged, are they?"

"What?!" She puffed an astonished laugh. "Did Clive tell you that?"

"Yes, something like it."

"It's a joke. Mum and Dad tease her about it. Olivia's much too young to entertain suitors. She's a sweet girl, Mannie, but I worry about her mind. She's dreamy and silly. Of course, you're a bit dreamy and silly too."

She kissed my forehead. Not for the first time. She ended most of her chats with me in just that way.

The costumed players for the pageant were called away, and I was taken to the vestry and fitted with robes. A young deacon reviewed with me the gospel passages I was to speak. I had already memorized them.

Ten minutes later, I was standing outside the cathedral door, lined up behind two dozen adult choir members and a seeming army of fidgeting choir boys, waiting for the moment we would enter the sanctuary to begin the pageant. Cathedral Square was alive with shoppers and passers-by, but from the cathedral steps, I could hear little noise from all the activity. The evening sky was still bright and warm. Our robes caught a slight breeze, and we all billowed gently as the choirmaster leaned by the entrance, waiting for the right moment to cue our procession. It was a moment of hypnotic serenity, soon interrupted by a confident blast of joyous music from within the church. The grand event was underway.

It was the most gorgeous Christmas pageant any of us had ever seen. A dozen acolytes carried banners of green, red, and gold. Some of them stretched out across the altar forming a billowing archway over the central manger. Six angels stood on a raised platform, beneath the star of Bethlehem, shimmering and silvery, reflecting colors from the stained glass windows. Three kings in elaborate bejeweled costume stood sweltering to one side. In the center of it all, there was the manger, with its own spotlight, and beside it, glorious Mary in her white and blue gown, and terribly handsome Joseph, who had one arm around Mary's waist. He had forsworn the fake beard. With his grinning face, he brought to mind a matinee idol. It wasn't hard to imagine the wedding pictures in some future album, with Olivia's adoring face gazing up at Nate's, perhaps in front of this very altar.

It was a pointless train of thought, and I still had my narration to deliver. I told myself to get over her, firmly decided that I had done so, and then I opened my mouth to speak.

"*And there were in that same country,*" I shouted, "*shepherds abiding in the field, keeping watch over their flocks by night!*"

My voice cracked as it thundered out across the sanctuary, bounced and echoed for a few moments. Faces turned and looked at me, some smiling, some shocked at the sudden volume. I quickly modulated my delivery, but it was too late. I could feel my ears warming up. I knew my face would soon betray my embarrassment by glowing red. I pressed on with the text.

"And lo, the angel of the Lord came upon them, and the glory of the Lord shone round about them!"

Olivia looked up to find the source of this raging voice that pierced the holy silence. For the first time since I had arrived, her eyes met mine, and her face did something altogether unfair and wondrous. It transformed, from Mary's serene demeanor to Olivia's own unvarnished surprise. She smiled so broadly, with such evident pleasure at finding me at the center of the room. And I have to mention, she laughed, just for a moment. I smiled back, from where I stood, dead center, with my own spotlight, she with hers, and we were the only two people in the world. Then I remembered that several hundred men, women and children, and presumably God Himself, were watching as a young boy stood center sanctuary, gawping.

I found my voice again, and as I continued, I turned to face the back half of the congregation. I spoke like a great orator, lifting my arms, making long, slow gestures, just as I had seen my own father do when he was rolling with a good sermon.

I don't know if the assembled throng found my performance inspired, or merely astonishing, but when I finished, there was applause, loud and sustained. I turned back to the manger, and Olivia was laughing with apparent delight, beaming at me. Was that a show of admiration, or had I just made a priceless fool of myself?

The applause faded, and the small orchestra began to play. I knew the song, for it had been composed by Rex Palmer, who lived in Clarketon, and led the choir at my father's church. I had already heard the anthem in our own sanctuary, and thought it lovely.

Olivia began to sing. She had a beautiful voice, low and rich.

In darkened cave, in freezing wind and winter
From every place of comfort turned away
Against his skin, coarse cloth and wooden splinter
His bed a broken crib of straw and hay

When she got to the first chorus, a second vocalist joined in. It was a boy soprano with a perfect voice, pure and lilting, singing a refrain in counterpoint with Olivia's melody.

> *From this emerged a kingdom, from this a prince of light*
> *From here we turn our hearts and lives around*
> *Oh let our humble song turn back the endless night*
> *With heaven song and angel sound*

It was Olivia's younger brother, the holy terror Clive Murney. Anyone who didn't know him would have thought he'd just been fitted for a halo.

It was a night for surprises. I sat down at a bench seat near the choir, looking out into the pews to find my parents. They were in the second row, my mother and father, and next to them, someone I hadn't expected to see. My Aunt Audra sat beside my mother, her sister. My mouth opened in silent astonishment. Audra lifted her eyebrows, and smiled in a conspiratorial kind of way. I could read her expression. *This is the last place you'd expect to see me, isn't it!* She gave a little wave and mouthed several words. I couldn't read them all, but *love* was one of them. Then Audra crossed her hands over her heart and her mouth pursed into a kiss.

It's a night of miracles. The thought ran in my head, repeating itself as I held Audra in my gaze. Her presence was like a miracle. It was so unlikely that I didn't want to look way from her, lest she vanish. The sanctuary settled into restless silence. Then the choirmaster cleared his throat. He was looking right at me. So was everyone. It was my turn to speak again.

"The concluding passage . . ." whispered the choirmaster, in such a way that everyone could hear it. "Go on, lad!" A ripple of laughter passed through the congregation. I shifted my attention to the audience, and felt that remarkable sensation, like a great iron door slamming shut in my mind. I had forgotten every word I was now supposed to say.

"It's a night of miracles!" I yelled. Not knowing what else to do, I threw my arms outward in a triumphant gesture and smiled for all I was worth. Then I repeated the only words I could muster. "It's a night of miracles, everyone! Happy Christmas!"

Chapter Two
Audra's Advice

The orchestra master shrugged his shoulders, and cued the organist to begin playing the postlude. One of the church priests, unable to bear the absence of the printed conclusion, began reading it out of his own script, but he was drowned out by the surge of music. The congregation had already stood, and there was no reigning them back in. The event was over. Order gave way to amiable chaos. It wasn't how the pageant was supposed to end, and the disorder was my own doing. If I had blushed before, by now I felt like I was running a fever.

Aunt Audra beckoned me to her side, and I broke ranks from the choir to jog down to her. She pushed past a couple of strangers so she could be the first to embrace me.

"Mannie! My favorite only nephew!" She squeezed me tight.

Audra LaPoore was my aunt on my mother's side, and sometimes a thorn in it. Not that she meant to be. Audra had no malice, though she had mischief. Everything that Audra cared about, my mother disapproved of. Audra was a free spirit, an anarchist, sometimes a Buddhist, sometimes an atheist. As a child, I didn't know what any of those things meant, but I heard my mother moan about them. To me, Audra was an energizing presence, a guarantee that boredom and unhappiness were banished. How improbable to find her here, in a church pew next to my mother.

"Audra! Nobody told me you were going to be here."

"We kept it a surprise," she said. "Look at you. You're a grown-up!"

"Not quite," I said.

"Oh, but you are. And what a command you took of this church! Didn't you think so, Georgina?"

My mother smiled, but in a controlled way. "It was an impassioned performance, Emanuel." So, I knew right away she didn't entirely approve of it.

"I completely forgot what I was supposed to say at the end," I confessed.

"I'm sure no one noticed," Audra answered with compassionate dishonesty.

"The Murneys are hosting a reception party at the Botanic Gardens tonight," I told Audra. "Will you be able to come?"

"No, I'm afraid not. But I would like to ride along with you on the way there."

"All right," I said. "I guess Dad will be driving."

"I don't think so," Audra said, arching an eyebrow. 'I believe you will arrive by carriage."

I looked at my mother. She nodded. "It's all arranged. One of the horse-drawn carriages will take you to the gardens. Go and change your clothes, and meet your aunt out by the front of the cathedral."

"Thank you, Mum," I said, and I hugged her. She returned the embrace, but added "Hurry up, now. There's a lot going on tonight."

As I ran back along the corridors by the rectory hall, I cast an eye around for Olivia. No luck, but I knew I would see her at the party. A few minutes later, I arrived at the steps in front of the cathedral. My father took my tote bag and clothes.

"Audra's down by the carriage," he said. "I'll pick you up from the party at nine-thirty, so wait by the gate, will you?"

"Yes. Thank you, sir." I bowed my head quickly, then turned and ran for the open air carriage. Audra was already seated inside. The carriage driver stood by the door. He wore an old-fashioned top hat and a long coat that must have been uncomfortable in the heat of a New Zealand December. Two gorgeous black horses were hitched to the front.

"Hello, you handsome young man," Audra called out. "Will you sit with me for this trip?"

I climbed into the cab, and the driver shut the door.

"Thank you, Aunt Audra."

"No need to be formal, Mannie. Just call me Audra."

"All right by me," I said, and she put an arm around my shoulder.

"Surprised to see me?"

"My gosh, yes. Did Mum and Dad know?"

"Yes. It's a surprise we've been planning for a long time. I'll be staying with you this Christmas, if it's all right with you."

"It's *very* all right, Audra," and I hugged her hard. Once I let go, I saw that though she was smiling, her eyes were wet.

"Is everything all right?" I asked.

"Yes, Mannie Candler. Everything is wonderful. I am so proud of you," she said, and she couldn't resist ruffling my hair.

"I think maybe I overdid things a bit," I confessed.

"Nonsense. You made an impression. A grand impression."

"Until I forgot my lines."

Audra laughed and said, "Well, that was the best part."

So, you liked the pageant then?"

She gave a delighted gasp and all but shouted, "I loved it! It was extraordinary. Such beautiful music, too."

"I'm glad you liked it. Even if you don't believe in it, I mean."

"You don't have to believe in something to see the beauty in it."

"No, I suppose not."

Audra pointed out the window. "There's Hays Department Store. Have you been yet this year?"

"We haven't had time. I only got to Christchurch an hour before the pageant started. And I've got to go home tonight. Oh, do you remember that little shop on Worcester Street? Where you got me the sheets for my toy theatre?"

"Of course. You want to go there?"

"It's gone, closed up. I noticed on the way in today."

"That's a shame."

"A lot of places have closed. I guess it's the Depression."

"Things will soon get better. That's what all the papers say. Anyway, I've got a very nice gift for you this year. Would you like to know what it is?"

"Of course I would. But I bet you won't tell me."

"You've got that right. You'll have to wait."

"All right,' I said, and we both laughed. I was famous in my family for being impatient about presents. And Audra was good at keeping secrets.

The carriage went all the way around the city center, the full scenic route. For a little while, Audra and I said nothing, but looked out at the decorated storefronts along Oxford Terrace, and across the street, the strings of lights glowing in the trees on the shore of the Avon River. There was still soft light in the sky, just enough to melt the edge of shadows and tint the city with a pale orange glow.

After a while, Audra broke the silence. "Your mother tells me you're thinking of dedicating your life to the church, like your father."

"Sometimes. I don't really know. I'm terrible at maths, and I'm a disaster at sport. Ask anyone at our school. But, preaching, I guess I can do."

"You have a long time to work out what you want."

"If I ever did become a priest, I wouldn't be like Father Humboldt. Have you ever met him?"

"No, I haven't."

"If you're staying with us, you will. He goes in for the hellfire and condemnation stuff. I don't like that so much." It felt strange talking about such serious things in the open air, in earshot of the coachman.

Audra went quiet for another moment or two. Her face betrayed the weighing of something in her mind. When she finally spoke, her tone had changed. It wasn't as carefree.

"Does it bother you that I don't believe?"

It was a question I thought she might ask. I knew Audra's lack of conventional faith was a sore spot with my mother. I had seen how upset she could be whenever my father discussed Audra with her.

For that matter, I didn't know how to reply. On one hand, I wished Aunt Audra would come over to the faith so central to the life of her family. I couldn't really imagine why she wouldn't. On the other hand, Audra didn't seem in any way incomplete without the church in her life. She was unconventional, and that's how I liked her to be.

"You don't have to answer if it makes you uncomfortable," she said. "But I care what you think."

"I worry sometimes," I said, abashedly.

"Of course you do. It's only because you care about me. That's why the subject makes your mother so tense and miserable."

"It's just that, some people say that, well . . ."

"That people like me don't make it into heaven, right?"

"Or worse," I said, and suddenly wished the subject hadn't come up at all.

Audra took my hand.

"The bad word you're avoiding is Hell. You're a kind soul, Mannie. I don't ever want you to worry about that awful word. We aren't that far apart, you and I. We both believe in love, right?"

"Yes."

"We might give it different names, but it's the same thing whether we think it's from Jesus or the Buddha, or something else entirely."

"Yes, I know," I said. But I didn't really.

Audra slapped her knee and laughed. "Couldn't you just shoot me for being such a killjoy! I'm sorry, Mannie. Let's talk about something else, all right?"

"All right," I said, relieved to let that topic go.

"Let's discuss things like parties and presents, and secret crushes on Olivia Murney."

"Oh feathered bats! Is it that obvious?" I could feel the warmth of telltale blush across my face.

"It may be the worst kept secret in Canterbury province," Audra said, pleased as pistachios at my involuntary reaction.

"Well, it's hopeless anyway," I said. "Did you get a look at the fellow playing Joseph? From what I hear, he's practically made himself her fiancée."

"Believe it or not, I've met young Mr. Garrick."

"You have?"

"Through mutual friends. I know a lot of people. You may have heard."

"Mum always says you know everybody."

"Nate thinks more highly of himself than he ought to. Olivia may not be as impressed as all that. See if you can steal her away, just for a moment. I bet there's mistletoe all over the gardens."

"You think I should steal a kiss?"

"If you want to be polite, then ask her first. I bet she'll agree."

"That's the kind of advice that gets people like me into trouble, you know."

"It's the only kind worth taking, my dear nephew."

Soon after that, our carriage had arrived at the Canterbury Museum. Audra snagged another hug as the coachman opened the door. I stepped out, and she followed. I noticed my father's car across the street.

"Oh, Dad's here," I said.

"He's taking me back to my friend Sissy's house. My things are there. Now, promise me you'll heed my advice," she said.

"We'll see," I said.

"Oh, that's the same as admitting you're going to chicken out, Mannie!"

"All right, I promise, then."

"Good! I want this to be the best Christmas of your life," she said.

"It already is," I answered, not knowing these would be the last words I ever said to her.

Chapter Three
Meringue and Mistletoe

Audra hugged me again. She whispered a quick "See you soon, love," then went back to tip the carriage driver. In another moment, she was across the street and getting into my father's sedan.

I had kept my jacket on my lap during the ride, but now I slipped it on. It was really too warm outside for a sport coat, but I would be underdressed without it.

I walked past the museum with its grand windows and towers of grey stone. By the ornate peacock fountain, I saw a few of my schoolmates. Ted, Bernard and Mindy were in the upper form. They had come to Christchurch with Rex to sing in the pageant chorus. (Back at home, they comprised almost one third of our very humble church choir.) All three of them hailed and helloed as soon as they saw me, then cheerfully ribbed my over-the-top recitation.

"You rattled me awake with that speech, Mannie," said Bernard.

Mindy laughed and added, "You should take over back at home. You're louder than Father Humboldt."

"When you remember your lines," Ted added. I waved as I continued on my way.

Beyond the fountain, several wireframe arches covered with red and green banners spanned the walkway. Dozens of elegantly dressed people sauntered toward the footbridge on the south side of the gardens that led to the rotunda.

On a well-kept lawn, a large canopy sat over a serving station. Even from a distance, I could see there would be no shortage of food and drink. Beneath the rotunda, a live orchestra played graceful music. A dance floor was set nearby. Already, half a dozen couples were waltzing, or standing near to each other, face to face and talking with drinks in hand.

Attendants walked along the path dressed in Victorian costume. They had trays loaded with drinks in elegant glasses and crystal flutes. It was an elegant party, and rich. Cy Murney was paying the tab. Life at our family's country vicarage could never approach this kind of opulence. I felt out of place within it, though glad to be near it for a while.

I often forgot to think of the Murney family as rich. To me, they were simply friends. I saw them at church events in the city or on holiday. Cyrus Murney was the founder and owner of Murney Wool and Textile. If it weren't for the fact that he was an avid patron and supporter of the cathedral, my father would never have met him. I would have been nobody to the Murney family. It was hard to imagine.

Annabella found me and led me to a table where several of her family sat. Cy Murney wore a Santa hat. In a large basket next to him was a pile of small wrapped gifts.

"Mr. Candler!" he exclaimed. "A happy Christmas! Won't you please take a gift. Each one is different, each a mystery. Take one for you mother as well. Don't open 'em 'til Christmas."

"Thank you, sir," I said. I picked up two small boxes. For a moment, I stood with one in each hand, wondering how I could best avoid carrying them around all evening, without losing them. Then Joan Murney offered me a plate.

"Have you tried the pavlova?" She held it just in front of my nose. "It's the best I've had yet."

I set both the little boxes down on the table and took the plate. The pavlova was topped with thick cream, strawberries and slices of kiwi. I picked up a fork and took a bite, my first ever for that dessert.

"It's fine," I said. I bit into the crisp meringue and discovered the light-as-air texture inside. "Oh! I've never had anything like this." Mr. Murney gave an approving laugh.

"Have all you like. There's plenty."

Clive approached the table, notebook in hand. "Look who's hogging all the puddings already. Should have known."

"You sang beautifully, Clive," I said, hoping to strike the civil note. He wasn't having any.

"You shouted like you were a sergeant giving orders to the Royal Dragoons."

Joan Murney took the notebook from her son's hand and replaced it with a plateful of pavlova. "Here, my rude little boy. This will keep your mouth busy."

Clive squinted at the pavlova, then dug into it with his fingers. He scooped a chunk of it out with his right hand, and held it close to his eyes to examine it.

"It's for eating, Clive, not for excavating," said Mr. Murney.

"I don't trust it," he said. "How do I know it hasn't got bugs in it?"

"Because your mother gave it to you, you little worm." Joan laughed in disbelief at the endless challenge of interacting with her own son.

Clive crammed the meringue into his mouth and sucked on his fingers.

Joan Murney glanced at me. "Mannie, this is no son of mine." In a flash, she collared the boy and marched him away.

Cyrus Murney stood, took off his Santa hat and placed it on my head. "Here, Mannie, I'd like you to be Santa for a while. If anyone stops by, just let 'em take any presents they like." He moved away, half dancing to the music, and hailed a merry-dressed attendant with a drink tray.

I sat in the chair Cyrus had vacated and finished my pavlova. I had a good view of the party. For now, just watching the swirl of people across the dance floor, hearing the music, was pleasure I could never hope to find in my own rural home. I only hoped that Olivia might find me soon. Instead, Annabella came to my side.

"Mannie, did my father leave you in charge?"

"Yes, I think so. He'll be back."

Annabella sighed. "He's a little drunk already. This is kind of a farewell party, you know."

"It is?"

"He's selling the business. Murney Wool."

"Gosh, I didn't know. Is everything all right?"

"Oh, yes. He's going to get lots of money for it. He'll be staying on as an advisor, but the firm that's buying is based in Wellington. He'll be there as much as here."

"Are you all going to be moving then?"

"Most likely. But, we'll be back and forth. Here one week, away the next. Clive and Olivia, though, they begin in new schools at Wellington after the holiday. It's a big change."

It was unwelcome news. Already I saw the Murneys far less frequently than I would have liked.

"This may be our last annual Christmas party in Christchurch, though," Annabella continued. "So make the most of it."

"Maybe you'll have parties like this in Wellington too," Just saying it made that city seem far away indeed.

"We'll know when the time arrives." Annabella shooed me off the chair. "Now, don't you sit here all night. Run along and enjoy yourself." She plucked the Santa hat from my head. I got off the chair and joined the party, leaving behind the two packages I had picked from the basket. I never recovered them.

The paths of the Botanic Garden were lit with paper lanterns, and in a dozen tented pavilions, candles burned in the center of evergreen wreaths. By now, the sky had darkened enough that the gentle glow of the lights entranced my eye. Every stranger's face was suffused with soft hues. Faces appeared and disappeared back into gentle shadow. Those in the distance were silhouettes against the shifting patterns of light and dark, the shadows of trees and the lights of the city street beyond them.

A welcome voice called my name. It was Olivia, at last. She was on the other side of the Avon River, but she ran to the footbridge and crossed in no time at all.

"Mannie!" she called, "Mannie, don't you move!" Her step went from fast walking to flat our running, and she crashed into me. Her arms wrapped me in a forceful hug.

"There you are! I've been looking all over for you!"

She was in a white party dress, trimmed with light green, and she wore a crown of plastic holly leaves. She was still a little taller than me, but the difference wasn't as great as it had been six months ago. She was prettier now than anyone I had ever seen. I stammered out a hello. Like everyone else, she remarked on how I'd grown. Then I made the kind of stupid remark that young men with bad crushes so easily make.

"So, where's Captain Magnificent?"

She inhaled so loudly she almost wheezed. "Captain Magnificent? Are you talking about Nathan?"

"Yeah, sorry, I meant Nathan."

She was seized with a spectacular laughing fit. She walked off of the footpath and leaned on a nearby tree, bracing herself as she went on chortling. I followed her and stood by, waiting for the spell to pass. "Captain Magnificent!" she cried. "I'm going to tell him you called him that."

"I wish you wouldn't," I said. And in a while, she had settled down. As we walked back into candlelight at one of the covered pavilions, I could see wet streaks running from her eyes. She was still grinning.

"Well, Mannie, that's the best laugh I've had in some time," she said.

"So, where is he?" I said, unable to come up with any other topic.

"He's having a smoke with some of the older boys. I think it's disgusting. You don't smoke, do you?"

"Of course not," I said. It was true. I had tried a cigarette from my friend Anaru not that long ago, and I decided it wasn't for me.

"Captain Magnificent." She was still relishing it. "You know, that's the sort of name only a jealous mind would think up," she said quite accurately.

Her smile was so wide it must have hurt. That generous, big-toothed smile she got from her mother. (Clive and Annabella took much more after their father.) It crossed my mind, in the stupid way that young people's minds go, that if I married Olivia, I would one day have a wife who looked a good deal like Joan, and I decided that was fine by me. Fine, but awfully unlikely.

"You mustn't be jealous of Nathan," Olivia said, sounding more serious. "He drags me around from place to place, and he's very flattering. But if Clive told you we're getting married, that's not true. I'm not marrying anyone, not until I've finished my singing career."

"Oh, you did sound great, by the way. And I had no idea Clive could sing like that."

"He's very good, but please don't change the subject. Back to me. I'm also not getting married until I've been to India, Italy, France and Japan. And not until I've become a horse veterinarian."

"You're going to be very busy, then," I said. We talked like that for another half hour, breezy and lighthearted, saying nothing of importance, responding as if every word was vital.

We made our way to the Bandsmen's Memorial Rotunda. The orchestra had ceased playing formal waltzes. Now they played Christmas songs, with a light swing to them, jazzy enough that my mother would have disapproved. Olivia and I danced along to Winter Wonderland, not in a close embrace like some of the other couples, but politely touching hands. Nathan found us there.

"Hey, 'Liv. This must be Mannie, eh?" He gave me a sportsman's grin and put out a hand.

I broke away from Olivia and offered my hand in return. He gripped it and squeezed. It felt like an endurance test, or a challenge. I didn't respond, except to say "Nice to meet you."

"Heard a lot about you. More than I want to sometimes." He smiled, and so did I, in spite of myself. There was something coercive about that confident smirk, and the cheerful blue eyes that accompanied it. He had a winning smile, if by winning one meant overpowering.

Nathan clapped me on the back, hard enough to jolt, and said, "Mannie, old friend, it would be nice if you'd go find something for Olivia. I bet she's thirsty."

"Nate, that's horrible," Olivia said. "You're the one that's just chiseled in on us. How about you find me something."

"All right, but when I get back, it's my turn to dance with you." He looked at me and winked, then proudly ambled off.

"Come on," Olivia said, and she took my hand and started to run. I jogged after unable to keep up for long. She darted to the pavilion where Cyrus had sat, and where Joan and Clive were now passing out gifts. Olivia went digging through a sack behind a table, retrieved something and then beckoned me to follow her.

She led me back across the bridge, and to an out of the way pavilion not far from the peacock fountain. There was no one else in it.

"There's something I've been so anxious to talk to you about. I couldn't say anything with Nathan around."

She pulled me further in, and closer to herself.

"Did Clive say anything to you about Father Christmas?"

It wasn't what I was expecting her to say. "No," I answered, but then I remembered my first run-in with Clive, near the table of trifles at the cathedral. "Oh, wait, he said he thinks you're daft for believing in Santa Claus."

"No, not Santa Claus. Father Christmas."

"Aren't they the same thing?"

"Of course not. Santa Claus is a nice story people tell their children. Father Christmas is quite real. So, do you think I'm daft?"

I didn't answer that question, but asked on of my own. "If he isn't Santa Claus, who is he?"

Olivia rolled her eyes as if she couldn't believe she had to explain this to someone of my advanced years. "He's the descendent of Nicholas. He's the bishop of the strange magics."

"Oh, of course," I said, "but how do you know he's real?"

"I'm not supposed to tell. I'm sworn to secrecy."

"You've already told me this much. I'm curious, I really am."

"You sound doubtful."

"Of course I'm doubtful," I admitted. "But that doesn't stop me being curious."

"I'll just say that, I've been in contact with him."

"Got a letter, did you?" I said, and it sounded more sarcastic than I intended.

"How did you know?"

"I didn't. It was just a guess."

"Well, yes, as matter of fact, I have got a letter," she said, and she held up the envelope she had just retrieved. She handed it to me. It was made of a velvety paper, and carefully inscribed with dark green ink.

Confidential

To Be Delivered To
Olivia Murney
Seventh Moss Circle
Aotearoa

Father Christmas,
Very North

The wax seal bore a small crest with the letters VN. The seal had been broken already, and I started to unfold the flap, but Olivia grabbed the whole thing back.

"No, I really better not. I promised." She looked genuinely worried. "You can't say anything to anyone. Especially not my parents!"

"You're sure your parents didn't send it to you?"

Olivia's expression showed some petulance. "You're just as cynical as my little brother."

"Surely not," I said, for how could I be.

"Anyway, if you must know, it was delivered to me by a forest gnome." She said this quietly, looking at her feet. I couldn't blame her. It was a difficult thing to have to say looking someone straight in the eye.

"A forest gnome brought you a letter from Father Christmas."

"Oh, it sounds so stupid when you just say it out loud like that."

"I'm sorry?" I was getting a little anxious to know if this was a joke, or a lead-in to some kind of gift or surprise. "So, where is this Seventh Moss Circle?"

"It's in a field. It's not a proper address, but that's where the gnome told me . . ." She sighed and drooped her shoulders. "I shouldn't have said anything. Now you think I'm stupid. If I just had a way, I could take you to it. It's very strange. Like a fairy circle, or something."

She sounded a bit desperate, and it was unsettling. This change in mood made it seem she wasn't joking, and I didn't know how to respond to that. She began to walk away. "Anyway, you won't say a thing about it, will you?"

I followed after her. "Of course, I won't say anything. But look, have you told Clive about this . . ."

"No! "She stopped in her tracks and turned to me. "No, I haven't told him. Not about the letter, and not about the gnome. And you mustn't either!"

"But, he said you talked to him about Santa . . ."

"About Father Christmas! I only told him that I know Father Christmas is real!" She stopped herself, having worked up more of a dither than she had wanted. "At least, I'm convinced he's real" she said more quietly. "Though, I suppose until I see him, even I won't know that for sure, will I?"

"Right. I mean, maybe the gnome is just having you on."

Olivia gave me the withering stare I deserved.

"I'm sorry, Olivia," I said. "I'm not trying to make a joke of it. Unless . . . it's a joke, right?"

She gave a resigned smile. "Yes, of course it is, you silly young man. Let's say no more about it. Now, come over here."

She pulled me beneath a paper lantern and put her face very close to mine. Her brow furrowed as she leaned in and studied my eyes. "Your face is a little thinner than it used to be. And you've got the most amazing little gold flecks in your eyes. Have they always been there?"

There was nothing flirtatious in the way she spoke. But there was the undeniable fact that a sprig of mistletoe hung from the bottom of the lantern, and that we were directly beneath it. There was never going to be a better time to put Audra's advice into action.

I choked a little when I started to speak, then I got my voice. "Olivia, would it be all right if . . ."

And I heard my name shouted in the distance. A loud, booming voice, not familiar to me, was yelling "Mannie Candler! Has anyone seen Mannie Candler?!"

She heard it, too, and stepped away from the lantern, breaking the spell. "Someone's looking for you," she said. That much was obvious, of course.

We both started back down the walk in the direction of the voice, and soon two or three others joined it. By the time we were halfway to the bridge, another half dozen had joined in, and it was like my name had become the subject of an ominous chorus.

Cy Murney spotted us first, and ran to me. "Your father is here. He says you've got to go at once.

And with that, my idyllic Sunday was done, and a long night of grief lay ahead.

Chapter Four
Time of Trouble

There was no time to say goodbye to anyone at the party. My father ushered me to the car and took off as quickly as he could.

"I'm sorry, son. I've got to get you on the nine o'clock train," he explained as he pulled into traffic. Something was wrong, and no mistaking it.

"What's happened?" I asked.

"I can't really say, Mannie. Audra's things are in the back." Indeed, two suitcases were propped in the seat behind me, with paper tags identifying them as belonging to Audra LaPoore. "I want you to take them back to the house. So we have to make the nine o'clock. It's the last one to Springfield. Father Humboldt will meet you at the platform."

"But why do I have to go home? What's going on?"

"It may be nothing." He didn't want to say more than that, but he can't have thought I would be satisfied by such vague answers.

"Has something happened to Mum?"

"No, son."

"To Audra?"

"We don't know," he said, a bit angrily.

"What's wrong with Audra?!" I all but yelled back.

"Mannie, please! I don't know anything. She'll be fine!" It was so rare for my father to raise his voice. I said nothing else until we reached the train platform.

Just before I boarded, Dad put his hands on my shoulder and said, "I'm sorry I was cross with you. We had to take Audra to hospital. You're mother is with her now, and as soon as everything checks out, we'll bring Audra home. I want you to help Father Humboldt get everything ready, all right?"

I nodded and Dad clapped my right shoulder, then hurried back to the car. I knew things were worse than he was letting on.

I spent the forty-minute train ride in worried silence. The city slipped away outside the window. The plains and scrubby hills were only shadows, even harder to see because of the reflection of interior lanterns in the window glass. There were few passengers on the train. I sat at the back of a coach that held no other riders. I drew my legs up onto the seat and hugged my knees, a position I often took when I wished to be alone with my thoughts. Just now, they were chaotic. I had nothing tangible to worry about, except that something was wrong with Audra. A wisp of annoyance had begun, that instead of taking me to Audra, my parents had thought it best to ship me back home unattended.

Father Humboldt was waiting for me at the Springfield platform. His burly frame was easy to pick out, even in shadow. When I emerged from the train, he ran to me, with a kind of bouncy jog, and took both of the suitcases from the porter. His expression was grim, but I reminded myself that Father Humboldt's expression was always grim.

"Welcome back, Mannie. How was the pageant?"

"It was good," I said. "You would have liked it."

"And the party after?"

"Good," I answered, tonelessly. "I had to leave early."

"I know. I thank you for coming back so soon."

We rode to our church, St. John's, Trinity Parish, just outside of the farming village of Clarketon, in Father Humboldt's beat-up truck. He had a more dignified car, now in its sixth month of disrepair. Father Humboldt, stout, tall, with a proud, stern face, looked comical driving the wood-sided pick-up. It made him less intimidating, at least.

"Have you talked to anyone?" I asked as we rode along the narrow highway to St. John's.

"I spoke to the vicar. He must have told you the same that he told me."

"Dad didn't tell me anything," I said. "I had to pry it out of him that Audra was in hospital."

"I suppose he didn't want to worry you." The old man smiled at me. A smile from that face, so often austere, was more worrying than comforting. "Your aunt has long had trouble with her heart. This isn't the first time we've had a scare."

"Has she had a heart attack?" I had never heard this about Audra. Panic instantly made itself home in my mind. "Why wouldn't he tell me?"

"They don't yet know, Mannie! We must hope and pray that it's nothing more than a brief disturbance."

"I want to go back," I said. "Tomorrow morning, I want to go back to the hospital and see her."

"I think instead, we will hold out hope that she is able to board the train and come here, all right?" They were words of encouragement, but firmly spoken, with an unmistakable subtext. Don't make trouble!

The Church of St. John of the Trinity included a sanctuary, with small office building attached, a parish hall, and the vicarage where I lived with my family. My father also ran the church school that served our village of Clarketon. Physically, this comprised four classrooms and a chapel attached to the parish hall. In the yard beyond were a barn and stable, where we kept our horse, Joey Pete, and a coop of chickens.

Father Humboldt placed Audra's luggage on the porch of the house, and asked me where we intended to put her up. The house had no guest room.

"She can have my room, if it comes to that. I can sleep in the living room," I said.

"There are the guest quarters in the parish hall, but as you know, the archbishop could arrive at any time." This was Father Humboldt's constant refrain. The guest room must always be ready for surprise visits from the archbishop, whom I don't recall ever having stayed. In fact, Father Humboldt lodged himself there several nights a week, though he had a small townhouse in the village. He surely coveted that room for himself for the duration of the Christmas week.

Once inside the house, I put Audra's cases in my parent's room and went on to my own. I placed my small carrying bag on the chair at my desk. I changed into clean day clothes, knowing I would not sleep very soon. I wanted to wait up in case the phone rang.

Our only phone was in the parish hall, and it shared a party line with several homes at the edge of the village. I sat in the living room and kept the front door open. I would be able to hear the jingle of the phone from here.

I brought my toy theatre out into the front of the house. For three years, ever since Christmas of 1934, it had been my chief hobby. When

I was ten and visiting Auckland, Audra took me on my first trip to the theatre. We saw an elaborate pantomime complete with fairy princesses, trolls and pirates. I was transfixed by the sets and costumes, by the way the audience got caught up in the whole fantastic story. I told Audra it felt a bit like church, except fun. She laughed so loud I thought she would rupture something, and then she took me into the gift shop by the lobby, and bought me the most beautiful wooden toy theatre, complete with half a dozen sheet sets of famous plays. (It was called Little Lyceum, labeled in fancy script on the proscenium. It was a childish sounding name, and I kept meaning to paint it over with a new designation: *Candler Hall*.)

The previous Christmas, Audra sent me the sheets for a presentation of Aida. I wanted to have the many sets and characters fully painted, cut out and assembled on the stage when she got here. I imagined that if I could complete the job before morning, it would all but guarantee her arrival, like some totem of obligation. I worked on it, with paint and scissors, to occupy my mind, and to keep from worrying.

*   *   *

This is the hardest part of my story to tell. A little after midnight, I drifted to sleep, my back against the sofa, my little paper company not quite finished. I woke up when a knock came to the front door. It was Father Humboldt.

The instant I saw his face, I knew the worst had happened.

He sat down on a chair, across from the couch. He told me he had just spoken to my father. The ringing of the phone hadn't been loud enough to wake me up.

I still remember the way he phrased the news.

"Your Aunt Audra has passed into the next life. It happened about half an hour ago. I'm very sorry."

There was little else to say. That was all he knew. He asked if I wished him to stay with me, in the house, and I told him no. He returned to the parish hall, and the rest of that night is a merciful grey void in my memory.

It will not serve any purpose to dwell for too long on the miserable days that followed, for there were strange wonders about to begin. But the sorrow of that time was, in a way, the soil from which those joys grew, and so, I must tell a little about it.

My father arrived home the next morning. He asked me if I had slept. Since the moment I learned the news, I had not. I hadn't cried, either. I knew that I would soon enough, and that it was going to be terrible. My dad encouraged me to eat something, and then to try and rest. I asked him if we were going to return to Christchurch, and to Mother. He didn't yet know.

Anaru Rongo got to the house a little past nine, and I sat at the breakfast table with him. I had no appetite. Anaru was sixteen, a Maori boy who started attending our church grammar school when he was ten. My father paid him a weekly stipend to help with yard work and upkeep. (Father never said so, but his chief reason for hiring Anaru was that I was clumsy and indolent when it came to physical chores.)

Anaru ate and I didn't. He was always quiet, and I initiated no conversation. It didn't occur to me that Anaru had no way of yet knowing what had happened. I avoided his gaze. Before long, I hopped off my chair and returned to the living room, where my toy theatre still sat on the floor.

I returned to painting and cutting out the paper figures. I didn't know what else to do. For a while, it was a distraction, a way to avoid facing what I knew I must sooner or later face.

Sometime, maybe an hour later, maybe two, Anaru knocked at the window and beckoned me to come outside.

He met me on the front lawn. He stepped close to me, took the back of my head in one hand, and placed his forehead against mine. "I just heard," he said. "I'm sorry, Mannie." Then, in silence, we stood, head to head. I closed my eyes, and felt powerful emotion stirring, ready to surge. My shoulders began to shake, but then, I fought it back. *Not in front of Anaru. I have to look strong.* I squeezed Anaru's shoulder, releasing him from contact, and I thanked him, then turned and walked back into the house.

I spent the day in a pallid haze, doing nothing, afraid to let myself feel anything. That Monday morning seemed to last for weeks.

My mother came home in the afternoon. By then, I was out in the barn, brushing down our horse, Joey Pete. (My parents bought the horse before I was born. Dad wanted to call him Pete, Mum wanted to call him Joey. The double name was their eventual compromise.)

Father Humboldt drove mother in from Springfield, and when I heard them arrive, I walked out to the grassy field and watched her disembark from the old truck. Father Humboldt carried her bags, and the two of them walked up to the porch.

I was close enough to see her face. I tried to read her expression. She looked cross, and that made me angry for a moment. Then I stopped, told myself that I ought to greet her, and ran to the house. She had already gone into her room and closed the door by the time I got in.

I hardly spoke to anyone that day. There were a few restrained words over supper, and Father asked me if I was all right. I said yes, looked at Mum, who said nothing and did not look at me. It didn't seem as if she had been crying. I wondered how she could be so cold and indifferent. Then I remembered that I hadn't cried either.

On Tuesday, there was plenty of emotion, most of it anger. I set off the powder keg myself.

Through the night, I had pondered my last conversation with Audra. She had gently introduced the subject of her own disbelief, and asked if I was troubled by it. I had been evasive, politely on-the-fence. Now, I knew what I should have said. I should have told her I would never again worry about Hell, because surely there was no such place. There was no chance that Audra, or anyone, could go there. The idea was so obscene, so unjust. I was now ashamed that I hadn't told her so.

I knew it was the right and reasonable conclusion for me to reach. Audra did nothing but love others her whole life. Eternal punishment was now the most unspeakable idea to me.

And I said so over the breakfast table.

Mother was shocked that I would even introduce such a topic. Father was angry that I had upset my mother. I protested that, in fact, I was trying to comfort her. Nothing about that conversation went well.

Father demanded I talk to Father Humboldt. I found him in the fellowship room of the parish hall, and he greeted me with a warm, parochial smile.

"Ah, young Emanuel. Please do sit down."

I pulled up a rickety wooden folding chair, and he sat opposite me at one of our aging banquet tables. Behind him, I could see a paper sign that hung on the wall during the school year. It was a picture of an eye, radiating beams of light. It was captioned: *The eye of the Lord is ever upon thee.* Everyone in the school hated this sign, and it was frequently taken down and disposed of. Father Humboldt always managed to replace it. Students joked that he had a large stack of them locked away in a safe somewhere.

Father Humboldt cleared his throat. His smile morphed into a morose, hangdog expression that, in other circumstances, I probably would have found amusing.

"I have not yet had the opportunity to fully express my sorrow about your loss."

"Thank you, Father."

"I can only imagine how it must affect someone your age. And at Christmas, of all times."

"Yes sir." I could hear the dullness of my tone. So could Father Humboldt. After an awkward interval, he continued.

"There must be a lot of questions going through your mind. I want you to feel free to ask them."

I knew what questions he was alluding to. He had obviously talked to my father.

"No sir."

Father Humboldt sighed and shifted in his seat. "I hope you will not mind my saying so, Master Candler. I can't help sensing a certain anger, a somewhat disdainful attitude."

"No sir."

"Are you sure? Your father was struck by the same feeling, and I daresay your mother . . ." He grimaced. "I think your mother finds herself a bit wounded by it."

"I'm sorry, sir."

"You needn't apologize to me. It is your mother who ought to hear it."

"No sir."

Another terrible silence. I stared at Father Humboldt, feeling nothing. He became tense.

"I appreciate how difficult this must be, but can you really wish to hurt your mother at a time like this!"

"I don't wish to hurt her,' I said. "But I'm not sorry about what I told her."

Father Humboldt had no more patience, and he let me know it. "I cannot condone this insolence! You really think having your say is more important than the feelings of your grieving mother!"

"She's not grieving!" I shouted, and the old priest slapped his hand flat against the table.

"That's enough! How dare you presume to know what she's going through!" He stood and crossed to the kitchen door. "I am going to leave you alone, now. Our emotions are running too high for reason."

"I'm sorry, Father." The words came out of my mouth with no premeditation. He moved back out of the kitchen. "I'm sorry. I don't know how to feel right now. I haven't even cried, and I know I should."

He came back to the table. "That's all right, Mannie. You have to work that out in your own time."

"And so does she," I said, knowing that it was true, but not yet feeling it.

"Yes, good. Now, will you tell her you're sorry? Please."

I nodded and stood up. "Father, you never met my Aunt."

"No, lad. I'm sorry to say, I never did."

"She wasn't a Christian."

"Perhaps, when she was younger," he said, and it almost sounded like a plea.

"I don't know. Anyway, she was lovely. And sometimes I think Mother didn't like her very much. Especially because she wasn't . . ."

"Later, Mannie. Let this work itself out later."

I went back to the house, aware that at least one emotion, remorse, was peeking through the gauzy vale of emptiness. I determined to find my mother and apologize, fully and unconditionally.

But it didn't work out that way.

I don't know if the words came out of my own personal need, or curiosity, or spite. I only know that when I opened my mouth to say, "I'm sorry," something different came out.

"Did you love her?"

My mother was folding linens in the dining room. Her first reaction was to laugh, in disbelief. I shook my head, as if trying to deny what I had just said. "What?" my mother demanded.

"I need to know that you loved her," I said. She dropped the fabric from her hands and stared open-mouthed. "What an absurd thing to ask!"

"Well, did you?"

"How am I supposed to answer you. What do you think!?"

"I'm not sure. That's why I'm asking." I meant this as a reasoned defense of the question. Her eyes brimmed with tears. Without meaning to, I had made things much worse. I turned away and darted from the room, muttering the word 'Sorry' as I went.

I shut the door to my room and sat on my bed. Not ten seconds later, Mother opened the door. She yelled, with trembling voice, "I want you to go out there right now and pick up that damned theatre. I'm tired of tripping over it!"

I immediately got up off the bed, but this didn't stop her from adding, "Did you hear me, young man?"

"Yes, mother," I said under my breath as I walked past her. I hurried to the living room and began collecting up the many bits: sticks of balsa wood, tiny Egyptian soldiers and guards, a painted barge. I stuffed them all into the proscenium of the wooden stage. Mother stepped into the living room.

"You know, you aren't the only one who's troubled here!" She spoke with an urgency I had never heard from her before. "You aren't the only one who doesn't know how to feel or what to do! Now, don't you ever dare treat me like that again!"

And she vanished down the hallway and slammed her door.

I returned to my room, and in newfound rage, I hurled the Lyceum at my closet door. The stage burst into a dozen pieces, and clattered to the floor, amid a flurry of paper figures. Finally, I cried.

Chapter Five

West Lodge

Wednesday, December 22, 1937
Parish of Trinity Corners, New Zealand

I slept until ten thirty the next morning, and woke up a just a little more clearheaded. I dressed and walked into the den. The house was empty.

Audra's belongings were set by the front door. It was as though there had been a phantom visitor, now ready to go home. I sat on the floor next to the two cases for a few minutes. It was all the connection with Audra that was possible now. It occurred to me that somewhere within those two light-blue coloured boxes, there was probably a Christmas gift meant for me. I indulged a selfish moment of wondering what it might be, and if I would ever receive it. I drove that thought away as quickly as I could. Then, I let go of another passing and evil thought. *No one is here. You could open them.* I knew there would be no forgiveness for such a brazen offense. Not from my parents, nor from myself. I stood up and went outside.

I found Father in his office. He looked neither pleased nor vexed to see me. "Where's Mum?" I asked.

"She's gone to the village this morning. Have you eaten anything?"

"No, sir." Now that he mentioned it, I had at least a little appetite today.

"I haven't time to make anything for you. There should be enough leftover roast for a sandwich. Help yourself, and then I've got a chore for you. Come back when you're ready."

He bent his head to his work, so I left with a polite "Thank you, sir," and hurried to the kitchen.

Anaru stood by the back door. "If you're hungry, I've got permission to raid the icebox," I told him. Together, we improvised a satisfactory breakfast that included slices of roast lamb, savory biscuits, black currant jam and lemonade.

Shortly after eleven o'clock, a car pulled into the dirt lot by the parish hall, and two men got out. The driver was a member of our church, Mr. Prassler. The other man was nobody I recognized.

Anaru made a sharp hissing sound. "Look who's here," he said. "Probably going to tell your father to cancel Christmas."

Anaru didn't like Mr. Prassler. It had something to do with a lawsuit brought against Anaru's father a few years back. Prassler had been the solicitor in a lawsuit that left Mr. Rongo bankrupt and out of work. I had never pressed for details. The topic made Anaru miserable, so I avoided it.

"Come on," I said. "Let's see what they're here about."

"I have better things to do. I'm going to look at the chicken house roof, all right?"

I left the house and dashed to the parish hall. When I got inside, Father was just inside the door greeting the two men. They all looked at me as I entered.

"Hello," I said. Father cleared his throat.

"Is there something you need, Mannie?" Father said.

The stranger standing next to Mr. Prassler had caught my notice. He was tall, with a long head of brown hair, long enough that it might shock the upright citizens of Clarketon if they saw him in church. His face was thin and careworn. He eyes were red, as if he had been crying. I immediately wondered if this had anything to do with Audra. I knew that asking would be a terrible idea.

"I . . . you said you had a chore for me."

"Oh! Yes. Look behind you," Father said. Stacked against the wall near the door were several cardboard boxes, bundles wrapped in white cloth and filled burlap sacks.

"Deacon Herford dropped off the charitable collections this morning. I would like you and Anaru to go through them. Take what's needed to West Lodge."

I was glad to have the task. It meant a pleasant walk with Anaru and Joey Pete into the village. "Thank you, sir," I said. I should have moved right away, but my eye was drawn again to the sad-faced man. He smiled at me and then turned away.

"Is there anything else?" my father said, with a tone that made it clear there had better not be. I said a quick 'no, thank you' and ran outside to find Anaru.

West Lodge was a multi-family dwelling at the edge of Clarketon. Anaru and his family lived there, along with a dozen other families. Our church made an effort to collect provisions for them. Anaru and I sorted through the various goods: Dinty Moore stew, Colgate toothpaste, bags of flour and sugar, carefully weighed and sorted for ease of distribution, bolts of cloth, and a canvas sack marked in red-stenciled letters, DO NOT OPEN TIL XMAS. Of course, Anaru and I had to open it, an operation easily accomplished by pulling apart the drawstrings.

The sack held about a dozen toys, all of them either dolls or stuffed animals. "I guess this is it for toys," I said. "I don't think the boys in your house will want dolls."

"Oh, they're in lucky luck!" Anaru laughed. "They asked Santa for a football."

"I'll see if my parents can't find one for them. How many girls are there in the house?"

"In our house? None. But in the lodge across from ours, there are at least five."

"It'll be a nice Christmas for them, anyway," I said. I picked one of the dolls out of the bag. Its hair was ratty and sparse, and its dress threadbare. "Maybe not that nice." I dropped the sorry looking doll back into the pack. "Surely our parishioners can do better than this."

"Go talk to your friend Mr. Prassler. He's got plenty of money."

"He seems all right," I said. I didn't know him very well, of course.

"He never put your dad out on the street," Anaru said.

I couldn't square that idea with the soft-spoken man sometimes chatted with me after church. I liked him, because he was one of those rare adults who didn't talk to me like I was still six years old. It was hard to imagine him as someone cold-hearted enough to throw Tamati Rongo out of his own home.

And yet, it must have happened, because Anaru and his family had once lived in their own house. Tamati had been a foreman for a thriving construction company. Now, his family was poor, and for months at a time, Tamati was away working on public roads, living in shabby work camps.

Anaru and I loaded two saddlebags with goods. We dragged them to the barn, and saddled up Joey Pete. The horse was seventeen years old, and looked enough like a Highland Pony that I used to boast about his distinguished Scottish lineage. He was a strong and sturdy horse, if no longer so fast as he had once been.

Anaru helped me onto the saddle. I offered to pull him up behind me, but he preferred to hold the reins and walk alongside. We had no intention of making Joey Pete run to West Lodge as we were in no hurry ourselves.

The wide ranch yard behind the church belonged to Martin Seeger. He never minded us crossing through his field. His property was large enough, we rarely saw him or his hundreds of sheep. Joey Pete knew without guidance how to step over the half-fallen rail fence that led to the pasture. The rail had been broken in this way as long as I could remember.

"You seem better today," Anaru said half a mile or so across the field.

"I guess so," I said. "I slept late."

"Good." He fetched a pack of cigarettes from his shirt pocket, struck a match and lit one. "I hope you don't mind," he said.

"Go ahead," I said. "Just be careful not to blow the smoke at Joey Pete."

He stepped ahead a pace or so and took several long draughts, then dropped and snuffed out the cigarette he had barely started. He returned to the reins.

"I've been thinking about her all the time," I said out of nowhere. I felt comfortable with Anaru, and I wanted to say it. "I know there will be a day when I don't as much. But right now, everything makes me think of Audra."

Anaru nodded slowly. "The Maori believe that the spirit of the deceased stays near the body for three days. So, we stay with them and talk to them."

"Have you ever done that? Talked to someone who's dead?"

"No. Not yet. My mother's told me about it."

"I wish I could talk to Audra," I said.

"I suppose you can talk to her anyway. If you want to."

I thought about the idea, and wondered what I would have said if I had the opportunity. My eyes started watering, but I fought the emotion back.

"I wish I were Maori sometimes," I said after a minute.

"You say that a lot," Anaru said. "It's no misfortune that you were born *pakeha*."

"I know,' I said. "I just wish sometimes."

We reached the other side of Farmer Seeger's' property, and crossed onto a dirt road. We were silent for the last two miles of the trip.

West Lodge sat at the end of a cul-de-sac behind a row of warehouses and a construction supply depot. There were four identical two-story houses, each of plain cinderblock, topped with corrugated tin roofs. A chain-link fence surrounded the area. The gate over the dirt road was crowned with a wrought iron sign, complete with fancy scrollwork. It said West Lodge Family Housing. It might as well have said "No Greenery Beyond This Point." The lot was barren of trees or grass, but richly supplied with gravel, pieces of cracked brick and dry weeds.

Anaru's mother Rawinia kept a flower garden by the east side of their building. It stood out from its dismal surroundings, a patch of bright yellows and purples, daffodils and magnolias, with rows of green herbs in between, defiant in that lot of dusty brown and grey. She tended it constantly. I had never seen it look less than splendid.

Anaru and I carried the saddlebags to the back door by the kitchen. Tamati was smoking a cigarette and talking to an elderly Maori woman in the native tongue. She laughed at whatever he had just said, then looked my way and waved. I returned the gesture, but she shook her head and pointed past me.

"Not you. I was waving at Anaru! I don't know you."

"Be nice, Ruta," said Tamati. "This is Mannie Candler."

"I met you last year, Ruta. Last Christmas," I said.

"I don't remember," said Ruta.

"His father's the vicar over at the Anglican church."

"I've never been there," Ruta said. "We go to the Presbyterian church," she told me directly. "Anaru should go there too."

"I like it at Saint John's," Anaru told her. "I like the school."

"Hmm." The woman shrugged and walked out of the kitchen.

"Don't mind her," Tamati said. "She's losing her sense. She hasn't been to the Presbyterian church in years."

Anaru dragged the canvas bag of toys over to the table. "We should hide these here. Nothing for the boys this year, though. It's all baby dolls."

Tamati looked into the bag and shook his head.

"I told Anaru I'd try to find more" I said. "Maybe a football . . ."

"Mr. Prassler was at the church this morning," Anaru said. "I say he owes us."

Tamati nodded. "He's too proud."

I couldn't help my curiosity. "Is it true he put your company out of business?"

"He was just doing what his employers told him to do," Tamati said. He stood and turned on the kitchen tap, then doused his cigarette in the stream of water. "People like that can't afford to worry about people like us."

My heart sank, because I knew that at some level, I was probably in the "people like that" category, in spite of my sincere good will.

Rawinia Rongo leaned into the room from the hallway. "Mannie? One of the boys is riding your horse."

I followed her into the common room, where a dozen people were sitting on rickety chairs, or on the floor. Ruta had begun to pluck out notes on an out-of-tune piano. Out the front window, I could see Joey Pete clopping around in circles, with a blond boy, about ten, sitting on top, and two others following on foot, cheering.

"That's Lake Marson. His mom's not here or I'd have her go out and paddywhack him."

"That boy is a nuisance," Ruta added. "He cheats at cards, too."

"Joey Pete's too good-natured to mind," I said. I stepped outside. "Hey! That's my horse you're riding," I shouted.

"He's not very fast," Lake hollered back. His friends laughed.

"All right, you've had your fun, time to get down," I said. Lake gave me a smug grin and kept riding.

"He won't pay attention," said Anaru, running to my side. "He doesn't listen to anyone."

But then Tamati appeared in the doorway. "Lake Marson!" he called, in a firm, low growl. No other word was needed. Lake halted Joey Pete and clambered down.

"Well, he listens to my dad," Anaru added.

"Is he the one that wants the football?" I asked.

"Yeah. You sure you still want to find him one?"

I retrieved the saddlebags from the kitchen and went back outside to get Joey Pete ready for the ride home. Rawinia was kneeling by her flower garden. I waved to her as I threw the bags, now much lighter, over the saddle and started to lift myself up onto the horse. It's a skill I never fully mastered, and my attempt was as graceless as ever.

Anaru went to his mother and spoke to her. By the sudden change in her expression I knew Anaru had told her my sad news. She waved me over, so I walked Joey Pete to the little garden.

Rawinia held her arms open. "Mannie, I didn't know. Come here." She held me for a long time, and it felt like the embrace I should have shared with my own mother. "I'm so sorry, Mannie. I didn't know."

I felt comforted and loved. I didn't want to let go. She swayed and rocked, and said a few words of prayer under her breath. Then she stepped back, took my hands in hers, and began singing, quiet as a whisper. It was a Maori song of mourning. I couldn't help weeping, but they were silent tears, nothing like the agony of the night before.

"It's going to be all right," she said. "It's going to take a long time, but it will be all right."

Just then, and no sooner, I knew it would be.

As I rode Joey Pete back into the barn, I saw my father driving onto the grounds. I met him in front of the house.

"A word with you, Mannie," he said as I approached him. "First of all, you and Anaru forgot to put anything away in the kitchen."

It was true, and I couldn't deny it. "I'm very sorry."

"I had to throw out the meat. That's a terrible waste."

"Yes, sir. It was thoughtless of me."

"I've made the same mistake myself, Mannie." He smiled, to my great relief. "Just be glad I discovered it before your mother got back."

"Is she here?" I said, and it sounded wrong, like panic.

"I've just put her on the train to Christchurch. She took Audra's luggage with her, as well."

Instantly, resentment bled into my heart. I wanted to be in Christchurch, too, if it meant being nearer to Audra. I coveted whatever connection might still be possible. I stammered, fighting my incipient fury in search of any way to respond. This surge of emotions clearly showed. My father's face fell.

"Son, please pay attention. This is important." He looked non-plussed. "Are you listening?"

"Yes," I said flatly.

"Your mother is staying with Audra's friend, Sissy. They're making all the arrangements for the funeral. Now, I am sending you to join her there."

It was the last thing I expected to hear. "You are?"

"Yes. I want you to be with your mother, to help her in any way you can."

"Oh!" I said, astonished. "Okay." Angry emotion had flooded in on me so quickly, and was now dispelled by a rush of relief and surprise. I felt each of these shifts physically, in waves. I tottered where I stood.

"Are you all right, son?" I nodded.

Father squatted down so that he was eye level with me, and he put a hand on my shoulder. "Listen to me well. This is a chance for you to redeem yourself. You've got a lot of mending to do where your mother is concerned. I expect you to be as cooperative, as obedient, and as understanding as you can possibly be. You know what I'm talking about."

"Yes, sir," I said, still stunned at the news. "Thank you. I mean, that's better than I deserve."

"Perhaps, son." He gave a pat on the shoulder. "Now, I want you to pack your best clothes, and get to bed early. You'll be on the train tomorrow, and you'll have a long, full day."

That night, in my room, I sorted through the pieces of my ruined Little Lyceum. The damage wasn't irreparable. Some glue and tack nails, and some repainting would put it right. When I got back from Christchurch, I would fix it. And I would rename it.

Chapter Six

A Reindeer
at the Well

Thursday, December 23, 1937
Christchurch, New Zealand

I spent all of Wednesday morning being as helpful as I could around
the church. I fed the chickens and cleaned Joey Pete's stable. I helped
Father Humboldt print and fold the missals for Christmas services.
No one told me when I was going to be taken to the train platform in
Springfield.

The parish phone rang around one o'clock in the afternoon. I was
the only one there to answer it. A sweet, almost childlike voice greeted
me on the other end.

"Is this Father Candler?"

"No. It's his son, Mannie."

"Oh! Mannie, I'm so looking forward to meeting you. My name is
Sissy. I'm a friend of your Aunt Audra."

"Yes!" I said, delighted by the introduction. "She told me about
you."

"Your mother is here with me in Christchurch."

"How is she?" I asked.

"She's fine. This is a sad time, of course."

"I know," I said. "Father said I'm to come visit you."

"That's right. If you'll go fetch him, I've got the details for your
train. I'll meet you at the station. It will be easy to find me. I always
wear purple, and I look like a little porcelain doll."

I finally boarded the train in Springfield at five o'clock. That was a lot later than I had hoped, but I was glad to be going to Christchurch at all. This was my third trip along the Midland Line in five days, and the second time I had traveled by myself.

The journey was usually a short thirty-five to forty minutes, but this one took longer. We were delayed just outside of the city by a slow-moving freight ahead of us. "We're so close," said a man sitting across from me. "We could probably walk the rest of the way in ten minutes, if we were allowed to disembark." Instead, we sat for an additional and unbearable forty.

The view out my window wasn't the most charming. Above a ridge of trees, I could see the weathered and beaten upper half of a large, dilapidated-looking warehouse. A faded logo identified it as Marbury Meats.

The fellow next to me noticed it, and tut-tutted. "Twenty years ago, that was some operation. Another casualty of the economic downturn, lad. It wasn't always such an eyesore."

"I just wish we could have been stuck somewhere nicer," I said, and the kindly fellow laughed.

"It's ugly, but then, the trees are all right, eh?"

Stuck as we all were, the others dozen passengers in the coach began an animated discussion of how their own fortunes were improving, or not. I thought about the word everyone had used to talk about the recent hard times: *Depression*. It was a word that practically caused the very thing it described. Everyone seemed to agree that this monstrous thing was going away, but very slowly. *Just like my own sorrow*, I thought. It felt like a deep and grown-up thought to have had. I gave myself the satisfaction of feeling I was wise. Once the train began to move again, I took special joy in seeing the unpleasant face of Marbury Meats roll out of sight. *Begone and discourage me no more.*

We chugged to a stop at the first of several platforms in Christchurch, and I looked out the window for my mother. She wasn't there, but I located Sissy right away. She was wearing a purple sundress and a flowered hat. She was short, plump, and her face, round and delicate, looked like a porcelain doll, just as advertised.

"You must be Sissy," I said as I approached her, toting my small bag on my shoulder.

"Mannie Candler! What a delight!" She clasped her hands together and ran her eyes across my face several times. "Do you mind if I pinch your cheek?" she said.

"No, it's all right," I said, a little doubtfully. She grasped the flesh on the left of my face and wiggled it about, with a satisfied 'Mmm-mm!'

"Now that's over with, how was your trip?" she said.

"We got stuck for a while. Sorry we were late."

"It's just as well. I couldn't get my car to start. Oh, speaking of that, we'll have to walk a few blocks. I hope you don't mind."

"No, it's all right."

"Your things aren't too heavy?"

"No, Ma'am. Not at all. How is my mother?"

"She was lying down when I left. My friend Lettie is starting preparations for supper. You should know we'll be putting you to work."

"Yes. That's fine."

"Good. There are a few lights that need changing, and we've got an old pump in the kitchen that needs priming. The house is old. And up here, at this end of the city, well, we're practically still in the countryside. We haven't got modern facilities. If you know what I mean.

"An outhouse?"

"That's right. I hope it isn't too much of a shock. No modern plumbing, but we've got electric and a telephone. We aren't completely primitive."

"When I was six, we lived in a parish outside of Auckland. They didn't have plumbing either."

"Then it'll bring back memories for you. Isn't that nice." She smiled the daintiest smile I ever remembered seeing. Then she pointed to the next corner. "A left just ahead. We're nearly there."

The two-story clapboard house stood on one side of a cul-de-sac. Across from it was another home, similar in design, but abandoned and boarded up. Beyond lay a wide field of small rolling hills, scrubby and dry. I saw, in the near distance, a tree line, and irregular strips of forest. Sissy's house was on the very borderline between city and wilderness.

The house had a corrugated roof, and a gable at its center. It was painted a chalky pastel green, well washed by the seasons. A separate garage made of rough wood sat at the top of a short driveway. An antique Wolesely squatted in front of it. There was a pool of oil, like an unguinous shadow, spreading from beneath the old car.

The weathered gate by the street swung unevenly on its hinge. A post box, the only thing freshly painted, showed Sissy's proper name: *Cecilia Bremmer*. It stood out against the scuffed exterior of the rest of the house, much as Sissy, in her bright purple dress made her own contrast.

"It's in a state, I know," Sissy confessed. "I'm too old to climb on ladders and paint things."

"I could do it," I said, wanting to be as helpful as possible.

"Well, aren't you a blessing! We'll just see about that. But not tonight."

A woman in a floral print dress opened the front door and met us. She was as thin as Sissy was round. She smiled as we approached.

"Here's our little gentleman! Welcome, Gus!"

"Lettie, his name is Mannie!" Sissy shouted.

"Oh! Yes, of course it is. Mannie, I know that. I'm Lettie Maynes. Please come in. It's nicer inside than it is outside." Lettie stepped aside and held the door open as I passed through.

"Your mother is upstairs having a rest," Lettie added. "You're going to be staying in our guest room. That's upstairs, too. Let me show you."

I followed her upstairs. The guest room was small, with a narrow bed on a brass frame. A ceiling fan turned slowly above it. The lace-curtained window looked out on the back yard. I could spot the outhouse, and a well with a bucket. A half-finished stockade fence ran along the back of the yard, with plenty of gaps to the brush and grass beyond.

"I hope it will be comfortable for you. The nights have been warm."

"That won't bother me," I said.

My mother appeared behind Lettie. She stepped into the room, bleary-eyed, her hair disheveled. "Hello Mannie," she said, and then she leaned over and kissed my forehead. No embrace, but she was obviously tired. "Thank you for coming," she added. "Lettie, I'll be down as soon as I'm presentable."

"Take your time, dear. I'm going to put young Gus to work right away."

"Gus?" my mother said.

"Oh! There I go again. Well, he looks like a Gus to me, er . . ."

"Mannie," I said.

"Mannie. Of course. I'll remember."

Lettie took me back downstairs to the kitchen. It was quaint, with a cast iron stove, a metal icebox with oak paneling, and a hand pump over a deep copper sink. Sissy was working the lever, trying to draw water.

"Oh, Mannie. Thank goodness. See if you can coax some water from this pump, would you? Then we'll have a nice meal of cold sandwiches and iced cream as a reward."

"That sounds nice,' I said. "Thank you, Miss Bremmer."

"Please call me Sissy."

"Sissy, then."

I raised and lowered the lever a few dozen times, and nothing came up. Sissy sighed.

"We'll have to prime it. There's a well in the back yard. If you could fill a bucket and bring it back. I hope you don't mind."

"Not at all," I said.

A screen door from the kitchen led straight to the back. The well lay a dozen yards out, a round stone wall circling it, and a shingled wooden roof above it. It had a charming storybook appearance, rustic and sun-bleached. I enjoyed turning the handle to lower the bucket down into its twenty-foot depth. It was more difficult to haul it back up once it was nearly full of water.

When I got the bucket back to the kitchen, Lettie and my mother were seated around a small table. Sissy stood by the sink. "Well done, Mannie. I'll ladle water into the valve, and you do the pumping." Together, we tried valiantly but in vain to bring up a stream of water. Eventually, we had emptied the bucket.

"What you must think of us," said Lettie. "It isn't always like this. But as soon as there's company."

"Mannie," Sissy said with her sweetest smile, "we need to try just one more time. Could you take another trip to the well? We'll feed you the instant you get back, all right?"

I dutifully went back outside. Early evening was fading into late. The colors of light shifted to warmer tones, enriching the landscape. The well stood in a shaft of ochre-hued light. It made for an enchanting scene, complete with one reindeer.

Spotting a wild animal is always a nice surprise, especially when it's close enough to allow a really good look. I saw the antlers first, then its muscular frame. The shoulders were at least five feet off the ground, and its head reached at least seven, not counting the long, thin antlers, covered in a natural layer of downy velvet. But this wasn't a wild deer, after all. There was a harness around its neck and shoulders, and a rope attached, tied to one of the well posts.

I gazed at it for a good minute, then stepped directly back inside. "There's a deer out here!" I hollered.

The kitchen was in chaos. Sissy had opened the icebox, and Lettie was looking over her shoulder, distressed.

"Oh, Mannie, don't look. It's a mess!" Sissy sounded ready to cry. "Everything that's supposed to have been frozen is melted, and everything that should have been fresh is wilted. Oh, I'm so upset, I could scream."

"It's a shame," Lettie said. "Gus must be very hungry by now."

"Oh, his name is Mannie!' Sissy said with exasperation.

My mother stood and pointed at the kitchen door. "Mannie, just go back to the well, please."

"But, there's a deer . . ." I started.

"No argument!" Mother snapped. I stepped back outside.

The deer was still there. I hadn't imagined it. But the animal wasn't alone. A small man wearing a coat of dried leaves, a harvest bag and a long pointed, feathered hat stepped into view from around the well. He had a chestnut colored beard, and a wild tussle of hair fell from his hat. His brows were bushy, and his expression was all furrowed frowns of consternation. He was smaller than me, perhaps two and a half feet tall.

"Psst!" he whispered. "Do you see me?" His voice had a nervous quiver.

"Yes," I whispered back. "I see you just fine."

"Do you see the deer?"

"Of course I see the deer. It's hard to miss." I was still whispering.

"Blasted heaths!" he shouted. "I thought it was just old biddies living here!"

"Who are you?" I asked.

"I don't have to tell you that."

"I guess not, but you are on somebody else's property."

"Says you! We've a difference of opinion on that! You tall and awkward folk may think you own this land, but you don't. Not really. We're letting *you* live here. You might want to thank us for it."

"*I* don't live here," I said.

He gave me a suspicious glare. "Then what are you doing here!"

"I'm sure I'm wondering the same about you," I returned.

"I am on official business." He folded his arms and did his best to look preeminent.

"What kind of business? And for who?"

"Official none-of-*your*-business, for nobody you need to know." He peered past me to the house. "You say you don't live here, but you came out of that door." He pointed with a sharp thrust at the kitchen door, to make sure I knew he had seen.

"I'm a guest. I'm staying the night."

He considered this answer for a tick. "Good. I accept your reply, and if I have seemed rude, I regret it."

"Don't worry about it," I said uncertainly.

"Excellent," he said. "Now, I ask a favor. Please turn around, go back into the house and pretend you never saw me."

"I've got to draw a bucket first, if it's all right with you."

"Yes, yes! Be quick about it."

I tied the bucket and lowered it in. The great antlered beast stepped closer and began sniffing the top of my head. I laughed, out of shock as much as amusement. Joey Pete liked to snuffle my hair in a similar way. The little man pulled the reindeer back. "Easy there, Trimble," he said.

I gave the fellow another glance. "Are you in a holiday pantomime of some kind?"

"What do you mean?" he said defensively.

"It's just that, it's almost Christmas and . . ."

"And I look like an elf to you," he snipped.

"Yes. That, and, you know, the reindeer."

"Not an elf, thank you very much. Gnome, I can accept. Call me one of the forest folk. Or, if we must make conversation, just call me Lem."

"Lem?" I said, lifting the bucket back over the rim of the round stone wall.

"Yes! Lem, as in Lemuel. Lemuel Greenleaf. Now, if you've got your water, please return to the house and forget this conversation. A fine evening to you, sir."

"Yes, of course. Good bye." I walked sideways a few steps, unable to stop looking at this unlikely pair of intruders, if intruders they were. Then I turned and headed for the kitchen door.

"Wait up a second," Lemuel called after me. "If it isn't a breach for me to ask, who are you?"

"Me?"

"No, the reindeer. Yes, you! I'd hope you have enough manners to return a name when someone gives you theirs."

"I didn't think you were interested."

"I'm not! But now you know who I am, I ought to know who you are, in case anyone asks."

"I'm Mannie Candler. Who would ask?"

"Important people." He took a few jogging steps toward me, and lowered his voice a bit. "Look, I mean what I say. My purpose here is crucial. And confidential."

"Is there anything I can do to help?"

"Yes. Go back in the house and keep quiet." He put a finger to his lips to reinforce the idea.

I took his advice and carried the bucket back into the kitchen. Sissy was speaking into the phone. Mother and Lettie were at the table. I set the bucket down by the sink and waited for Sissy to finish her call.

"There you are," she said after she rang off. "You took your time."

"Yes. I thought I saw something."

"Well, I've just called the Brixton Garden Room. They're two streets away, and they're open for another hour. We can get something to eat. I'm sorry we spoilt everything in the house."

Sissy and I began again trying to prime the pump. Lettie joined us.

"You aren't going to get anywhere that way," she said. "Let me have a try."

"Now, what makes you think you'll have any better luck?" Sissy asked.

"Because I know what I'm doing. Here, Gus, let me at that handle."

I didn't correct her. I stood aside and let her pump the lever up and down. Within five strokes, water began to surge into the sink. The first gush or two were pale brown, but then clear water came up, and Sissy gave a short sigh of exasperation.

My mother beckoned me over. "Are you feeling all right?" She put her hand to my forehead. "You look a little strange. Has something happened?"

"Would you believe me if I told you that a gnome has tied a reindeer to the well outside?"

"Of course I wouldn't," she said, and a perturbed look passed across her face. "Why don't you go upstairs and lie down until we're ready to go."

"I'm all right," I said. "Really."

"Well, go sit in the parlor, then. You're warm. Cool off by the fan, all right?"

I did as she suggested. Inside of three minutes, everyone in the house had joined me.

My chair was small, pinching at my hips along the wooden back. It had fading upholstery and torn lace. Sissy and Lettie were on an equally tatty looking loveseat facing me, and my mother was in a wooden rocking chair.

"I've never felt so ill prepared for entertaining guests, Sissy," Lettie said. "It used to be so much nicer here," she said to me. "I hope you don't think we're low class louts, Gus."

"Do either of you know a little man named Lemuel?" I said.

Lettie looked surprised by the question, as who wouldn't. "What has that to do with this house?"

"Nothing, Lettie," said Sissy. "He's changing the subject, because you're making him uncomfortable."

"Well, do we know a Lemuel?" Lettie asked.

"His full name's Lemuel Greenleaf.' I said. You'd remember him right away."

"No one around here by that name," Lettie said.

"Mannie," my mother broke in, "is this the gnome you just mentioned to me a moment ago?"

"Yes, Ma'am. Sorry."

Mother looked to the other two. "I am sure Audra told you. Mannie is blessed with a lively imagination."

"She certainly did. Loves books and plays, and I hear he has a magnificent toy theatre."

"Yes. And sometimes, he seems to be living in it." There was a hint of a smile as my mother said this, but beneath it, a clear warning signal to drop the matter.

"If he's going to ask us about imaginary people, I'm sure I won't know how to answer," Lettie said.

And that's when we heard a knock at the back door.

"Perhaps that's him," Sissy said, and she quickly strode to the back door to check.

"You did hear that, didn't you?" I asked the other two.

"Yes, Mannie, but it was probably just the screen door," said Mother.

"It sounded distinctly like a knock to me, Gus," Lettie said.

Sissy reentered the parlor. "No one there at all." She started for the stairs. "I'm going to get ready. We should all change into something nice, don't you think?"

My mother stood and joined her. "That's fine," she said. "Mannie, come upstairs and get into your clean clothes."

"I'll be right there," I said. "I need to use the . . ."

"All right, but hurry up. And if there really is someone out there, come right back inside. Don't talk to any strangers."

So she at least entertained the possibility I wasn't making things up.

I stepped out the back door, and looked left and right. The well stood, all by itself, before me. No reindeer, and no Lemuel. A sense of unreality swept over me. (Not for the last time that night.) Had I really hallucinated my conversation with that little man? It was frightening to think that I could misperceive the real world so dramatically. Then I noticed the hoof prints in the sand. They proceeded to the left, so I followed them.

Lemuel and the deer were hiding at the west side of the house. As soon as he saw me, Lem put a finger to his lips and made a shushing hiss.

"This is very important, young fellow. I need a place to hide Trimble. I want to use that little barn over there."

"That's not a barn. It's a garage."

"Whatever it is, it's perfect. But I need your help. Can you get away from those others for a while?"

"What do you mean?"

"I need you to help me stow Trimble before anyone sees him. Can you get away?"

"We're supposed to go out somewhere to eat."

Lemuel snapped his fingers and his eyes brightened. "That's good. Tell them you're not feeling well. Pretend you've got digestive upset. See if they'll shove off without you."

"If I do that, I'm sure my mother will stay here and fuss over me."

"Won't know until you try. Just do whatever it takes, then come back here as soon as you can."

"Mannie!" my mother's voice shouted. "Where did you go?!"

"I'm right here!" I said, and then wished I hadn't. I heard her shoes grinding in the sand. She was walking right toward us. I raced around the corner so that I could forestall her discovering Lemuel and the reindeer. I got to her just inches before she would have rounded the bend.

"What's going on over there?"

"Nothing," I answered, and in saying so, discovered my own intent. I meant to go through with Lemuel's foolish plan; pretend to be sick and help hide a wild animal in the little shed next to Sissy's house. *Completely crazy and irresponsible*, one part of my mind acknowledged. But other thoughts countered. *Once it's done I can show them I wasn't crazy. Then we can alert someone who handles wild animals. Really, it's the responsible thing to do.* I was expert at kidding myself.

"Is there someone there?" she asked, now patently worried.

"No one," I lied. "I thought I heard something. Listen, Mum, I don't feel so well after all." I was instantly appalled with myself for so easily telling such a whopper. I was also impressed with how readily she accepted it.

"I knew it! Well, that settles things. March upstairs right now!"

"I've still got to visit the loo," I said.

"Mannie, you're behaving erratically. I don't like it. Now hurry up."

I beat a path to the outhouse, and while I was there, made use of it. When I was finished, I emerged to find Lemuel not five feet away. From any window at the back of the house, he would be perfectly conspicuous.

"Well?" he asked. "When are they leaving?"

"Be careful! They're going to see you!"

"No they aren't," Lemuel said with a laugh. "I'm surprised *you* can see me!"

"What do you mean?"

"I mean, most of your people can't see my people. It's rare."

"Mannie!" My mother's voice carried well across the yard. "Mannie, hurry inside!"

I told Lemuel to keep the reindeer out of sight, and I ran back to the house.

Mother and Sissy walked me upstairs and to the small guest room. A pair of felt pyjamas was laid out on the bed. "I hope these will be the right size," Sissy said. "They should be comfortable. Now, Mannie, you just rest until we get back. We won't be long, and I'll bring your food right up to you. Then perhaps we can heat some water for a nice hot bath."

"Thank you, Sissy," my mother said. "Now, young man, I want you to change, and get into this bed. And I expect to find you right here when we get back. Do you understand?"

Ten minutes later, I was in the pyjamas, too large by at least a size. As I sat on the bed and gazed at the back yard, I heard Mother, Sissy and Lettie go out the front door. I worried that they might spot the deer before they got far enough away for me to sneak back down.

I allowed a couple of minutes, then I put my shoes on over my stockinged feet, went downstairs and out the back door. Lemuel and the deer were right where I had first seen them, at the well.

"Nice work getting them all away," he said. "Now, let's see about that barn."

It wasn't locked. He really wouldn't have needed my help getting in. I fumbled and found a switch on the wall. I flipped it, and a single dangling light bulb came on. There were wooden shelves on either side with old tins of oil, a few rusted tools, and a length of chain. Lemuel had to coax and pat the reindeer before it would step into the shed. It was wide, but just barely tall enough to accommodate the fleecy antlers.

"Now that you've got me mixed up in this, could you at least tell me where the reindeer comes from, and why we're hiding it?"

"Those are good questions, and it's confidential."

"But, you didn't find him just wandering around."

"Of course I didn't find him just wandering around. You ever see reindeer around here? Wetas and lizards, yes. Moreporks and kiwi birds, to be sure. No end of cats, to which, I must add, I am allergic."

"Yes, well, how did it get here?"

"He has a name," Lemuel said.

"Oh, right. Trembler, or something."

"Trimble," said Lemuel. "His name is Trimble!"

"How long do you plan to lodge Trimble here?"

"Until the F.A.B. has given up and gone back to Switzerland," said Lemuel.

"That didn't make any sense at all," I said.

"Of course it did." Lemuel gave a dismissive wave of his hand. "There's too much you can't understand, and I'm not authorized to tell you."

"Then I'd best get back inside," I said. No use making trouble for myself.

I was about to open the door and walk back to the house, when I noticed the mark on Trimble's forehead. Amid a patch of light gray-brown fur were thin lines of darker brown. They appeared to form a symbol; two letters, VN, inside of a circle.

"Oh, look at that!" I said. "It looks like a brand mark. What's VN?"

"That's confidential," Lem said, predictably. "And it's not a brand mark. That would be a cruel spot to burn a poor reindeer, don't you think?"

"Of course," I said. "It's just strange."

"Where we come from, everything is strange," he said.

"So, this mark just grew on him?"

"That's right. Ever since Kris adopted him."

"Who's Chris?" I asked, but I knew what the answer would be, and I said it along with him. "That's confidential."

The inside of the garage went dark. At first I thought the bulb must have burnt out, but then it lit up again. Then it went dark, then lit again. Lem had found the wall switch.

"Oooh, I do love these!" Lemuel gazed at the bulb. He hit the switch again, shutting it off, then back on. He rapidly flipped it, on-off-on-off. "It's like a thunderstorm!" he said. He commenced to making the sounds of a tempest with his mouth. "Boom! Crtzckch! I can feel the howl of the wind and the sting of the rain!"

"I'm glad you're so suddenly amused, but could you leave off that a minute?"

"Oh, sorry," he said and took his hand off the switch. "We don't have those, you know. I keep saying we should, but . . . human ways are not our own. You understand."

"I'd better go back in," I said, and I left the garage. Lem followed me.

"Don't you want to know about the F.A.B.?"

"Sure, but I doubt you'll tell me."

"It's the Forest Abduction Brigade. They capture animals, for a price. Thieves and kidnappers, I say."

"And they're from Switzerland?"

"This team, yeah. Specialize in reindeer. Rotten muck-slugs!"

I was at the back door now, and eager to go inside, where I was supposed to be. I was feeling disconnected from reality out here, conversing with a gnome about Swiss reindeer hunters.

"Can I come in, too?"

"Of course not. It's not my house. I'm just a guest. I can't invite others in."

"I thought we were friends," he said. He couldn't have seemed more disingenuous.

"How do I know you're the good guy," I said.

"What do you mean?"

"I mean, here I am helping a complete stranger to hide a reindeer. For all I know, you've stolen it from its rightful owner."

"I am aghast at your unprovoked accusation!"

"I don't mean anything personal by it. It's just that, well, if you're going to keep saying things are confidential, how am I supposed to know I'm doing the right thing by helping you?"

Lem paused. "You make an intriguing point."

"Have a good night, Lem. I'd stay with Trimble if I were you." I stepped inside and closed the door. Almost immediately, Lem began knocking on it.

I climbed the stairs and returned to the bedroom, where I had promised to stay in the first place.

Within seconds, bits of gravel hit the window. I looked out, and there stood Lem in the back yard, tossing small rocks at the second story and making wild gestures. I pulled up the sash and hollered down.

"I can't help you!" I said. "I'm already going to be in enough trouble."

"Trouble and rubble! I'm going to be dead!"

"What's wrong?" I shouted down. Lemuel pointed at the ground around his feet.

"Look at this! Prints! Everywhere, hoof prints! And they go all the way back beyond the fence! Oh, what a stupid scout I am! What a nincompoop! Our enemies will find us!"

Sure enough, Lemuel was surrounded by hoof prints. Deep, clear, unmistakable hoof prints

"Brooms. Do the biddies in that house . . ."

"I wish you'd stop calling them biddies. They're very nice."

Lem gave me the hand wave again. "Yes, yes, they're angels, I'm sure. Do they keep any brooms in the house?"

"Probably."

"Well, find them! We've got to sweep these prints! Hurry!"

There was one broom in a small closet by the entrance to the kitchen. At least a third of its bristles had fallen out. As the floor itself was perfectly clean, I reasoned that there must be a better specimen of broom somewhere in the house. I opened the back door and tossed this one out to Lem.

"Here you go," I said. "I'm going to look for another one."

"Have you got feet?" he said.

"Of course I have."

"Then get out here and start kicking these prints. Bury them with your shoes, all right?"

And so it was that found myself, under a darkening evening sky, with a quarter moon near the horizon, in baggy pyjamas with anchors and boats printed on them, kicking up dirt next to a gnome with a broom.

The more we kicked and swept, the faster we went, until we were nearly frantic. The prints led back toward the wooden fence. Lem and I were about halfway across the yard when my mother walked around the east side of the house.

"Oh no!' she shouted. "Emanuel Gregory Candler!" Even from this distance, and with fading light, I could tell Mother was as angry as I'd ever seen her. I felt my knees go a bit weak, and I let out a sigh.

"Oh, great," I said under my breath.

Lemuel dropped the broom and dashed behind me.

"Look at you!" my mother went on. "You're filthy! Just look at what you've done to those nightclothes!"

"I'm sorry," I started, hopelessly.

What are you doing out there!?" She came closer, just a few yards away. "What could possibly have possessed you to leave that bed!"

"I heard something out in the yard." I couldn't believe how feeble my response sounded.

"Don't you dare tell me it was a gnome!"

"Well, as a matter of fact . . ." I said, and I moved aside, hoping to reveal Lem to my mother's sight. "Look, here he is, right here."

"It's no use. She can't see me," Lemuel said.

"What?!" I cried to Lemuel. "You can't be serious!"

"I told you! Here, what's your mother's name?" he asked, and I told him it was Georgina Candler.

"Watch," he said. Then he hopped out in front of me. He ran a few steps, until he was mere feet away from my mother.

"Hello my dear Georgina!" he sang, and he began to dance a ridiculous little jig. "*Candler-wandler, How d'ye do, Here's a merry dance for you.*" He wrapped up his merry tune with a screechy refrain, "*Ain't it a lovely eeeve-nin!*"

She looked right past him. Before he had even finished, she shouted, "Where did you get that broom!" She hollered it right over Lemuel's silly routine, as though he weren't there at all.

"It belongs to Sissy. We were trying to wipe out the deer tracks."

Mother's hands went to her face, and I heard a sobbing sound. She turned around and ran into the house, slamming the door behind her. By this time, Sissy and Lettie were standing in the kitchen doorway. Sissy stepped outside.

"Mannie, what's going on?" She asked. "I think you've upset your mother very badly."

"I'm sorry. I didn't mean to. It's just that . . ." I looked at Lem, who was no longer dancing. He was looking at me and rolling his eyes. "I don't suppose you can see this gnome, can you?" I said hopelessly. 'He's standing right here."

"I'm sorry, Mannie," Sissy said, in a calm, measured tone. "There are a lot of things I have trouble seeing these days. But no, I can't see any gnomes in my yard."

I turned to Lem. "Will Trimble be invisible?"

Lemuel shrugged. "I don't know. He's a magical deer. But then, your type has been known to hunt and kill magical deer without knowing it."

"Who are you talking to?" Sissy asked. Lettie opened the kitchen door behind her.

"Sissy, this poor woman needs a drink. Can't we please get going?"

"In a moment, Lettie." She turned back to me. "I really was hoping you would stay in bed," Sissy called to me. "I didn't expect you to get into any mischief."

"I'm sorry," I said. "I didn't think you'd be back so soon." I had that awful feeling that I had chosen my words poorly, and that it was evident the very instant I spoke them.

"We hadn't really left yet. We walked a block and a half, and I realized I'd forgotten my coin purse. We came back to retrieve it."

Lettie cleared her throat. "I really think we should drive," she said.

"You know perfectly well we couldn't get that old heap to start."

"*You* couldn't get it to start! You didn't let me try!" Lettie sniffed a bit to get across her deep feelings on the matter.

"All right, Lettie. I'll let you try."

Lettie jumped and clapped her hands twice. "Hooray! I'll crank the engine, and you shall steer!" Lettie bounced through the door and straight for the garage. "I'll just get the crank," she said. Before I could think what to say, she had opened the small door into the garage and stepped in. I held my breath, wondering if I would hear a shriek when she discovered Trimble.

A moment later, she walked out, metal crankshaft in hand, smiling gladly.

I asked her, "Did you see anything strange in the garage?"

"Strange? Like what?"

"Like a reindeer," I answered. Lettie waved off the idea with a 'pshaw,' and went back inside. Sissy placed a hand on my shoulder and began to lead me in as well.

"Young man, it's time for you to go back upstairs and stay there!"

"Yes, ma'am," I said.

"Oh, please call me Sissy. Now, up you go!"

My mother was sitting on one of the parlor chairs, her back to Sissy and me. She was hunched over, her head in her hands. Just before I started up the steps, I said to her, "I'm sorry, Mother." She didn't respond, just slumped over a little further.

"Now isn't the time," Sissy said. "I'm sure we'll have an awful lot to talk about tomorrow."

In the guest room, I sat on a little wicker chair and tried to dust off the pant cuffs of the nightclothes. Sissy brought in a small oil lantern and lit the wick. "It's going to be dark soon. I'll leave this here. Don't go out again unless you really need to, all right?"

"Yes, I promise," I said. Even then, I wasn't so sure I meant it. I wasn't so sure about anything.

"I know I've been a terrible guest,' I said. "I promised my father I'd be cooperative and helpful."

"You've had a stumble on the way, that's all. A good rest is the first step to making everything better." She stepped into the hallway, then turned and addressed me in a soft whisper. "I should tell you, Mannie," she said. "I've never seen a gnome. But you're not the first young person I've met who said they'd spotted one around here. Good night, for now."

And she gently shut the door.

Chapter Seven

The Moss Circle

Lettie had no trouble starting the old Wolesley. From the upstairs guest room, I heard its motor sputter to life, choking and popping as it went into gear and drove my kind hosts and my mother out of the driveway and down the block.

I couldn't see Lem from the window. I opened it and leaned out. The side door of the garage was open, the light bulb still burning. No reindeer stood within. Trimble was missing. *Or was never here at all*, I thought. All was still and quiet. For a few minutes, I lay back on the bed and closed my eyes. It was possible the whole episode was just a mad hallucination. I had heard about such things happening to others, especially at times of stress or grief. Was that it? I couldn't discount the possibility.

I might actually have fallen asleep for a minute or two. By now, I was tired enough. But I was shaken by a loud thump, and the voice of Lem crying out, "Dire Damnations!"

That thump and cry came from downstairs. Lem was in the house!

I grabbed the lantern and loped down the stairs. I found Lem in the kitchen. He was standing on a chair. A wooden shelf, formerly attached to the wall, now lay on the floor, its contents scattered everywhere.

"What are you doing!" I yelled.

"Oh! I thought you were gone."

"Of course not!"

"But everyone else, is, right?"

"Oh, I *sure* hope so," I said. "Now, what's happened here?"

"I need rations. Provisions."

"Whatever for?"

"For running away!" Lem shouted. "Trimble's gone! That means the F.A.B. got him! I know when it's time to make myself scarce!"

He hopped off the chair, picked up his cloth sack, and began stuffing items from the floor into it: a tin of sardines, a jar of black currant jam.

"You can't just raid Sissy's kitchen!" I protested. "That's stealing!"

"Look, you ought to go back upstairs. If she shows up asking questions, you don't want to be held responsible."

"She? Who do you mean?"

"My Lady, the Sorceress of the Southern Snows." Then, Lem rapped himself on the forehead. "Oh! I did not say that. Pretend I told you it was confidential!"

"A sorceress. You think she's coming here?"

"If she is, she won't find me!"

PAK! PAK! PAK! Three loud knocks sounded on the front door of Sissy's house. Lem raced for the kitchen door, ran straight into it, rebounded and landed on the floor. A tin of soup rolled out of his canvas bag.

"Lemuel! Are you in there?" I heard a voice say from outside. It didn't sound like any sorceress to me.

"Oh!" Lemuel sighed with relief. "It's only Flutterbold! Go see what he wants." From the floor, Lemuel waved me on imperiously.

I peeked through the parlor window and saw another gnome standing at the door. This man had mottled gray hair and a bulbous nose. He wore spectacles and a green vest. A watch chain dangled from his breast pocket. This attire made him look altogether more sensible than Lemuel. I opened the door.

"Hello," I said. "Lemuel's here all right."

"Are you human?" the formal-looking gnome said.

"Of course I am. And yes, I can see you."

"So it seems. Are you a candidate?" he asked.

"I have no idea."

"Oh. Then you aren't. You would know if you were. May I come in?"

"I suppose. Not for too long, though. I don't live here, and the people who do could be back any second now."

The man Lemuel had called Flutterbold sauntered into the house, looking around with clear curiosity. He nodded and made approving *hmm* noises.

"A candidate for what?" I said, as soon as I caught his gaze.

"Sorry?"

"You asked me if I was a candidate. What does that mean."

He made a sound that was half cough, half chuckle. "Highly confidential, young man."

Of course.

"I hope Lemuel hasn't been any trouble," Flutterbold said.

"As a matter of fact," I began, but then Lem was with us, answering for himself.

"If the boy says anything about me stealing, it's nothing but slander. Or a misunderstanding. Whichever you like."

"Lemuel!" Flutterbold peered over the top of his spectacles. "I don't want to have this talk again. What is fit for humans is . . ."

"Not fit for us, I know. I've put everything back."

I glanced into the kitchen and saw that this was not quite true. The shelf still lay on the floor, assorted tins and jars in disarray. I left the two of them to talk, and I went to the kitchen to put things right. I heard Flutterbold excitedly say to Lemuel, "So, rumor has it you've captured Trimble!"

I put the shelf back up, and started replacing its contents, when I heard Flutterbold, from the nearby hallway, shout an aggravated "*What!?*"

"How could you have let him out of your sight! Lemuel, you'll be arrested for this! And you'll deserve it!" Flutterbold continued to harangue Lemuel as I left the kitchen, stepped past the two of them, and opened the front door.

"Gentlemen," I said, "I don't want to be rude, but . . ."

"Oh," said Lemuel, "I guess we're not wanted."

"*You're* not wanted," Flutterbold said. "He knows a troublemaker when he meets one."

"It's not that," I said. "But I've already upset my mother, and . . ."

"Say no more. I will get this nuisance out of your hair." Flutterbold marched Lemuel out the door.

"It was nice meeting both of you," I added as they walked down the porch steps. Neither of them said anything. They looked ahead to the street, looked at each other, shook their heads, and both ran toward the back yard. I went to the kitchen door and watched two small shadows scamper away, past the well, and the wooden fence. The sky was now nearly dark enough to hide them.

I sat in the parlor for a while, watching the pattern of light from the lantern flicker against the wall. I couldn't decide if I should tell anyone about this home invasion or not. I knew mother wouldn't believe me. I had the sense that Sissy might at least give a sympathetic ear, but then, no one is going to be pleased to learn that their pantry has been raided, even if by friendly gnomes.

PAK! PAK! PAK! The front door again. I looked out the window and saw that it was Flutterbold. I cranked the window open half an inch and whispered to him.

"What are you doing here?" I said.

"Ah. Hello again. It's getting dark."

"Yes, I know."

"Lemuel and I need to find our way to the Moss Circle. It isn't far from here. Not far at all."

"That's good, then" I said.

"But, we . . . ah" Flutterbold was giving me the oddest look. I couldn't guess what he was trying to get at.

"Is there something you need from me?"

"Yes! I'm glad you offered!"

"I didn't offer anything. I only asked."

"That's just as good, and awfully kind of you." He smiled at me.

"Well, what is it?!" I sounded just as impatient as I felt.

"The lantern! You have that lovely lantern, and it's dark. We just need to get to the Moss Circle. It's so close by."

"I can't let you have the lantern. It doesn't belong to me."

"And I wouldn't dream of taking it from you! No, no, I was hoping you might accompany us with it. We're very close."

"How close?" I said. By even asking, I knew I was letting myself in for it.

"You won't be gone five minutes. I promise."

I closed the window, picked up the lantern and went to the front door. When I opened it, I found both Flutterbold and Lemuel standing side by side, smiling.

"There's a condition," I said.

The two looked at each other, then at me. "Name your condition,' said Flutterbold.

"I want to ask a few questions, and I don't want the answer to be that it's confidential."

Flutterbold removed his spectacles and held them to the side of his mouth. "I see. What do you think, Lemuel?"

"We can't tell him everything!"

"But we could tell him a few things . . ."

"A few, to be sure. But we'd have to be careful. He's not a candidate."

"No, indeed, he isn't." Flutterbold placed his spectacles back atop his nose, cleared his throat and said, "Three questions. Choose them wisely. And ask them while we walk."

"Five minutes," I said.

"That's right," answered Flutterbold, smiling broadly. "We won't be five minutes."

I ran back upstairs and traded the dusty flannel trousers for a pair of short pants I had brought with me. I kept on the nautical nightshirt. I put on my socks and shoes, then returned downstairs, lantern in hand. I had no key with which to lock Sissy's front door behind me, but I trusted Flutterbold's word that I wouldn't be gone long enough for it to matter.

The two little men led me through the backyard, and past a fallen post in the stockade fence. Not far around the other side, we found a footpath. There was enough fading dusk that I didn't need the lantern to see it. The path was narrow and twisting. I guessed it was mostly used by forest gnomes. Here and there, I spotted hoof prints. "The reindeer must have come by this way," I said.

"Yes," said Lemuel. "This is the path I took after I caught Trimble. I got hold of him by the Moss Circle."

"What's the Moss Circle?" I asked.

"Is that your first question?" said Flutterbold.

"Would it be confidential?" I asked.

"Yes," said Lemuel. "But as that's where we're going, you'll be able to see it for yourself."

"Good. Then I withdraw that question," I said. "Instead, I'll ask this one. What is a candidate?"

"Fair enough," Flutterbold said. "You may be aware that very few humans can see us, or hear us. The fact that you and I are talking right now means that you are exceptional."

"Thank you, I think." I wasn't sure if it was a compliment.

Flutterbold continued. "Mostly, when a human spots us, it's somebody very young. And most times, when that young person grows up, the ability to see us fades away."

"Maybe it's because they have a harder time believing in you when they're older," I said.

"Belief doesn't seem to have much to do with it. Did you believe in forest gnomes before tonight?" Flutterbold stopped in his steps and gave me a hard look.

"No, I didn't. Actually, I can't say I'm a hundred per cent certain even now."

"An honest answer," said Flutterbold. "Admirable enough." He ran ahead a few steps and looked into the distance. The path was taking us closer to a copse of trees. On our left, the meadow swelled up to form a ridge. The path branched off onto a second trail that went up to the top of the small rise.

"We should go this way," said Lemuel, pointing at the branch in the trail. It was a gentle slope, and the path went laterally up the side, never at too steep an angle.

"So," Flutterbold continued, "our invisibility is part of a spell. It's a defense, conjured from the strange magics. And among those humans who can sense our presence, we select a very few in whom we place our trust and confidence."

"Candidates," I said.

"Yes. Specifically those approved by our boss. He's human, by the way."

"All right, then that's my next question. Who is your boss?"

Lemuel held up a hand. "Think twice before you answer this one, Flutterbold."

"I must decline." The gentle-gnome adjusted his spectacles and gave a polite bow in my direction. "Technically, it is an offense to answer that question. I could be arrested." He resumed walking, several steps ahead of me. He spoke loudly, as though to the air around him. "But sometimes I can't help talking out loud to no one in particular! To the air itself, right?"

"Right," Lemuel said, and he snickered.

"We work for a powerful wizard, whose name is known, but I will not name him. You have heard of him. He is famous, but not well understood." He paused and looked my way to be sure I was listening. I gave an affirmative nod. "He lives far away, in a frozen fortress. He has dedicated his life to the causes of joy and merriment."

The events of that Thursday evening had so far taken me utterly by surprise. At thirteen years old, there was still so much I didn't know about the world, but I had been pretty confident about its lack of forest gnomes. I could never have foreseen that this night I would find myself asking, in all seriousness, my third question.

"Are you talking about Santa Claus? Santa Claus at the North Pole?"

"He is not Santa Claus. And it isn't the North Pole. It's something far more mystical and grand," said Flutterbold.

"But it *is* very north of here," added Lemuel. "And it is cold."

"And that is your third and final answer," said Flutterbold. "We're almost at the Moss Circle."

We stood at the top of the ridge. The path continued down the other side, into a field of wildflowers. I could just see the rooftop of Sissy's house back in the distance. From here, I just might be able to hear the chugging of the old Wolesley. If I did, it might even be possible to run back within a few minutes, perhaps sneak into the house and up the stairs, unnoticed. Alas, I knew my chances of getting in further trouble were much greater than my chances of pulling off such an exploit.

In the field ahead, I could make out an open area beyond the rows of flowery grasses. A dirt road connected several patches of tall trees half a mile beyond. I perceived a dim green glow, faintly illuminating some of the nearby flowers. Suddenly, a bright, yellowish ball of light bounced and moved, then shone directly into my face.

"Candlewax? Is that you?" The light came from an electric torch. The voice proceeded from none other than Clive Murney.

He was standing at the bottom of the ridge. I ran straight down the small hillside. "Clive! What are you doing here?!"

"I'm under orders not to tell," Clive answered. "Besides, I should really ask you the same thing. I live here. You're a long way from home."

"You don't live *here*," do you?" The Murney house was on another end of the city. I knew that much.

"No, not right here, Sherlock Holmes. I'm on a family outing."

"So where is your family?"

"I can't talk about it. So, shove off already."

Lemuel and Flutterbold kept following the winding footpath, but they ran in order to catch up to me. "Who's that!" shouted Lemuel. Flutterbold followed with an out of breath, "We've been discovered!"

"Watch out, Candlewax! I don't know if I trust those two. Probably with the F.A.B."

"Wait a minute! Who is this?" demanded Lemuel, nonplussed at finding another human here.

"This is Clive Murney," I said. "I have no idea what he's doing here."

"Tracking an animal, if you must know. So are those two, I'll wager. You had better believe I'll be writing this all down, Mister Mannie Candlewax."

"Write down all you like. If you've seen anything like what I've seen, no one is going to believe it."

"And just what have you seen? And who are this lot? And what are you doing here?" Clive was doing a remarkable job of sounding like an inspector in one of those crime thrillers from the cinema.

"These gentlemen are named Lemuel and Flutterbold. They're not F.A.B."

"You're sure of that?"

"Pretty sure," I said.

"Of course you're sure!" Lemuel burst out. "You helped me to hide Trimble, remember?"

"You helped this little rustler hide Trimble?" Clive said, with a palpable rise in tone.

"How do *you* know Trimble's name?" said Flutterbold.

"I'm on orders to help protect him," Clive said, sniffing with pride.

"You mean to say you're a candidate?" Flutterbold looked completely stunned at the prospect.

"That's what the letter says," Clive returned, adding a lift to his chest and a note of hauteur to his voice.

"*You've* got a letter?" Flutterbold said, not hiding a hint of contempt. "Let me see it, please!"

Clive reached into the pocket on the left front of his red flannel shirt and produced a little white envelope. He waved it with a flourish. The little gnome swiftly snatched it from Clive's hand and examined the address.

"Be careful with it, and don't spend all day looking at it."

Flutterbold gave it a once over, then handed it to me.

"It's got an official seal. He seems to be a candidate."

I took one look at the envelope and immediately saw the truth of the matter. It was not addressed to Clive.

"You give that back, then!" Clive said, and he moved to take it out of my hand. It wasn't hard to keep it out of his reach.

"This letter is for Olivia!"

"She gave it to me!" Clive said.

"Wait a minute!" Flutterbold cried. "Do you mean Olivia Murney?"

'Yes," I said. "Clive is her younger brother."

"But, I was supposed to meet her here!" Flutterbold stamped his foot into the dry weedy ground. "*She's* a true candidate. I don't know this blight!"

Clive rounded on Flutterbold and stuck out his tongue.

"Clive," I said. "Do you mean to tell me I could have been talking to your sister right now instead of you?"

"I'm telling you she gave this letter to me. Said she couldn't be bothered trying to round up magic reindeers. She's a little old for that kind of thing, now that she's got to spend every waking moment with her fiancée."

"Nate *isn't* her fiancée," I said, suppressing the urge to inflict harm.

"Shows what you know, old man."

I removed a folded note from the envelope and opened it. In the light of my lantern, the ink on the page glinted with hints of gold. I read it to myself.

Dearest Olivia,

How delighted I was to learn from my spies that you would make an ideal candidate. I will require your help very soon. Certain forces are planning to heist my friend Trimble, the reindeer I wrote you about last month. I am readying my best agents for a counter-effort, but there is a task I think you would be best qualified for. My trusted agent Flutterbold lives in a forest near the Seventh Moss Circle. You must visit this mystical place. I know you've already been shown the way. Walk to the center of the circle, and you just may find a key. If you get hold of it, keep it with you. It may open a passage that will hide and protect Trimble.

I look forward to meeting you face to face very soon. I scarcely need mention that this matter remains Highly Confidential.

With Joy,
Kris

"You stole this from her, Clive." I put the letter in my pocket.

"You give that back."

"I'll give it to Olivia." I said, walking steadily toward Clive. He backed up as I did so. "Where is she?"

"She's off canoodling with Nate. I followed them . . ."

"Good. Then you can lead me to them now. Where are they?"

"They're at some café. Never mind that. They caught me, and they were awfully annoyed. They told me to go away."

"I believe that," Lem said.

"Don't you start!" Clive said. "I don't even know you and already you're casting aspersions."

"Fancy talk!' Lemuel said. "I don't trust thieves."

I had to laugh. "Careful there, Lem," I said. "Your record isn't exactly spotless."

"I'd like that letter back," Clive said. "I need to find this mossy patch. I want to get my hands on this key."

"Is he talking about the key to the crossway passage?" said Flutterbold.

"Of course!" Lemuel cried. "That's brilliant! If we can get a key from the Moss Circle . . ."

"Then we just might intercept Trimble!" Flutterbold finished. "My friends, we may not be beaten yet!"

"Didn't you say you already caught Trimble?" Clive said, in the snottiest way he could manage.

"He got away, you opprobrious little brat!" Lemuel waved his arms about his head as he shouted.

"Opprobrious! I know that word!" Clive said.

"I'm not surprised. It was probably coined with you in mind!"

Flutterbold stepped between the two of them. "All right, that's enough. Let's keep our focus." Then he turned to Clive. "Now, young man, I personally delivered no less than four communications to your sister over the last several weeks. Have you seen any of the others?"

"I've got *all* of 'em," Clive boasted. "That's what she gets for not being more careful. She should do a better job of hiding things from me. Blame her, if you want to blame anybody."

Flutterbold flinched, as if pained by Clive's attitude. It was a common response. "Did you read all of them?"

"Of course. Why do you think I'm here?"

"Why indeed. Did any of them contain a verse?"

"Yeah. One of 'em had a soppy poem in it. *Eeaugh.* It was rotten."

"Nonetheless, we need it. By any chance, did you bring the other letters with you?"

"No."

"Blast! Lemuel, we can't get the key without our *actual* candidate." Lemuel shrugged his shoulders at this.

"Oh, I *know* the awful poem, if that's what you need," Clive said.

"Do you," replied Flutterbold.

"The worthy snows of Very North, so on and so forth . . ."

Flutterbold's expression perked up a bit. "He does know it! All right, quick! Let's get to the Moss Circle!"

We had only to take a few steps. The Moss Circle was embedded on the ground, a layer of fine green moss that emanated a faint glow. The edges were scraggly and uneven, but the overall circle, some thirty feet in diameter, was perfectly round. Within the circle were the outlines of a labyrinth, formed by weeds and short grass. Toadstools sprouted here and there along the inner path. They, too, gave off their own faint light. Instinctively, I turned down the flame of my lantern. I wanted to see the luminescence of this enchanted circle as clearly as I could.

"It's quite a thing to see, isn't it," Flutterbold said. "Let's hope it will yield a key to the crossway passage." He then motioned Clive to come over to him. "Young man, we don't have time to retrieve the *true* candidate. So, we must rely on you." He turned to Clive. "This is very important. Do you understand that?"

Clive was digging through his small knapsack. He got out his notebook and began to write in it. "Hold up a bit," he said. "I want to get a few things down before I forget."

"For goodness sake, do it quickly!" Flutterbold was reaching the breaking point where Clive was concerned.

"Called . . . me . . . opprobrious," Clive said as he scribbled away. Lemuel seized the book, taking it from Clive in a lightning fast nab. "You give that back!"

"*After* you walk the circle!" Lemuel said.

Flutterbold pointed to a gap near the southernmost point in the circle. "This is where you enter. Just follow the path of the labyrinth. It will take you to the center. It's very simple."

"Then why don't you do it?" Clive said.

"I can't. The labyrinth is under enchantment. The keys it holds are human magic, Kris's magic. Hands off for us gnomes. This task was meant for your sister. I don't know if it will work with you."

"Of course it will work!" Clive shouted. "Do I look like an incompetent?"

"You don't want to know what *I* think you look like," said Lemuel.

Flutterbold interrupted. "Enough. Listen. I want to impress upon you the laws of the Moss Circle. Never jump across lanes to shorten your path. If you do, there will be no key."

"And if there's no key, we lose all hope of finding Trimble again," said Lemuel.

"That is right." Flutterbold cleared his throat. "Once you begin, you must walk at an even pace all the way to the center, without stopping. If you stop, you must go back and begin again."

"Why'd they make it so complicated?" Clive said.

"To keep scallions like you from getting the keys, of course!" Lemuel mumbled.

"Recite the verse, word for word, and the ground will yield your prize," Flutterbold continued. "Once you are at the center, you may not try again. You have only that one chance. Please don't take this lightly."

Clive muttered something about getting it over with, and stepped into the glowing path of the labyrinth. He looked askance at all three of us as he began plodding along the winding trail within the circle.

There were no split paths or blind corners. The single lane curved and looped along seven concentric rings, now closer to the center, now back at the edge, now to the center again. I could trace the entire route with my eyes. The pattern was simple, beguiling and beautiful.

When Clive had clomped with heavy foot through about half of the course, Flutterbold called out to him. "Say the verse."

"I'm saying it in my head," Clive hollered.

"That won't do. You've got to say it out loud."

"Fine," Clive said, and he made his strides a little longer. He started chanting, bouncing his cadence with each large step.

"Poor Napoleon Bonaparte
Lost the fight at Waterloo
All his generals blown apart
While he dawdled on the loo!"

"What are you saying!" Flutterbold looked near to panic. "You'll ruin everything!"

"It's better than that codswallop about snows and love. I hate that!"

"I don't care if you hate it. You've got to say it."

"I don't remember it."

"You knew it two minutes ago!"

"It's slipped my mind."

By now, Clive had been stopped for several moments. "He's going to have to start over," I said.

"No chance!" Clive countered.

Lemuel ran straight to Clive, just steps shy of the middle of the labyrinth. "Oh! This is too much!"

"Lemuel! You've broken the law of the circle!"

"Don't see how I could make things any worse!" Lemuel said. "I just want to help the lad see reason!" He growled that last bit, making it clear that he was considering severe measures.

"Just stop where you are," Flutterbold called. "Let the boy complete the circle. You, lad, try your best to remember the proper verse. You're supposed to be helping us, right?"

"Right, but I wish you'd let me do it my own way," Clive said. He stepped around the close rings of the inner portion of the circle.

"The worthy snows of Very North
Are something something . . . Love and Joy
Bla bla bla, Happy Christmas"

Clive now stood at the center of the circle. "What happens now?"

To himself, Flutterbold muttered, "The ground opens and we're all consigned to perdition." More loudly, he said to Clive, "Is there anything lying on the ground at your feet?"

Clive stooped down and pawed at the ground. "Just weeds."

"You don't see a key?" Flutterbold said.

"No." Clive stood up and folded his arms. "Don't pretend this is *my* fault."

Lemuel walked directly to the center and began digging into the soil. "Maybe it's buried!"

"Stop that!" Flutterbold commanded. "Lemuel, get out of there at once! You too, lad."

"Wait a minute!" I shouted. "Lemuel, toss me that notebook."

"Don't you dare!" shouted Clive. "That's mine!"

But Lemuel had already sent the little book sailing through the air. I caught it and knelt down next to my lantern. I turned the flame back up, and flipped to the back of the book. Several pages were still blank, but not far from the end, I saw what I was looking for.

"I knew you'd write it down," I said out loud. "The verse is right here."

"It's too late!" said Lemuel. "He's already made a mockery of it."

"Let *me* try," I said. I took a close look at the verse. It wasn't hard to commit it to short-term memory. I stood, walked to the labyrinth and began pacing my way through it.

"He's going to mess it up," Clive said, and Lemuel asked him, not too gently, to put a sock in it.

Halfway through the twists and turns, I slowly spoke the verse. I kept the book open in my hand, in case I needed to glance at it.

"The worthy snows of Very North
Compel the stars and moons above
To shine more brightly back and forth
Their earthly message—Joy and Love"

I stood at the center of the circle. Clive was still there, looking disgruntled. I handed his notebook to him. "Thank you, Clive," I said.

Lemuel was now next to Flutterbold. "Do you see anything?"

I looked down at my feet. There were several clumps of weeds and wildflowers. I knelt down and parted the largest clump with my hand. In brighter light, it would have been easy to see the key. In the near-darkness, I felt it before I saw it.

"There's a key!" I shouted. "No, wait! There are two!"

For in fact, as I tried to grasp the one, another came into view. I picked them both up. They were almost identical. They were about the length of my palm, made of brass. They had cylindrical barrels, and the letters VN adorned the bow of both keys. There was a single difference. One key was straight, and the other was bent, its barrel at least forty-five degrees askew.

"Er, one of them is bent out of shape," I said.

"So, the little guttersnipe *did* cast a spell," Lemuel said to Flutterbold. "And he got what he deserved." Then he shouted to me, "Give the bad key to the knucklehead!"

Flutterbold turned to Lemuel. "Please, Lem, be kind." Then to me, "I fear he's right. The young man did conjure a key. Let him take it. You, sir, may keep the fit and proper key."

"How do you know that one's mine?" Clive asked.

"Call it a hunch," answered Flutterbold.

I handed the crooked key over. "Here, Clive. Don't know what you'll do with it." Clive opened his knapsack and dropped the key into it. I caught a glimpse of the other three envelopes he had swiped from Olivia.

"I would have got it right if you lot hadn't turned up," he sniveled.

"But you were embarrassed to say the verse out loud in front of others," I said, not without some sympathy. Clive made an unpleasant grunting noise.

"Shush! There's somebody coming!" Lemuel was leaning to his left, cocking his ear. "From the trees," he whispered. "Along the old road. Keep still a moment." He ran over to crest of the hill and craned his head forward, looking like the mast of a fanciful ship.

I heard the clomping of hooves and the clatter of wheels against the dirt road. A wagon appeared from amidst the trees, and an electric lantern put us in its spotlight. A deep, rough voice shouted "Whoa," and the wagon came to a stop, just yards away from us.

The wooden cart was covered with ornate carvings, curlicues and figures of forest animals. Two reindeer, with antlers shorter than those on Trimble, pulled the cart. The electric lantern was housed in a wooden case crowned with a carefully sculpted goat's head. The driver, as large as a grown man, wore a black robe and cowl. A black mask in the shape of a deer's head covered his face. The effect was disquieting. Sitting next to the driver was a little gnome, smaller than the others. He wore a kind of officer's uniform. Epaulets sat perched on his shoulders, and a pointed blue cap crowned his head. His face was clean-shaven, unlike the two gnomes I had already met. Once the carriage came to a stop, he stood up on the bench and gave a salute to Flutterbold.

"Old friend!" The gnome in uniform shouted.

"Drillmast! *Guten abend!*" Flutterbold said in return. "I had no idea you were on this island."

"It's a new appointment," the official-looking newcomer said. He had a slight accent. German, I presumed, given the words with which Flutterbold had greeted him. The little man jumped down from the driver's bench, whisked over to Flutterbold and shook his hand rigorously.

"We got word that Trimble was captured, on this spot. I must congratulate you!"

Lemuel spoke up, smiling with pride. "That was me! I caught him just a few yards away, over there!" He pointed to his left. "I got the harness on him. He was no trouble at all. Trusted me completely."

"Aha! This is *gut*! Where is he?"

"Ah!" Lemuel said, his brow suddenly knit in a tense mien. "Yes. You see, I took him to the well behind the old house."

Drillmast looked at Flutterbold. "The well! That was *your* post tonight, yes?"

"It . . . it was . . ." Flutterbold stammered, "It was supposed to be. I arrived a bit late."

"I secured Trimble in the small barn," Lemuel continued, "where they usually keep the stink-wagon."

"Stink wagon?" Clive said.

"Motor car," I told him. "We put Trimble in the garage."

"So he is there?" Drillmast said, his voice getting faster and higher pitched. "Why are you hanging around here if Trimble is over there?!"

"He isn't there anymore," Lemuel said. "He got away."

"No! This is impossible!" Drillmast was so keyed up, he was practically dancing in place. "You had him and Trimble is gone! We are going to be pickled! In jars!"

"But, he can't have gone far," Flutterbold said. "And we've worked the spell on the Moss Circle. We have a key now. Two of them, in fact!

"Though the one is probably rotten," added Lemuel.

"We might find the F.A.B. if we get to the crossway passage. But we've got to go now!" Flutterbold pointed toward the tree line.

"Who! Who has the key?" Drillmast said, nearly frantic.

"I do," volunteered Clive. "I've got the good one, anyway."

"Don't listen to him," said Flutterbold. "That child is an interloper. He has illegally taken the place of a trusted candidate."

Drillmast began to spin in circles. "Oooh! Every time one of you says something, it gets worse and worse! Silbersee! Silbersee!"

The large figure in black cloak turned his masked face to Drillmast and made a low, guttural growl.

"Silbersee, do you see any reason I shouldn't arrest all of these felons right now?"

The deer-masked head moved slowly back and forth.

Drillmast stood stiffly and squared his shoulders. "Silbersee has authority as the voice of the law. I hereby arrest you, Flutterbold, for dereliction of duty."

"Fair enough," Flutterbold said.

"Lemuel, I arrest you on the charge of letting our precious quarry out of your sight."

"We can get him back if we hurry," Lemuel said.

"And you, little boy, what is your name?"

"Aristotle," Clive said.

"Aristotle, I arrest you for impersonation of a trusted agent." Then Drillmast turned to me, leaned in and poked my chest with his finger. "As for you, what is *your* crime?"

"I don't think I have one," I said. "I've got one of the keys. You can have it."

"Sounds like a bribe to me," said Drillmast. "Right, you're arrested too. Everyone get on board!" Under his breath, I heard him say "*Ja*, pit roasted *und* pickled, that's what I'll be."

Flutterbold and Lemuel climbed into the back of the wagon. Clive followed after them.

"Wait Clive," I said. "Don't get on. I've got to take you home."

"But I've been arrested," he whined.

"Let's just leave these people to their own business. Our families are probably in a panic already."

"I haven't been gone that long. And Olivia *told* me to make myself scarce."

"I believe that," said Lemuel.

"You've *got* to get on," insisted Drillmast.

"Have I?" I looked to Flutterbold. He seemed to me the most sensible of this group.

"I don't know what to tell you," he said. "Technically, I don't think Drillmast has any authority over humans. On the other hand, Kris may need your help."

"Careful there!" said Lemuel. "You've already said enough."

"He has a key," Flutterbold half whispered. "We need it, and we can't use it. We'd better keep him around."

"I can't go with you," I said. "I'm sorry, but I'm in enough trouble already."

"But you've seen Trimble yourself!" said Lemuel, almost hollering. "Don't tell me you weren't fond of him!"

"He's lovely, but I'm more worried about Clive right now."

"Figures," said the boy. "No spirit of adventure at all." The black-cloaked coachman laughed at this. It was a deep, sinister cackle. I didn't like it one bit.

"Clive, please come with me," I said. "Let's at least let the others know what's going on."

"No time, I'm afraid," said Flutterbold. "Listen, we just need to find the Crossway Passage. It's hidden in that forest. Your key may open it. And we just might rescue Trimble in the process."

I sighed. "So, you're saying I'm the only one who can help you."

"Yes, it looks that way."

"And you don't know where this passage is."

"Close by," said Lemuel.

"We won't be five minutes," added Flutterbold.

"You said that before we came out here, and it's probably been half an hour."

"So, he didn't lie," said Lemuel. "Definitely wasn't five minutes."

"I'll tell you what, lad. Join us for one drive-around on the old road," said Flutterbold. "We keep our senses on alert. Maybe the strange magics will show us the passage. We take one circuit, no more. The road bends around and meets up with the noise boxes and ugly huts over there." He pointed in roughly the direction of Sissy's house. "If we find nothing, then we give up and drop you off. All right?"

I looked at Clive. "I'm going wherever you go. You need watching, and I won't rest easy until I see you back with your family."

"Poached roaches," said Clive. "The last thing I need is *you* for a guardian."

Drillmast stepped in to the conversation. "Everyone put your arms out to your sides. I don't like to be intrusive, but I've got to check you all for weapons and illicit goods." He went to Flutterbold first and patted his pockets. Then he rifled through Lemuel's burlap sack, and made a few dubious noises.

"*Ach!* Human things in here. You are a thief. There *are* laws, Lemuel."

"There's nothing in there I can't defend," Lem said.

"I don't know," said Drillmast. "You make me uneasy."

After Drillmast had patted down Clive's pockets and checked his knapsack, he came to me.

"I haven't got anything at all," I said to him.

"Just a formality. No use getting snippy" He made quick work of his inspection, and then everyone got on board the wagon.

"One circuit," I said to Flutterbold. "No more than that. And you can drop Clive and me back by Sissy's house." Flutterbold nodded his agreement, then placed his arms together behind his back, wrists held close. "Drillmast, you have not bound me, but I will act as if I am bound."

"*Danke.* I appreciate it," said Drillmast. "Not every prisoner is so courteous."

"I hope you will pass word of my good behaviour on to her ladyship," said Flutterbold.

A few moments later, Silbersee took the reins and started the two deer on their course. We, two gnomes and two children, rode in the back of the strange wagon. None of us looked too certain about the night ahead.

Chapter Eight
Secrets of the Forest

The sky darkened fast as the strange coach bounced along the rough dirt road and into the thick strand of trees. The electric lamp at the front of the wagon brightened only a few yards of uneven road ahead. Irregular lines of shadow crowded out the stars and built a canopy of airy blackness. In the forest, the chirruping of bugs and trilling of frogs sounded loud and close to the ear. It was an atmosphere that lent itself to a stirring sense of adventure, if tempered by trepidation.

Lemuel and I sat at the back of the wagon, facing forward. Flutterbold and Clive sat opposite us, with their backs to the driver and Drillmast. To each other, we were now faceless shadows. Even without benefit of seeing his expression, I didn't have to guess how Clive felt about my presence.

"It's just like you to show up and spoil my fun," he said.

"Fun is not our aim, young man," Flutterbold pointed out. "This may seem a lark to you, but it's deadly serious to us."

"What's serious to you is damned silly to me," Clive said.

Lemuel nudged me with his arm. "Is there no way to silence this overgrown turnip?"

"Clive!" I said, as forcefully as my thirteen-year-old voice could manage, "You're not making any friends here. Button it!"

"Thank you," Lemuel said.

"So, if you're under arrest, who is it that's arrested you?" I asked.

"Agents of Mother Solstice," answered Flutterbold. "We will be subject to her judgment."

"Unless we find Trimble first," added Lem.

"Will you be put in prison?" I asked.

"We will be banished from our homes for at least a year," said Flutterbold. "We will most likely be confined, and placed in her service."

I heard a low growl from the driver's bench. It was the cloaked man.

"Perhaps our driver is currently under such a contract," Flutterbold said.

"I don't like him much," said Clive. "Why can't he show his face? I don't trust him."

The driver made another noise, an animal roar, inhuman and frightening.

"Clive's got a point," I said. "We're in the company of strangers here, and we don't know where you're taking us."

"I can assure you that Silbersee is trustworthy," Drillmast interjected from the front bench.

"I hope he is," I said. "But his manner is a bit unnerving."

"Don't put so much polish on it," shouted Clive. "He's horrible!"

Silbersee pulled back on the reins and brought the wagon to a halt. The cloaked man turned around, stood and set his gaze on Clive. From behind the black deer mask came a series of snorts.

"Calm down, Silbersee! They can't be expected to understand!" Drillmast made placating gestures, and Silbersee sat back down. He did not start the reindeer resuming our journey. We sat in silence for a beat or two.

"Splendid!" Flutterbold interjected. "This will be a perfect place to stop and give a listen." His upbeat tone heightened rather than quelled the tense atmosphere. "Everyone keep silent. The Crossway Passage has to be nearby."

"We need to touch the earth," Lemuel said. He jumped out of the back of the wagon. "Come on, everyone. Feet on the ground. It's the only way we can feel the vibrations."

Drillmast turned off the electric lantern, and I lowered the gas light of my own. The three little men stood well apart from each other, closed their eyes and raised their faces skyward. Clive wandered over to me, and sat on the ground, then got out his notebook and tried to write something by the dim light from my lantern.

Flutterbold began to whistle, a sound like a birdcall. Lemuel joined him, and then Drillmast. They then stood very still and listened. I heard the call of an owl, myself. Clive tore a page out of his book and handed it to me.

This is bonkers!

I made no reply, but folded the page and put it in my pocket, next to the key. I patted my pocket, and remembered something. When I had first put the key in my pocket, it had been long enough that the end stuck up just beyond the edge. Now the entire key fit snugly within. Had the key shrunk? As soon as I began to wonder about it, Flutterbold shouted.

"Counter spells! Does anybody else feel it?"

"No. I don't feel a thing," said Lemuel.

"Oh, I don't like it at all!" Flutterbold's whiskers twitched. "I've only sensed this once before. When I came up against the Grim Frost."

"Oh, I do wish you wouldn't say that!" Lemuel put a few steps between himself and Flutterbold.

"There's no need to fear him here. He couldn't possibly visit a place this warm."

The others began to talk amongst themselves.

Drillmast approached Clive and whispered something to him. He pointed to Silbersee, who was still seated on the wagon. The cloaked figure made a beckoning gesture to Clive. Clive said something back to Drillmast, and then the two of them went to the front of the cart. Every one of these actions made me uneasy.

What happened next went quickly. Flutterbold shouted again. "Wait! Stop! Something's wrong! Someone here is a traitor! I can feel it!" He hopped into the back of the wagon just as Clive hoisted himself up onto the driver's bench. "One among us has made a deal with the Grim Frost! I hear it in the earth. I see it clear as Polaris." From the back of the wagon, Flutterbold stared at Lemuel. Lem looked a little cowed.

"It isn't me," Lemuel muttered quietly.

Silbersee leaned over to Clive, right next to his ear. I couldn't hear if the masked fellow actually said anything or not. Then he reached up and flipped on the electric lantern. Drillmast hopped quickly onto the wagon.

Clive stood, and turned to face Lem and myself, still standing on the ground a couple of yards away. He grinned. "Hey! Candle Wax! Look what I've got!" He put his hand into the beam of electric light. It held a key. My key, the unbent key.

Then Drillmast hollered to us, "We're off to the Crossway Passage! Long Live the F.A.B."

Silbersee shouted a deep, raspy "Hoooah!" prompting the two reindeer to take off. Soon, the wagon was rolling away, with Clive laughing happily, pleased to have joined the opposition. Flutterbold, meanwhile, was hollering from the back of the wagon.

"Drillmast, you traitor! Stop at once and let me off!" The wagon rolled along, and just as it disappeared into the dark mass of trees, Flutterbold shouted at Lemuel. "I'm sorry, Lem! I thought it was you!"

The cart was gone, carrying Flutterbold away with along with its nefarious party. Lemuel kicked up a small cloud of dirt in the direction of the departed wagon. "Bolts of Bilious Brimstone!" He jumped up and down a few times for good measure. "May a north wind blow down their backsides!"

I put my hand to my pocket and drew out the bent key. No wonder it had felt strange. It hadn't shrunk. It had been stolen and replaced. I showed the key to Lemuel.

"We've been tricked," I said. "I don't suppose this is worth anything."

"Hang on to it anyway," said Lemuel.

"Lem, I need to get back to Sally's house. I need to call Clive's parents and tell them what's happened. Or try to, anyway."

"Yes. I can walk you back." Lem looked around him. "I know exactly where we are. You light the way, eh?"

I turned up the flame of the lantern. The thing was beginning to feel heavy in my hand, so I switched to the other. "Which way?" I asked Lem, and he pointed back in the direction from which we had come.

"There's a foot path near here that will be easiest for us. Look, I know you're worried about the boy. But, these gnomes, traitors though they may be, they won't harm him. In fact, they're not going to want him around for very long. As soon as he opens a passage with that key, they'll be ready to be rid of him."

"All the same," I said, "I need to do whatever I can."

"Of course," said Lem. "In the meantime, be of good cheer. And keep that light closer to the ground. I need to find that path."

The footpath lay parallel to the dirt road, and closer to the ridge, where the trees met the valley beyond. There was more starlight, and a sliver of white from the quarter moon.

"You must be reeling from all of this," Lemuel said. "Before tonight, did you even know our kind lived here?"

"I didn't know anything," I said. "It doesn't seem real."

"Well, you're young, and human. Can't expect you to have experienced much. The world is stranger than you might have imagined. It's rich and grand. Still, you can't trust everyone."

"I suppose it's the same in my world."

Lemuel stopped and raised his face again, eyes closed. "Did you hear anything?"

"Like what?"

"Like her. The sorceress." He lowered his head again, and quickened his step. He was now moving so quickly, I had some trouble keeping up.

I shouted, "Do you mean Mother Sol-"

"Don't say it!" he said, stopping suddenly. "You could summon her!"

"Just by saying her name?"

"She's had all year to amass her powers. She can move through oceans, through ice and snow. She can disappear into the mist and frost, then reappear solid as you please, in no time."

"Is she dangerous?"

"She's powerful. And temperamental. And when she finds out I had Trimble and then lost him . . . she'll ask, and I'll have to answer."

"Are you sure she'll ask you about Trimble?"

"Of course she'll ask me about Trimble!" Lem burst with a shout. "Trimble is her pet, don't you know anything!?"

"Sorry, no, I don't."

He stopped himself and lowered his voice. "Oh, of course you wouldn't. Sorry." He spun on one heel and began walking off the path. "Let's just say, it's best if she doesn't find us."

"Is Trimble in any danger?"

He didn't answer that one. He just kept walking.

"Where are you going?" I asked. "Is this the way?"

He didn't say a word. I couldn't find my way back without him, so I followed.

Not a quarter of a mile further on, he finally spoke. "I believe I can trust you, Munnie."

"It's Mannie."

"Mannie, of course. And you can trust me, right?"

"I hope you won't mind if I say I'm not so sure."

"Look, if it's about the soup . . ."

"It's not that. I just can't work out who's on what side. That officer fellow, he arrests everyone, and now he's the enemy."

"A two-faced cheat, yes! No doubt he was trying to rein in his opposition by capturing them."

"But why?"

"I can only guess. He must have been corrupted by . . ." He went silent. He frowned as he kept walking.

"By who?" I kept following, but it became clear he wasn't going to answer me.

"Mannie, there's someone I'd like you to meet," he finally said, and he stepped off of the path and into a small clearing, circled by trees.

"Who?"

"As it happens, we're just a couple of steps from my own front door. Would you say hello to my wife and child? I'd like to let them know what's happening."

We stood by the trunk of an evergreen tree, formed of a mass of twisted roots, braided around each other. "Do you see the door?" Lem asked.

"No," I answered.

"Try knocking on it," he said, with a proud smile.

I tapped my knuckles gently against the rough bark. It hurt my knuckles, but I did hear a hollow clack from within. This section of the trunk was not as solid as it looked. Along the ridge of one long strand, I saw a trace of light, very faint. Soon, an oblong section of striated roots opened out, as if on a hinge, and there stood a little woman in a green and white apron. She was lovely, with soft coils of red hair framing her round face.

"Lemuel! How pleased I am to see you home already!"

"Not home to stay, not yet." Lemuel's stepped in, and waved a beckoning hand back at me. I followed him into the trunk of the tree.

"Shut the door behind you," he said, and he hurried into a tunnel-like opening that sloped down from the tiny entryway.

"Please, come in," said the lady forest gnome. I followed her down into a cozy, cave-like room. The floors were rough, unfinished wood, and the roof was dirt and wooden beams. Along one side, wood trim and wallpaper were hung to provide a semblance of hominess. A lantern dangled from a tree root overhead. Opposite was a door covered with a curtain. Another narrow corridor branched off from near the fireplace, currently hosting a modest blaze.

"Sara, this is Mannie," Lem said, presenting me with an open-armed gesture.

Sara gasped at the sight of me, then beamed. "What an honor to meet you, Mannie."

I didn't know if I should extend a hand, so I bowed instead.

"And what a gentleman," Sara said. I could hear a subtle accent in her speech.

"He's been very helpful," Lemuel said. "And discreet."

I looked at the fireplace for a few moments, and as though she had read my thoughts, Sara spoke. "There is a chimney, of course. It carries the smoke to the very top of the tree. You wouldn't see it from the ground. At this time of year, we only burn a few small logs for cooking. We have to stay as well hidden as we can."

"Has no one ever found your front door?" I asked.

"It's almost impossible to see," Lemuel answered. "By daylight, you'd swear it was just wood and moss."

"Lemuel is very clever making such things," Sara said. "Please excuse me for a moment. I'm going to look in on Elvira." She disappeared through a curtain into another chamber.

"Elvira's our little girl. She's not seven months old, and already almost too large for Sara to carry."

Sara reappeared, holding a baby girl in her arms, and indeed, the baby looked to be nearly a third her own size.

"She's growing far too fast! Why, she may one day be as tall as you, Mannie."

"Mannie here is just a boy himself," said Lemuel. "He'll be a lot taller one day."

"You must be at least fifteen years old, Mannie," Sara said.

"Only thirteen," I answered.

"Just a baby, then. Why, I'm more than five times that old."

I tried to do the math in my head, but Lemuel saved me the trouble.

"She's sixty-four."

"Lemuel!" Sara cried, but then she smiled at me. "That's still very young for us forest folk."

"You don't look anything like that old," I said.

Lemuel is seventy-three."

"And I'll probably live to be at least one hundred and fifty."

"Really . . ." I said, astounded to have learned this about both of them. "So, you live a lot longer than . . ."

"Than you humans, yes," said Lem. "But no matter. The time goes too quickly, no matter how much of it you get."

Sara cleared her throat, in a way that reminded me very much of my own mother when she intended to squelch a topic. "May I get you something to eat or drink?"

"Oh, I . . . I am a bit thirsty." In truth, I was feeling ravenous, but I didn't want to say so.

"You're in luck!" Lemuel said with a broad smile. "We've got some freshly brewed holly punch!"

"Lemuel!" Sara gave him a reproachful look. "We can't give him that!"

"Why not?"

"Forgive my husband, dear. He's forgotten that holly is poisonous to humans."

"Oh! Of course. Sorry, my friend. You're not in luck, then."

"Not even in lucky luck," I said, much as Anaru might have. "Thank you anyway."

"I've got a nice herbal tea that you will find refreshing," Sara said.

"I'll fetch it for him," Lemuel offered. He walked briskly to the curtained doorway. As he passed through, I could glimpse a small iron stove and two wooden cupboards.

Sara brought Elvira to my side. "Here, you can hold her," she said, and she handed the infant over to me before I could reply. She quickly followed Lemuel. I hear their exchange from the other side of the curtain.

"What have you got there?" Sara asked.

"Nothing, my dear," Lem replied.

"It's very pretty. So, you must have stolen it."

"Not quite. It was given to me."

"Oh! You don't expect me to believe that!"

It was uncomfortable listening in on such a discussion, but I had no choice. They were standing only feet away, on the other side of a thin cloth.

"Lemuel, this has magic in it!"

"Yes, Sara . . ."

"Powerful magic! Who gave it to you?"

"I'd rather not say . . ."

Then I heard a sound of tin cans rattling around.

"Oh no!' Sara's voice shook with anger. "Stolen gems are one thing, but not this!"

"But Sara!"

"Not in this house! Take it out of here! Now!"

All the while, as they had their spat, I tried to find somewhere to set Elvira down. As yet, I had no experience holding infants, and the baby looked puzzled and unhappy to find my uneasy face looking down at her.

Lemuel reappeared, smiling sheepishly. "I've got a little something for you, Mannie."

"Don't give it to the boy!" Sara shouted as she reentered the room. "Throw it out!"

"But he might like it!"

"It's against our law, Lemuel. Not in this house!"

"What is it?" I asked as I handed Elvira back to Sara. Lemuel presented two tins of soup. I knew the label at once.

"Kramer's Kream of Asparagus Soup?"

"We are not ever to bring human manufactured food into our forests," Sara explained.

"It's a weakness," Lemuel confessed. "I first had it at a tavern in the Lapland forests, and, well . . ." He offered the cans to me. "Perhaps you'd take 'em?"

"No, thank you. I don't much care for it."

"Where did you get them, Lemuel?" demanded Sara.

"I found 'em," Lem answered with a nervous glance my direction.

"You stole them, more likely," Sara said.

"Wait a minute." I narrowed my eyes at Lem. "These are from Sissy's kitchen!"

"That shelf fell by accident. A few items must have landed accidentally in my harvest bag. It wouldn't be the strangest thing that happened tonight, don't you agree?"

"You may not be F.A.B." I said, "But you seem to be a thief."

Lemuel's face fell, and his voice trembled a bit as he spoke. "That I am. It's true. I am deeply sorry, Mannie." Lem backed away from me a step or two. "I've taken something that wasn't mine to take. But, please understand what a severe temptation I faced . . . I mean, soup!"

"You never eat *my* soup," Sara added. "Young man, you must take these cans back to their rightful owner, with our apologies."

"Except you really can't say anything about us."

"Yes, it's best if you don't. So, make the apology anonymous."

Elvira began to fuss, and Sara excused herself, taking the baby into another room by way of the smaller corridor.

"We should be on our way," I said to Lemuel. "My mother and Sissy must be home by now, and I wouldn't be surprised if they already alerted the police."

"I have caused you trouble. Let me just go say a word or two to Sara, and we'll be off."

Lemuel went into the baby's room, and I heard him briefing Sara on the events of the evening, how Trimble was lost, and Lemuel arrested, and then how Drillmast had turned traitor.

"So, you're not really under arrest, then . . ." I heard Sara say.

"Not if Drillmast is a traitor." And they conferred like this for a minute or two, then reentered the room.

"Are you ready to go?" I said to Lemuel.

"Oh, but you haven't had any tea," Sara said.

"I'm really *very* worried about getting home."

"Of course you are. Lemuel, get this young man safely home and hurry back."

And then came a pounding knock at the door, then a muffled shout. "Lemuel! Lemuel, Sara! Please open the door!"

It was the voice of Flutterbold. Lemuel went up the corridor to the entryway and shouted back. "*Winds of the North!*"

"*Spells of the South!*" the voice at the other side called back.

"*If you can't keep a secret . . .*" said Lemuel.

"*Don't open your mouth!*" came Flutterbold's voice. Lemuel opened the door. Flutterbold hurried in, and all but collapsed against the earthen wall.

"Sit down, Mr. Flutterbold," said Sara. "Sit down and relax."

"I got away. I jumped out of the wagon and ran," Flutterbold said, between gasping breaths.

"Can you believe that traitor Drillmast!" said Lemuel.

"I am sorry, Lemuel. As I was listening to the strange magics, for a moment, I thought the traitor was you."

"Ah, yes, well . . ." Lemuel looked uncomfortable.

"You're not, are you?" I said. "I mean, it seems to me you're hiding *some* kind of secret."

"Isn't everyone?" asked Lem.

Flutterbold looked at Lemuel closely. 'You can't possibly be on the side of the F.A.B."

"Indeed I'm not!"

"But the lad is right. Something is out of sorts with you. You're afraid of something."

Sara took Lemuel's hand. "Tell them, please."

"I can't," he said.

"Lemuel made a bargain. It's something he should never have done. But he's saved poor Trimble's life."

"Sara!" Lemuel covered his face with his hands.

"Well, you have!"

"How can this be?" Flutterbold took Lemuel and guided him to a chair. "Come now, you're among friends."

Lemuel looked miserable, slouching on the chair and pulling at his beard with his hands. "I've got to find the passage, old friend. I made a deal with the Grim Frost."

Flutterbold's eyes seemed to grow twice their size in astonishment. "Lemuel, that's worse than joining the F.A.B. That's high treason!"

"I got a promise from him. If I for my hands on a certain treasure, I was told the Grim Frost would spare Trimble's life. But, I've got to get it to him before the F.A.B. gets there."

"What treasure would this be?" I said. Before I could get an answer, a great sound came from outside. It was something like a trumpet blast, but much louder; a minor chord that swelled in volume, and left the ears ringing. Then came a woman's voice, loud and strong. It shouted "Lemuel Greenleaf!"

"Oh, I meant to tell you." Flutterbold smiled weakly. "Mother Solstice has materialized on our island. I believe she is at your door."

Immediately, there was another knock, and Lemuel pushed me into the next chamber. Sara and Flutterbold followed.

"Lemuel, what's wrong with you? This is an honor."

"It's a life sentence in confinement, is what it is!"

The swell of noise came again, this time accompanied by three forceful knocks at the door. "Lemuel Greenleaf. You cannot hide from me!" The voice seemed to penetrate the wood and earth. It seemed to swirl around the room.

Little Elvira began to cry and Sara knelt and moved aside a wood panel on the floor. It exposed a ladder that extended down into a tiny cellar.

"Downstairs, Lemuel. I will talk to Mother Solstice."

"She'll know," said Lem.

"I can handle her."

Lemuel lowered himself down the ladder. He motioned for me to follow. Sara took a candle lantern from the nearby wall and handed it down.

"Be careful," she said. We heard another hammering strike at the door. "I'd better go!" Sara nervously motioned to Flutterbold, and he began his descent into the cellar as well.

Then I heard Lemuel gasp. "Sara! What is this!?" The faint light of his candle lamp had revealed a secret. Three chocolate bars lay on a small wooden bench, still in their wrappers, bearing the very human trademark of Chidley Chocolates.

Sara gave a little shrug and a guilty laugh. "All right, so I've got my weaknesses too." She quickly lowered the wooden panel, leaving Lem, Flutterbold and myself trapped in near darkness in a damp, earthy pit.

Chapter Nine
At the Tavern

As the little wooden door closed above us, I heard again that strange musical chord, but this time, it sounded as though it was coming from within the confines of the Greenleaf house. An edge of bright white light bled through the edges of the cellar door just as Sara shut it.

"She's already in the house," Lemuel whispered.

"You mean, that's Mother Sols . . ."

"Don't say it, boy!' whispered Lemuel sharply. "You don't understand her powers!"

"What's the use? She must know we're here anyway," Flutterbold asserted. The sound of kicking at the wooden door above us seemed to confirm this.

"Lem, there's someone here to see you," we heard Sara call out.

"I'll be right there, my dear, just a minute or two," Lemuel shouted.

"You'd better come now," Sara said, her voice muffled through the door. "She's asking for you."

"See?" Lem whispered to me. "My wife couldn't keep a secret from her for ten seconds. No one can. Now, you two, you should go."

Lemuel grabbed my left hand and placed something in it, then closed his hand around mine. "Take this!"

"I don't even know what it is!"

"Don't worry about that, just take it." With that, he held his lamp aloft and pulled me along after him to the other side of the little cellar. He pointed to a cellar door overhead. "That will take you back outside," he said. "Just get under it and push up. Head for home, and don't show anyone what I just gave you. I'll be back for it later."

I crouched beneath the cellar door, then stood, arms above my head, to open it.

"How will you find me . . ."

"No time to discuss. Very nice to meet you, Mannie." Lem gave a move-along gesture.

I climbed out the door and back out into the forest. Flutterbold followed after. He threw shut the cellar door and then beckoned me to run.

"I can barely see," I said. My lantern was still inside, in the den of the Greenleaf household.

"Let your eyes adjust, then," the gnome said. "What did Lemuel give you?"

I hadn't looked yet. I knew it was metal, attached to a small chain. I opened my hand. In the darkness, I couldn't see it very well. It was a medallion, with a gemstone set in its center. I told Flutterbold.

"Is the stone blue?" he asked. It was. Icy blue. It caught a glint of moonlight.

"An outrage!" Flutterbold bellowed. "It belongs to Trimble. How did he come to possess that!"

"He had Trimble, out by Sissy's house."

"Of course! So, that's why he wanted that post! He wasn't trying to protect Trimble. He just wanted to steal the medallion. Tell me, young man. When you first saw Trimble, was he wearing that broach? You would have seen it on his forehead."

"No. I've never seen it until now."

I heard noise from the tree nearby. Lights began to dance on the other side of it. I could hear voices.

"It's time for us to go," said Flutterbold. "Lem is facing the consequences of his choice. You and I must seek the advice of the council. Come on!"

I followed Flutterbold into another clearing among the trees. He stopped to catch his breath. "I can't run far, not like I used to do." He sat on the ground. "Give me a moment, lad. I need to take stock."

He sat and stared up at the sky for a while. The non-stop cycle of wild noises filled the air. Behind the calls of crickets and cicadas, I thought I heard the faint hum of machinery.

"Must be troubling for you, getting tangled in this business."

"I don't even understand it," I said.

"How could you? Until now, I didn't grasp it myself. The Grim Frost. It's got to everyone. Drillmast. Lemuel. That poor brute in the black cape. I'll wager each one of them made a deal with the Frost. I bet they all had a promise from him that Trimble would come to no harm." Flutterbold struggled back to his feet. "There is only one thing left to do. I've got to find the council and report on this."

"What about this medallion?"

"Keep it to yourself for now. The Grim Frost can't show up here, not on this island. But his agents seem to be everywhere. And that gem is what he wants most, or I'm a kettle of mulled molasses."

"What if I give it back to the lady? To Mother Solstice?"

"I wouldn't advise it. She's at the height of her power. Her touch might destroy it."

"Is she good?"

"Hmm?"

"Mother Solstice. Is she good or is she evil?"

"She's powerful," said Flutterbold. "And good. Terribly good. I'm not ready to have a conversation with her just yet. Not now. Follow me. Let's go to the council."

"Where are they?"

"Where any sensible council would be. The Tavern!"

Flutterbold tugged at my sleeve and began to run.

"Slow down," I said. "I don't have a light to see by."

But Flutterbold just kept running. He made plenty of noise, so I followed as best I could.

Ahead, the forest rose onto a slope, and in our way stood a great, gnarled oak tree. I could hear music coming from within it, and along one or two ridges, just above eye level, I saw a warm yellow glow coming from inside. There was noise, muffled, like the sound of gears turning and steam hissing. These were the machine-like sounds I had heard in the clearing.

"Here is the tavern, lad. Hidden away in this mighty tree, undiscovered for centuries."

"It's a little conspicuous, actually," I said. "If I came walking along here, I think I'd notice it."

"You're gaining an eye for the strange magics. That's rare. It'll probably wear off as you get older." He kicked twice at the base of the tree, and then shouted, "*Seven Boughs of Holly!*"

A voice came from within. "*Seven Draughts of Beer!*"

"*Seven Secret Wishes.*"

"*Never Spoken Here!*" And the door opened, seemingly by itself.

I had to duck to get through the short and narrow opening in the trunk of the tree. Inside was a comfortable candle-lit room. Seven beer barrels were arranged behind a long wooden bar. Each had a bough of holly perched above the tap. Above each tap was painted a name in red letters, Wish Number One, Wish Number Two, all the way through Wish Number Seven. At the far right of the barrels hung a painting, as tall as one of these little men. It depicted a reindeer, and riding on its back, a discreetly naked Lady Godiva, crowned with holly and holding aloft a mug of beer. Nearby, seven tables were scattered near the fireplace.

A little man stood behind the bar, helping himself to a tin mug of Wish Number Three. He smiled at me, and I saw that, unlike any of the gnomes I had met so far, he had pointed ears. So did his two companions, sitting at a nearby table.

When Flutterbold came in behind me, I heard him gasp and utter a word so foreign I cannot now recall it. "I am sorry, young friend. I have led you into a trap."

"Close the door behind you," said the one behind the bar. "It *is* a trap. But an agreeable one. Have some holly beer!"

"No, Wheatbrew. I'm on duty," said Flutterbold.

"Suit yourself. We're on duty as well but that ain't going to stop us," said the barkeep. His long-curled moustache wiggled as he laughed. "Who's your friend?"

"I'm Mannie Candler," I said, as politely as if I were addressing the archbishop.

"The name is Wheatbrew. Care for a mug of Number Five? Holly Lager."

"None for me, thanks," I said. If holly punch would be poisonous, holly beer would surely be worse.

Wheatbrew whistled at his two companions, and they stood up from their chairs. They wore identical leafy garments that looked like military uniforms.

"I want you to meet my battalion," said Wheatbrew.

The other two gave a kind of salute, their hands flittering to their brows, then fluttering back down. "Branchstaff, second in command," said one, and the other followed with, "Copper, *second* second in command."

Wheatbrew concluded, "I'm number one, of course. Chief Commander of the Forest Abduction Brigade!"

"You're the F.A.B." I said in disbelief.

"And you're invited to join us," said Wheatbrew.

I turned to Flutterbold. "Did you know that . . .

"That they would be here? No, but it doesn't surprise me. They've always been underhanded, duplicitous . . ."

"You flatter us with your great big words, Flutterbold." Wheatbrew raised his rusted mug. "We're all impressed. Aren't we boys?"

Branchstaff and Copper raised their own holly beers and shouted in unison, "All hail Flutterbold!"

"*Und* here's to big words," Copper shouted out in a gravelly high-pitched voice, with an accent so pronounced, 'words' sounded like '*virds.*'

"Big words *und* a big stomach," said Branchstaff.

The F.A.B. are from Switzerland, I thought. Lemuel had mentioned before I could have known what he was talking about.

Flutterbold cleared his throat. "I will have you all know that Mother Solstice is only yards away, in the home of Lemuel Greenleaf."

"Poor Lemuel," said Copper.

"He'll be incarcerated for sure," added Wheatbrew.

"*Ja.* Incarcerated and put in jail for the season!" shouted Branchstaff. "All hail Lemuel!"

"And all hail to the jail!" added Copper. He and Branchstaff tipped their heads back in unison and quaffed the remainder of their holly beers.

"My point is, her ladyship is likely to stop here next."

"And she's welcome to my very best Number Four." Wheatbrew tapped the wooden keg proudly.

"I don't think she'll be so keen on holly beer. She will demand to know where you have taken her dear pet."

"Dear pet! Zat is a good one," shouted Branchstaff.

Copper joined in. "*Ja!* Her pet is a deer. Dear pet! All hail Flutterbold, the jester!"

Wheatbrew walked around from behind the counter and approached me. "What's the matter with you, boy? Don't you like Flutterbold's joke?"

"I don't care about that! *I* want to know where Clive is!" I surprised myself with the force of my reply. It startled all four denizens of the tavern.

"Clive?" Wheatbrew said. "I don't know any Clive."

"Is Clive your pet reindeer?" said Copper.

"Clive is another human child," Flutterbold said. He pulled up a chair at the closest table, then sat down with a sigh.

"Now that you mention it, there was a human child here just a while ago," said Branchstaff.

"Very recently," added Copper. "Didn't care much for him, if you want to know the truth."

"Very rude," added Branchstaff.

"That was Clive," I said.

"Hmm. I've got some good news, then." Wheatbrew began a slow saunter back to the bar as he spoke. "And I've got some bad news to go with it."

"Careful," said Flutterbold. "He's going to speak in riddles."

"Fine," I said, not in the mood for games, but resigned to this one. "What is the good news?"

"The good news is that your Clive is safe and sound, and probably still in Trimble's company."

"All right, what is the bad news?"

"The bad news is, they're both so far away, you have no hope of catching up with them."

"How far away could they be?"

"Have you ever been to New Zealand?" Copper chirped.

"Of course I have. We're in New Zealand now."

"Well, Trimble and your silly little friend aren't," said Wheatbrew, and all three of the F.A.B. laughed.

"Aren't in New Zealand? That's absurd."

"It certainly is," said Copper, nodding. "But it's true."

"If it isn't so, my name isn't Branchstaff," said the other. "*Und* my name *is* Branchstaff, so there's your proof!"

"Though, actually, when he is at home, his name is *Zweigstock*!" Copper laughed, then added, "*Und* I am really called *Kupfer*. But when we are in this forest, we speak the language of the locals."

I sat down next to Flutterbold. "This is making my head hurt."

"These elves have that effect on all of us."

"Not elves! Root folk," said Wheatbrew.

I sighed and then said, "If they aren't in New Zealand, where are they?"

"In another forest," Wheatbrew said airily, as he drew a mug of Wish Number One. "I don't know which."

"If your friend chose the West door, he is in a rainforest in Brazil," said Branchstaff.

"If your friend chose the East door, he is on a mountain in Bhutan," said Copper.

"If he chose either of those, he's among friends, and Trimble is safe," said Wheatbrew.

"But if he chose the other door," said Copper.

"As we instructed him to," said Branchstaff.

"Yes, if he followed our instructions . . ." added Copper in turn.

"And we doubt it, because he doesn't seem the type that follows instructions . . ."

"Then he has gone north," said the two of them together. "*Very North.*"

"*Und* he is probably *very* sorry," added Copper.

I noticed a grave look on Flutterbold's face. "This is worse than I thought. You had better brace yourself, lad. Our mission has already failed."

"And it's a good thing, too!" said Wheatbrew. "You may not realize it, but we're a force for good. You should join us in our victory celebration. We've delivered Trimble to our master, and all is well."

"I don't understand," I said to Flutterbold.

Copper and Branchstaff came over to our table and sat down with us.

"That is because we haven't explained it."

"Your friend Clodhopper," said Branchstaff.

"Clive," I said, though I did like the alternative he had just proposed.

"Well, however you say it, he had a key."

"A key with the mark of VN."

"That wasn't his," I said. "It was more properly mine, or really, I think it was meant for his sister."

"Irrelevant detail," said Wheatbrew. "The thing is, only someone with a key like that can get anywhere close to Very North."

"And we really wanted Trimble to get there,"

"As quickly as possible," said Copper.

"So, we told Cloppy to take Trimble through the North door."

"But we don't know if he did."

"News travels fast, but not quite that fast."

"We'll know inside of the hour."

Flutterbold put a hand on my shoulder. "It's our greatest secret, young man. The forest passages. With the right key, we can cross oceans and continents in a matter of moments. These ancient tunnels can link us to other tunnels in other forests throughout the world."

"But you have to know where to look."

"*Und* you have to have a key!"

"And those are hard to come by," said Wheatbrew. "We led your friend to the Crossway Passage. We let him make up his own mind."

"If only *we* had a key, we could try to follow," said Flutterbold.

"But we have a . . ." I began to say, but Flutterbold cut me off.

"*If* we had a key. But we don't." I understood at once that the key in my pocket, bent though it might be, was best kept secret.

"If what you say is true, what will happen to Clive?"

Wheatbrew whistled casually, then smiled. "Honestly, there's no reason to fret."

"None *vhat*-soever." Copper made a carefree hand-waving gesture.

"*Vhat's* done is done!" Branchstaff brushed his hands off against each other in a "job finished" motion.

"I'm sure he will be back in a month or two," said Wheatbrew.

"Until then, it will be a treat for his family, *ja*?"

Flutterbold stood. "Don't you care about Trimble? Have you thought what could happen if he's captured?"

"It's beyond our control now. We'll get word soon, if . . ." and Wheatbrew gave a small chuckle.

"You laugh at the thought of Trimble lying dead. Is that the sort of elf you are?" Flutterbold was turning red.

"I hate that word. We are root-folk."

"You're criminals," Flutterbold cried. "And you are aiding our common enemy in the destruction of that innocent animal."

"We aren't *aiding* the enemy. We are *appeasing* him. And you should be glad we are."

I began to understand what had been at stake for poor Trimble all along. "Are they saying Trimble is going to be sacrificed?"

"To an unholy monster, yes," said Flutterbold.

"That's awful!" I turned and looked at Copper and Branchstaff, who were smiling as merrily as if I had just recited a funny limerick. "How can you smile?"

"It's our job."

"Merriment, it's what we root-folk are known for."

"It's all very well to be merry, but killing an animal for a sacrifice . . ." I could feel indignation rising to the surface and taking over. "You mean to make merry over that?!"

"We do and we will! And if you knew our reasons . . ." said Wheatbrew.

"I don't give a damn about your reasons!"

Flutterbold took my shoulder and drew me aside. "All right, young man. I salute your strength of feeling, but it's prudent not to let it govern you."

"The boy needs a drink," Wheatbrew said. "I have a harmless crabapple cider. It's sour. Perfect for him."

"Are all human children zo impolite?" asked Copper.

"Wait!" said Branchstaff. He lifted his nose and sniffed the air. "I smell something." He moved closer to me. "Human child, I smell the faintest whiff of strange magics. Are you hiding something?"

I didn't answer, which proved answer enough.

"What is it?" said Wheatbrew, running over from the bar counter to our table. "Did you steal something?"

I looked at Flutterbold, hoping for some guidance. He shook his head in resignation and said, "Go ahead and show them what you have in your pocket."

I had two objects, of course, a bent key, and a medallion. I took out the key and set it on the table. All three elves burst into raucous laughter.

"How in the seven realms did you manage to do that?!" Wheatbrew said, and he followed with a bellowing guffaw. "Did you walk the Moss Circle while reciting the Tin Bird's Lament?"

"Oh, it's precious!" said Copper. Branchstaff echoed this. "*Ja,* precious *und* pathetic!"

Suddenly, Wheatbrew shouted, "Wait!" He froze in place. "He's got something else. He's got something . . . rather powerful." Wheatbrew's look hardened as he stared at me. "Empty your pockets, boy."

Flutterbold looked frightened, but he nodded. "Go ahead. Let them see."

Standing by the little table, I reached into my left pocket first. I turned it inside out. It contained nothing but a bit of lint. From the right pocket, I brought out a folded slip of paper and set it in front of Wheatbrew. He unfolded it and read the slip out loud.

"*This is bonkers!*" He frowned. "What is that supposed to mean?"

"It's nothing," I said. I then held open my hand and showed the stolen treasure. It was the first time I got a good look at the medallion myself. It was a small bronze cross, encircled with metallic scrollwork. The four equal arms were joined at the center by a bright blue gem, round with seven facets.

"Sacred Sunflowers!" said Wheatbrew. "That's Trimble's medallion."

"Oooooh!" Copper's eyes went wide. "I didn't know you were such a master thief, boy!"

"*I* didn't steal it,' I said.

"You must have done! Trimble didn't just give it to you." Wheatbrew appeared to be awed by the gem. The other elves were staring at it with comparable wonder.

"If there are any takers, I'll gladly give it to you," I said.

"No, Mannie! Don't let them have it!" Flutterbold placed his hand over mine to cover the little prize.

"We wouldn't dream of touching it," said Wheatbrew.

"*Nein!* We may be criminals, but if her ladyship found us with that? There would be no mercy!"

"But I don't want it!" I shouted.

As if responding to my outcry, the musical blast came again, like the trumpets of a pipe organ. White light bled through the cracks of the knotted opening to the tavern.

"The lady is here," said Flutterbold, as he let go of my hand. "She will arrest us all."

"Best get to the brewery," said Wheatbrew, and he cocked his head back to the picture frame. "She'll arrest you, for certain. We've got alibis. Air tight."

Flutterbold stepped to the portrait. "Come along, Mannie. There will be a right time to face her ladyship. Now is not that time." He stood in front of the lascivious painting and scanned it. "There must be a switch somewhere," he said.

"Press on the pretty lady's mug of beer," Wheatbrew said, and then he motioned me toward the portrait. I pocketed the medallion and joined Flutterbold.

The old gnome had to jump up to reach the mug in the painting. He slapped his hand against it. The portrait swung forward on hidden hinges. Flutterbold and I stepped into the passage behind it. As he pulled it closed, the tavern was flooded with light, and the musical chord, beautiful and frightening, sounded louder than I had yet heard it. My hands went to my ears. I caught a last glimpse of the F.A.B. turning their heads to the tavern entrance and holding their arms up to their eyes against the bright light.

Once the portrait doorway was closed, we turned around and groped our way in darkness, until Flutterbold struck a match. In the glow, he found a tiny candle lantern and lit it.

The passage went down into the roots of the tree, and into a room at least as large as the tavern above. Five metal vats were arrayed in a circle, and on one wall, a row of wooden barrels. Each vat had its own distilling machine, with steam-powered pistons that chugged and gears that turned to stir the vats. This had to be the source of the mechanical noises I had heard outside.

"The distillery! Of course. It's the perfect hiding place." Flutterbold was highly excited.

"If we must hide,' I said, "it better not be for long."

"I don't mean a hiding place for us! I mean, this is where they've been hiding the Crossway Passage! We found it!"

Flutterbold lit three more lanterns that hung along the walls opposite. Each wall had a painted inscription: East Door, West Door, and opposite to where I stood, the letters VN. Beneath each inscription was a keyhole.

I noticed that the noises of blasting chord and chatter had died away from the chamber above us.

"Is Mother Solstice gone?" I asked.

"I believe so. And I'll bet everyone else is, too. She wouldn't have had to ask. When she possesses full power, she is persuasive. She can take a prisoner without a word."

"So if we had stayed up there . . ."

"We would have followed her as well. Against our own will. She is a powerful sorceress. And good! Good, but . . ."

"Frightening?"

"Powerful."

I looked at the door marked VN. "The key, the good one that Clive took from me. It would have opened that door, right?"

"It would have opened any of them. I just hope that, if Trimble came this way, he went through either the West door or the East door. Though Very North is Trimble's first home, he is not safe there. Not tonight."

I looked at the floor, and saw hoof prints pressed into the dirt. "Trimble's been here, all right" I said.

Flutterbold held the candle lantern closer to the ground and followed the tracks. They led straight to the VN door at the north end of the room.

It was a picture of a door painted as a fresco against the smooth north wall. A fissure in the rock was surrounded with a depiction of a keyhole. The opening was large enough to accommodate a key much larger than the bent specimen in my pocket.

"I don't know if it will work," said Flutterbold, "but you could try the key. It's imperfect, but it did come from the Moss Circle."

"You want me to go through?" I asked.

"You need to find your friend. While he could have gone through any door, I feel sure he chose this one.

"And Trimble went with him?"

"Oh yes." Flutterbold's expression spoke the dread that his words did not.

"Is Clive in danger?"

"I don't know. More likely in trouble than in danger, but . . ."

"I should go to him," I said. "Unless you . . ."

"The key is Kris's magic. You walked the circle. I did not. Only you can go through that door. So, will you?"

"I guess I have to." I stood for a few moments, and thought my way through it. "Can I get back?"

"Some way or another, but it won't be this passage."

"Where will it take me? Where, really?"

"North. Very North. I can't be more specific than that."

I fetched the key from out my pocket, and the bronze cross on its chain came out along with it.

"What about this medallion? It's trouble, I bet. I don't want it."

"Return it to Trimble, if you can."

"And if I can't?"

"Then be on guard. The Grim Frost will be looking for it."

There were so many things to be uncertain about. I had more questions than I could count. Was I really about to go willingly into an underground passage, on behalf of strangers? Could all these gnomes and elves truly be real? Or was this an elaborate trap? Perhaps I was about to be kidnapped, by way of the most fanciful conspiracy. That was troubling, too. But when it came down to it, I had to follow Clive.

"My mother, can you tell her where I am? Can you tell her I'm safe?"

"She can't see or hear me."

"But you could leave her word. You could write something down."

"Yes."

"Let her know that I've gone to find Clive. I'll contact her the first instant I can."

"Sensible lad," he said. "All right. There is no time. Try the key."

I pushed the key into the hole, about halfway, and then something unseen grabbed it away. It vanished through the hole, as if under its own power. Then the wall opened just a tiny bit, at it's left end. There was barely enough room for someone my size to squeeze through.

Flutterbold handed me the candle lantern. "You'll need this," he said. "One day, if our fortune is good, we may meet again. You'll have a tale to tell. I'll be interested to hear it."

He stepped back and waited as I wriggled my way through the opening. On the other side, all was dark. Flutterbold leaned against the wall on his end and pushed the rocky panel shut. I could still hear the machines of the distillery clanking and hissing. I could smell the wet, earthy scent of the underground tunnel. My tiny light flickered in its iron cage. I took a breath and turned around to find out where this adventure was taking me.

Chapter Ten

The Passage to Very North

The other side of that wall held no handle or latch. I pressed back against it and felt only cold stone. If I had second thoughts about going further on this journey, it now seemed clear there was no going back.

The cave narrowed and hooked to the left. Around that bend, I found a second keyhole. Brass hooks hung on the wall on either side of it. On the left hook was the bent key. On the right hook hung a jacket, lined with fur. A note was pinned to the collar.

WEAR THIS—YOU WILL NEED IT.

I took the coat down off of the hook and tried it on. It was too small for me, forcing my arms and shoulders into an awkward shrug. Whoever had provided it must surely have been expecting a gnome or root-dweller, not a thirteen year-old human. I took off the coat and hung it over my left arm. With my right hand, I put the key into the keyhole, and once again, it was pulled from my grasp. It vanished just as before. With a rumble the wall opened, this time inward. Again, barely enough to allow me access. I wondered if the unbent key would have opened a wider doorway. It must have done, if Trimble had passed through. A draft of cold air rushed from the new opening. Not just cold, but frigid. I put the coat back on. I felt very silly, just as I no doubt looked.

I squirmed into the new passage, almost burning my sleeve with the candlelight as I did so. Once I had got all the way through, the wall closed itself, and I was trapped in a dark, misty corridor. It was bitter cold. I pushed against the wall. It was heavy, fixed and unmoving. With no way to turn back, I faced the chill. It settled on my skin and instantly burrowed deeper, making my teeth clench.

The haze of icy mist put an aura around the lantern's glow. The warm, clear skies I had left behind in Christchurch must surely lie just two doorways back. Yet I knew I must be somewhere else, someplace impossibly distant. I could literally feel it in my bones. My shaking, shivering bones.

The aggressive cold energized my steps. I noticed a dozen points of light around me. Other lanterns, I thought, but it was only the light of my own lantern, reflecting off of mirrors stuck along the walls on both sides of the tunnel. Each was framed in rough, unfinished wood, hung with twine on wooden pegs. The reflections amplified the light, and I could see well enough to turn my quick steps into a near run, until I reached the other end of the long, twisting passage, and yet another keyhole. On a small, crooked table next to the wall was set the now-familiar bent key, and a pair of boots with another note: *YOU WILL NEED THESE TOO.*

The boots were too large. I could slip my feet, shoes and all, into and out of them. I wouldn't be able to walk so much as drag and lumber along in these. I thought it might make more sense to simply carry them until they were really needed. It took both hands to lift them, leaving me no way to carry the lantern. So, I slid my shod feet into the hulking things yet again, picked up the lantern, slid the key into the hole, watched it vanish, and stood back as this third wall opened.

The stone wall swung my direction, a little further this time. A gust of wind carried a flurry of snow through the new opening. There was enough leeway to allow me to step through without wriggling. Once I was past it, the wall shut tight. Now it was just a rocky ledge, jutting from the ground, surrounded by snow. I turned around and faced an unfamiliar world, dark, and cloaked in terrible weather.

The wind pressed firmly into my uncovered face. I stepped, or schlepped, into it, pulling the jacket up over the top of my head. The wind sang a slow, eerie harmony in the air. Beautiful if it weren't for the accompanying sting of cold.

A drift of snow lay just beyond, and there were tracks, deep enough that the wind had not yet erased them. I could not see beyond a few yards. I detected the shadows of trees not far off. In the flickering spotlight of my lantern, I saw that the tracks traced the steps of a hooved animal and a young child. Trimble and Clive, it must have been. I kept my head down and followed these tracks.

I stood by the branches of a snow-covered evergreen where the tracks divided. Trimble's went off to the left, and Clive's led around to the other side of the tree. I followed Clive's trail, and to my dismay, saw that it vanished, as if he had been caught up into the air.

There were shouts in the distance. I turned my body away from the wind, and saw a morphing orange glow from the other side of a dark rise in the ground. It looked as though at least three electric torches had been switched on in the distance, and their lights were moving and scurrying, making beams in the dark. I heard the voices of men hollering through the breeze, in a language I didn't recognize.

Suddenly, between the torch lights and the place I was standing, an enormous shadow came into view. It looked like a giant wearing the antlers of a reindeer on its head. The shadow passed quickly by, and I heard a brutish roar. A chill went through my already cold frame.

Another shadow came into view, outlined by the beams of light in the haze. It was a reindeer. The torches projected its shadow against the snowy air, so that it loomed over me. It just about had to be Trimble. I wanted to shout out for its attention, but nothing came from my mouth.

Suddenly, the deer bucked up on its hind legs. I heard it make a terrible noise. The deer's shadow fell and rolled, and I saw, too clearly, the shaft of an arrow protruding from its side. Men's voices called out in triumph. I saw the dark forms of two more arrows sail through the air and land with horrible accuracy in the deer's neck and haunches. Then I turned away. If it was Trimble, I was too late to save him.

I was not alone. Someone stood just behind me. He cast an imposing shadow. I gasped as the man spoke.

"Don't be afraid," he shouted. Then he leaned closer and said in a low voice, deep and calm, "I hope you didn't see what just happened."

I nodded my head.

"Such an awful turn of events." He stood straight again and raised his voice to be heard above the melodic howl of wind. "Follow me! You need the warmth of a fire."

He wore a thick coat of dark brown fur, trimmed with fur colored a light beige. The coat tapered to a fur-trimmed hood. He also wore a thick leather belt and heavy boots. I tried to see his face, but he turned away and started to walk. I moved awkwardly after him, only a step or two. Then I found myself stuck. The boots had buried themselves as I tried to move ahead.

"Wait," I said, and he turned back around.

"Try to lift your feet as high as you can. You get stuck if you drag them. We only need to get a few more yards," he said and he pointed into the darkness. "You'll be safe and warm in a moment."

I finally had a look at his face. He had gentle blue eyes, and a white beard. Above his brow, but beneath his hood, he wore a crown of entwined holly branches.

"Father Christmas?" I said. He didn't answer, but turned and kept walking.

Soon enough, we arrived at a small cottage, almost completely buried in drifts of snow. A lantern hung by its large wooden door. The roof and all beyond it were in shadow, or lost in the grey rush of wind and fine fragments of ice. My host pushed open the door and hurried me through. As soon as I walked into the warm interior, I shivered. The shudder ran along my spine and through my entire body. I had never been so cold, even if for just a short while.

"Into the den, young man," he said. He took the tiny, ludicrous coat off of my shoulders, and asked me to step out of the gargantuan boots. These he picked up and carried as he showed me into a cozy room. There were three large, cushioned chairs. A fire burned in a stone fireplace, and the hearth above it was decorated with a crèche.

"I'm happy you arrived safely. And I'm glad I went outside when I did. You could have caught your death of cold," the imposing man said. He lifted the coat in his right hand and looked at it. "Oh dear, is this the coat they left for you?"

"It was hanging on a peg . . ." I began, but found myself unable to say more.

"And those boots. Really, who could they possibly have been expecting? Someone with tiny shoulders and enormous feet."

I was still shivering, though the room was very warm. The flannel pyjama shirt was wet, as were my half-bare legs.

"I'll have warm drink and dry clothes brought to you at once. Please take a seat by the fire. I must go back outside, but I'll return soon."

I sat in the chair nearest to the fire. The bearded man in the great coat disappeared down a hallway. I heard him say a few words to someone. He reappeared not a minute later. He gave me a smile, warm but weary, and a nod. Then he opened the front door and was gone back into the freezing darkness.

A gnome with a long nose, topped with wire-rimmed glasses, appeared from the hallway pushing a teacart. He wheeled it to me, and gave a bow.

"I don't know who you are, but a friend of my master is a friend of mine."

"Where am I?" I asked.

"You are at a scouting post just a short distance from Very North. My name is Clement, and I am posted here until New Year's Day. This is usually a quiet post, but there seems to be an awful lot happening tonight."

"What country is this?" I said.

"Country? I guess I don't know. I'm no good at keeping track of human borders. If it helps, you are at the edge of a forest we gnomes call the Ice Crown."

"It's . . . cold all the time?"

"Oh yes. This close to Very North, it's always cold."

"I've seen snow on the south island before, but I've never been in anything like this." It felt like my thoughts were coming out disconnected and dull. I was overwhelmed, and more than a little frightened. "I'm not sure I should be here."

"But you are here, and once you get to Very North, you'll like it." He poured some tea and set it on a small table beside my chair. "We're almost out of biscuits. I confess, I ate most of them myself. But there are these two left, if you want them."

"Sure," I said.

"They are crisp and taste of ginger cake. I do hope we will get more soon." He turned away and scuttered down the hall. "Don't go away," he said as he went.

The prospect of an evening meal had first been raised when I got to Sissy's house, and that now seemed like a very long time ago. Since then, I had not eaten anything. The ginger and spices of the biscuits tasted better than any sweet I ever remembered having. I devoured the two baked treats, and they were rich and filling. The tea warmed my throat. The sensation of hot liquid running into my body was soothing. I wanted to drop off to sleep in that chair. Yet I wondered if I could possibly go to sleep. Surely, I was already doing so, and dreaming. Then, there was the troubled part of my mind, the one telling me that I had just seen an animal slain, an animal that must have been Trimble.

Clement reappeared with a stack of clothes. "I don't know how well these might fit, but they're warm and dry, so, please try them on. I'll go back to my quarters, and you can change. You'll be on your way again in a short while."

The clothes fit well. There was a pair of trousers, a dark pine green in colour, and a white undershirt. A red wool pullover, graced with a knitted image of a reindeer, completed the ensemble. As soon as I put them on, I was very glad to have them.

Once changed, I took a minute to look around the room. Several pictures hung on the wall opposite the fireplace. One depicted the face of a priest, surrounded by a wreath. Another looked like a portrait, drawn long ago, of a young girl, surrounded by a heart-shaped bough of holly.

Presently, the front door opened. I felt the rush of cold air, and heard the insistent moaning of the wind. The tall man had returned. I heard him stomp his boots in the entryway, and soon he was in my presence.

"I hope you're feeling more comfortable, and relaxed," he said as he reentered the room.

"Yes, sir."

"You may call me Kris." He removed his coat and hood and hung them on a hook. The crown of holly stayed atop his partially bald head, above his bright silver-white hair.

"Are you Father Christmas?" I said.

He lifted his head and glanced at me sideways. "At just this moment, not quite. But, in a little while, yes. By all means, yes."

"So, does Kris mean you're Kris Kringle?"

"Sometimes. I have a lot of names. I like Kris." He strolled to the chair I had been sitting in, and took his place there. Then he looked back at me. "You aren't still feeling a chill, I hope."

"No sir, . . . Kris," I said. "I'm . . . happy to meet you."

"Likewise, but you have me at a disadvantage. I still don't know who you are."

"Oh! I'm Mannie."

"It's a great privilege to meet you, Mannie."

"Mannie Candler."

"Superb. Please, have a seat." He gestured toward a smaller wooden chair. "Mannie Candler. I usually know who my guests are going to be ahead of time, but I am always happy to receive surprise visitors."

"You were expecting Olivia, right?"

"She is one candidate I was especially eager to meet. Apparently, her invitation was usurped."

"Have you met her brother Clive, then?"

"I have seen him, briefly."

"Is he . . ."

"Safe? I hope so. My agents took him into custody."

"Sounds as though he's in trouble."

"That will depend a great deal on Her Ladyship."

"Am I in trouble?"

Kris gave me a quizzical look. "Is there some reason you should be?

I didn't say anything. I thought about the little trinket I had carried with me. When changing, I had transferred it into the pocket of these new pants. All I knew about it was that it had been stolen from Trimble, and was reputedly filled with potent magic.

"If I can put you at ease, young man. You look troubled."

I almost told him about the medallion, but changed my mind as quickly. I was sure he could read the racing of mixed emotions on my face.

"You have no experience of the strange magics. I was the same way, once. They flow through the earth, and connect distant shores to one another. I have learned to detect the shifts in the magical tides. The forest people and the root-folk, they are far better attuned to that stream. But now, we have business to attend to, some of it joyous, some of it sad."

"Yes." My voice shook a little. Kris's presence was at once reassuring and intimidating.

"This world must seem very different from the one you woke up in this morning."

"Very."

"We are close to the world you know, but only barely a part of it. Tell me, Mannie, do you daydream a great deal?"

"Yes." I smiled. "Everyone who knows me can tell you that."

"It's a common trait among those humans who can see the fair folk."

"Lemuel told me, um . . . Do you know Lemuel?"

"I am well acquainted with that rascal, yes."

"He told me that once I'm older, I won't see such things anymore."

"That's probably true. You must be twelve?"

"Thirteen."

"It's unusual for boys your age to see us any longer. But not unheard of." He leaned closer to me. "I was once a boy much like you, a human child, and prone to fanciful dreams. I stumbled into this world much as you have done. But that was a long time ago. I am very old, much older than I look." He glanced down at the empty biscuit plate and shook his head. "That's the last of those," he said. "Did you enjoy the biscuits?"

"Yes, very much."

"They are made by a forest gnome in the Bavarian woods. He has customers around the world, and he permits only two dozen biscuits each year per customer. No exceptions, not even for me. You've had the last of them, so I am glad to hear that they gave satisfaction."

"I'm sorry if I had yours," I said.

He stood and moved closer to the fireplace.

"Tonight, you have found yourself in the middle of an operation, led by me. The aim was to secure the safety of a reindeer named Trimble. That operation has failed. Trimble has been shot and killed."

I said nothing, but lowered my head. The news came as no surprise, but hearing Kris say it so bluntly made my heart sink.

"This is a sorrow," he continued, "but there was always some risk that it would come to this."

"I saw it happen, just before you found me."

"It was a terrible sight. I'm sorry you had to endure it."

"Who shot him?"

"Hunters in the service of a powerful sorcerer. Have you heard of the Grim Frost?"

"Yes, sir." I couldn't stop myself from addressing him that way. "They talked about him in the forest."

"He is a magician, feared by many. He demands loyalties from his subjects, and he expects frequent gifts. If these are not delivered, he is able to cause a great deal of misery."

Kris walked to the hallway and motioned me over. He drew a book off of a small shelf and opened it, then handed it to me. It featured a woodcut illustration of a giant creature with a goblin-like face emerging from an ice cave. A whirlwind of frost issued forth from its bellowing mouth.

"This is a depiction of the Grim Frost, etched by an explorer from the Scoresby Expedition to the Polar Sea."

"Is this accurate?"

"It is a little drastic, but this is how many think of him."

"Is he your enemy?"

"We are at odds with one another, but without him, I would have died long ago. I am dependent on his powers. I disapprove of the way in which he wields them. I do not think of him as an enemy. I think of him as a prisoner."

"Is Trimble . . ."

"His sacrifice, yes."

"That's horrible."

"Trimble's life was his demand, and he had many agents in place to make sure it happened. I had my own agents. I did my best to prevent it. Well, I tried to do my best."

"I'm sorry."

"Oh, please don't blame yourself. You weren't an agent."

"But I had Trimble, for a moment. In a garage."

"There is no need to explain. We have much to accomplish. There are other children here, you know. They arrived by very different means. By invitation."

"Candidates? Like Olivia?"

"Yes, that's right. Each one of them carried messages or helped the effort in some way. They have no idea what has happened here at this outpost. They are, most of them, hoping to meet Trimble. That would seem to be impossible now, yes?"

"Yes," I said, and my voice shook.

He leaned in close. "May I trust you?" But as soon as he came within a few inches of me, he closed his eyes in a wince, and tilted his head slightly, as if he had sensed something. "What have you got with you? You're holding something, a powerful object."

"It's a medallion," I said. I dug it out of my pocket. "Lemuel gave it to me."

Kris's face grew stern. "Has anyone else held it?"

"Flutterbold put his hand on it, for a moment." I said.

"It belongs to Trimble!" he shouted. "This could have protected him!" He stepped away angrily and crossed to the fireplace. For a few terrible moments, he looked into the flames. I wanted to disappear. I felt my throat clutch.

"I never wanted it," I said. Kris heard the emotion in my voice. He turned.

"I'm sorry, Mannie. This isn't your fault. You couldn't have known."

I extended the medallion by the chain. "Will you take it?" I asked.

"I don't dare," he answered. "In my hands, the Grim Frost will find it too quickly. It's probably safer with you."

"But then, am I safe?"

"Not here. Very North must be your fortress. I will take you there immediately."

Clement entered the room. He held a fur coat. "This belonged to a forest tracker named Lastbear. He was a giant among gnomes. So, it might fit you." I tried it on, and the coat fit perfectly around my frame. The sleeves were slightly too short. It didn't matter. It was a vast improvement over the coat I had recently tried to wear.

Kris led me back out the door of the outpost and into the snowy cold. A sled now stood nearby. It was carved of wood, similar in its ornaments to the wagon that had brought Drillmast into our presence back at the dirt road. Two reindeer were harnessed to it, and I saw, with instant grief, that another reindeer lay in the back. It was the body of Trimble, unmistakable from the VN on its head. The arrows had not been removed from his body, but they had been broken off. I couldn't look for long.

"What a terrible thing," Kris said, almost shouting to be heard over the sound of wailing wind. He placed his gloved hand on my shoulder for a moment. "Take this end, will you?" He handed me one side of a green tarp, and together, we threw it over Trimble's body. I stood by for a moment as Kris secured it.

"Try not to dwell on this," he said. "You carry a powerful charm. It might change everything. Remember I said it looked impossible that my candidates might meet Trimble?"

I nodded, while stamping my feet to ward off the cold creeping into my toes.

"I now think it might be possible. Not easy, but possible."

Then he turned and walked over to the bench of the great sleigh. "Get on board, and keep your head down. The wind is picking up."

I walked around the front of the sled and climbed up next to Kris. "It will be dark and very cold, but where I'm taking you is not far. Banner and Lina know the way. I hardly have to guide them. Keep your head down. Shield your eyes. You don't want them to freeze."

Clement was standing by the two deer. He slapped the flanks of Banner, the deer on the left, and both began to move into the darkness.

The wind picked up in intensity almost as soon as we took off. I huddled and kept my head down against it, though once or twice I peeked over at Kris, and saw that he too had trouble looking into the snow and ice rushing at us. The oncoming flurry of tiny white flakes against the blackness looked like a tunnel of shooting stars. I couldn't glance into it for more than an instant, and then I buried my face again. I put my gloved hands against my ears, as the cold made my lobes ache.

The trip took only a few moments, and then Kris brought the sleigh to a halt. "Stay put," he instructed. "Keep your eyes closed." I waited as he dropped down to the ground, his boots making a soft thump against the snow. He walked around to my side, took me by the shoulder, and guided me into a sheltered opening. It looked like the entrance to a tunnel, with walls of rock and ice.

"I've got to go another way," Kris said. "This path will take you to Very North and I will meet you there soon enough." He handed me a lantern, opened it, and then struck a match against the side of the sleigh. He lit the candle within, and closed the glass door. "The passage is safe, and you won't have to contend with this wind any longer."

I lifted the light to the tunnel ahead. It sparkled with blue and white.

"Mannie, a word before I go. You will soon meet the young candidates. I need you to keep Trimble's fate a secret. Can you do that?"

"Yes," I said. "If anyone asks . . ."

"You simply don't know. And the secret treasure you carry. Don't mention that either."

"I won't. I promise."

"One last thing," he said, and he looked at me with a smile that was both weary and consoling. "Try to be of good cheer. Cultivate merriment, and share it with the others. I place my confidence in you." He stepped onto the sleigh and took the reins. In no time, it disappeared into the darkness, and the noisy rush of wind.

The ground inside the tunnel was solid, of hard earth with no ice or snow. I no longer wore the ridiculous boots, but my own shoes seemed thin and inadequate to the chill. I held the candle up, and saw before me an etching in the wall. It was a labyrinth, carved into the stone. It looked to be a perfect match to that of the Moss Circle. Just to the right of it, there was a rough-hewn doorway. The instant I stepped into it, a soft glow began to emanate from the ground. Patches of ice along the sides caught a soft illumination that seemed to spread like the gentlest of fires. Blue light pulsed behind sheets of ice. My way was being lit, as if by fireflies beneath the surface of the frozen path. The trail curved away, and I knew I would be walking the same pattern I had already traversed in a warm field not so long ago.

A few steps in, I saw one word etched along the right hand wall. *The*

A few more steps along, a second word. *worthy*

Then another few steps. *snows*

It's the verse, I thought. I'd best read it out loud. I backtracked to the beginning, and called each word out as I practically raced through the labyrinth. The verse was not entirely the same.

> *The worthy snows of Very North*
> *Protect this ancient hidden place*
> *If you but banish cares henceforth*
> *The magics here will thee embrace*

By the time I reached the last word, I was in the final, concentric spirals of the labyrinth. At its center, I found steps, rising at a gentle slope, to a doorway above. It was open. As I stopped to catch my breath, a face appeared from behind it.

"Hello! Welcome to Very North," said a man with a pointed black beard. "You must be Mr. Candle Wax."

Chapter Eleven

The Chapel and the Den of Friendship

The man had called me Candle Wax, so that told me one thing. "Clive must be here," I called to the man at the top of the steps.

"Yes, very much so." He spoke energetically.

"He calls me Candle Wax, but it's not my name," I said.

"That's fine. Please, ascend, and we'll make introductions."

I stepped up. At the top of the rise was an arched doorway, crowned by the VN symbol, within the outline of a stone tower. The man reached out and pulled me up the last couple of steps.

He was a little taller than me, slight of build, and his dark beard and moustache came to three sharp points. He wore an apron, decorated with symbols. Some I recognized at once, astrological signs, while others looked like they could be masonic. Others were simply odd; a laughing squirrel, a dancing fireman, a fish wearing a baker's toque.

"It's quite an apron, indeed. I would need a couple of hours to explain its designs." The man smiled. "My name is Martin Piper. Kris will be here, but I don't know how soon. In the meantime, will you follow me?" He bowed.

I returned the bow. "Thank you sir. My name is Mannie. Mannie Candler."

"I've been expecting you, Mannie. Though I didn't know your proper name. Your young friend is here. He's taking notes on all of us."

"He does that," I said, and I felt great relief at knowing this familiar nuisance was nearby. "Has he been any trouble?"

"He joined forces with the F.A.B. For that, I fear there may be consequences. Not severe, mind you. I will take you to him soon.

But first, let me to show you around our home at Very North." His gregarious attitude put me very much at ease.

We stepped through the arched portal, and up three steps. Martin led me down a hallway, along which were doors of differing heights. Some were as small as a few inches, others as tall as eight feet, and many increments in between. Martin smiled as he reached a door exactly his own height and knocked at it. The door opened by itself, and he stepped through, but put out a hand to bar my own entry.

"Find the door closest to your own size, and then knock." he said. His own door closed. It took me no time to find a door my own height, and I knocked. It swung open, and Martin stood on the other side. He waved me in.

"Quickly. If it closes, you won't get a second chance."

On the other side was a second hallway, running parallel to the first. "You had to come in by the proper door," said Martin, "and I through my own. It seems silly, but it would break an important spell to go through the wrong one. I hope you understand."

I nodded and followed Martin as he walked down the corridor to another arched wooden door at the end.

"You've got to remove your hat before entering here. You aren't wearing a hat, which means I've got to give you one."

Martin turned to a side table on which were scattered three or four hats, all of them pointed and bearing bells or feathers. The largest of them was tiny on my head, but Martin propped it there for a moment. He prompted me with a nod, and I removed the hat. Martin respectfully doffed his own, and the door opened.

Through the door was an exquisite little chapel, lined with stained glass windows, three on each side east and west. A rosette hung above the entrance door, and another larger one at the opposite end. Gothic arches were set within rough granite stone walls. A dim orange glow flickered through the windows. There was just enough illumination to make the stained glass images visible.

Martin began a slow walk down the center aisle. There were no pews, but five rows of small wooden chairs faced the front of the chapel. Before the altar, an elaborate crèche had been arranged.

"There isn't much sunlight this season, so we make do with lanterns, placed just outside each window," Martin said. "I wish you could see them in their full splendor."

I followed him and took a good look at the glass. In one window was a man dressed in Roman robes, riding a chariot. Below him was another, floating on a rough-hewn barge, wearing rags that made him look like John the Baptist, but for the holly branches in his hair.

"Each of these is in some way a predecessor of Father Christmas. Along the left, you may spot Ded Moroz, the Russian ice spirit. And there is Tomte the goat-rider," he said. Each was shown giving alms to the poor or leaving gifts in secret. On the right, I recognized Saint Nicholas. Next to him was a monk in Buddhist robes, offering a bag of gold to a poor widow. Martin said this was the compassionate Bodhisattva.

The next glass depicted a small man with horns, holding a bag of money and thumbing his nose at a plump, furious man in a waistcoat.

"Here is Hans Heilig-Teufel the trickster."

"He doesn't look quite so generous as the others," I said.

"Some of his pranks were merry, some of them were cruel. His name means "holy devil." According to legend, his targets got what they deserved. Here, he steals from someone who got his wealth by dishonest means."

I pointed to a glass showing a woman with a white horse, giving shoes and clothes to two children. "Who is the she?"

"She is Berchde, the companion of Woden. She was a healer, a caretaker for the poor and the sick. She stands beside Sliepnir, the horse. Children once left oat cakes outside for him. They hoped to attract Berchde's blessings."

"Are they all related?" I asked.

"It's said that each had an ability to see the invisible folk. As such, they were chosen, each in their own time, to reign over a very small portion of the strange magics of the world."

"Like here, at Very North."

"Yes. This place is one focus of those powers. Here, Father Christmas is sovereign, here and nowhere else. And only for a few months out of each year."

"So Lem was right, this really isn't the North Pole."

"No. We are very north, but we aren't *that* north."

"So, is Kris, is he . . ."

"Santa Claus? No. At least, he may easily be mistaken for that fanciful figure. But if such a gentleman exists, darting down chimneys and flying with reindeer, well, that is not Kris." It was clear from Martin's attitude that he didn't think there was any such man.

"And this chapel . . ."

"It's a sacred place. Each year, Father Christmas dedicates himself to a singular purpose."

"What purpose is that?"

"Don't you know?"

I shook my head once slowly.

"His purpose is joy, the rare, precious merriment of hope. Each year, he is granted the power to enrich the lives of a few fortunate souls. And they in turn are given the power to touch a few other lives with it."

"So, the candidates . . ."

"Yes. They are the lucky few. Soon they will celebrate the secret feast in our halls."

"Not me, though," I said. Martin gave me a curious look. "I mean, I wasn't invited. I'm here by chance."

"Perhaps," said Martin. "Very lucky chance. Do you play piano?"

It was an unexpected turn of topic, but I was ready with an answer. "Yes. A little. I'm not as good as I'd like to be."

Martin smiled and said, "Wonderful, though. I have a task for you. If you don't mind."

"Not at all," I said. Martin went to the corner behind the crèche, to the left of the altar, and pulled a grey cloth off of a small piano.

"Can you read music?" he asked.

"Yes. Slowly."

"Slowly will do just fine. Here, see if this bench will support your weight."

I sat down at the little keyboard. Martin went to a nearby box and began shuffling through sheets of music. "Ah! This one is perfect!" He brought the sheet and set it before me. "Can you figure out this song?"

I looked at it. The tune was simple, and the chords few. "Yes, this looks pretty easy."

"Good. You must teach it to one of our young candidates. And *he* is to sing it for Father Christmas. I was asked to teach him myself, but my schedule . . . let's just say it's a busy day. I am delighted to hand this task over to you."

"All right,' I said, without much certainty.

Martin turned for the door. "Your student will be here in a few minutes. Give it some practice until then."

Now I was alone, in this quaintly gorgeous chapel. A decent chill still gripped the air, and my fingers moved stiffly across the keys as I slowly plunked out the melody written on the sheet in front of me.

The Magpie's Christmas
A folk song for the season

The piece was simple, and I soon had the tune worked out. I read the words. They were ridiculous.

> *I have a little magpie*
> *I don't know what to do*
> *She tells me that this Christmas Day*
> *Has left her feeling blue*
> *Oh, speak, Magpie, what has made you blue?*

> *(and the magpie said)*

> *You brought me Christmas pudding*
> *To bless the holiday*
> *But just before I took a bite*
> *The pudding ran away*
> *Oh, who made my pudding run away?*

I had never heard this Christmas song before. I couldn't imagine it would be very popular. I continued to read.

> *You sang me Christmas carols*
> *You chose my favorite song*
> *But when I tried to join the tune*
> *The words came out all wrong*
> *Oh, who made my Christmas songs all wrong?*

> *You filled my Christmas stocking*
> *With candied fruit so sweet*
> *But when I tried to take a bite*

It smelled like stinky feet
Oh, who made my sweets smell just like feet?

I couldn't help but laugh. Had Martin really meant to choose this song for Father Christmas? I plucked out the accompaniment as I examined the final verse. The whole arrangement was easy to play.

Then in came Father Christmas
And said, oh magpie dear
These tricks I played were just a bit
Of merry Christmas cheer
I'll give you all my puddings
We'll sing the songs you know
There's lots of sweets, and we can take
A sleigh ride in the snow
Oh, what a cheery Christmas, Ho Ho Ho

Presently, I heard a knock at the chapel door. A muffled voice shouted Hallo. It was a young boy. I got up and went to the door, but couldn't open it.

He knocked again, and I remembered how I had first entered the chapel.

"Are you wearing a hat?" I shouted through the door.

"Yes," came the reply.

"Take off your hat," I yelled, and a moment later, the door opened. A boy with red hair and abundant freckles stood without.

"I forgot about the hat," he said. "Sorry."

"It's all right. Come on in. My name is Mannie."

"I'm Gordon," the boy said, and he hurried over to the piano. "Gordon Gibney. Are you going to help me with this song?" he said, looking impatient to get started.

"Yes. You're to sing it for Father Christmas."

"I know that," he said, with a tone. I returned to the piano bench, and Gordon hopped up beside me.

"Is this a real piano?" he said. "It's too small. I've got a much bigger piano at home. I'm supposed to be learning how to play it. But I never practice. Do you?"

"Not as often as I'm supposed to," I admitted. "Here, have a look at this. It's called The Magpie's Christmas. Have you ever heard of it?"

"No. I told the man I already know Away In A Manger. But he said no, it's got to be The Magpie's Christmas. Is this a real church? It's too small."

"It's a chapel. They're often small."

"We hardly ever go to church, but when we do, it's much bigger than this. I have a cat who's pretty big." Gordon wiggled nearly as much as he talked, which is to say, an awful lot.

"Do you want me to play the tune for you?"

"Yeah, you better. It's cold in here."

"Yes. I noticed. All right, here goes. I'll sing the first verse for you."

I have a little magpie
I don't know what to do
She tells me that this Christmas Day
Has left her feeling blue

"Is this supposed to be a sad song?" Gordon asked.

"I don't think so. It's meant to be funny."

"What's so funny about a sad bird?"

"Just wait for the next bit. You sing the first verse, and then, before you go on, you speak this phrase out loud. 'and the magpie said."

"Why?"

"So everyone will understand that the second verse is being sung by the magpie."

"Did you write this?"

"No," I answered. "Here, listen to the second verse." I sang it, ending at the line about the pudding running away. Gordon stared at me with his mouth open. "Do you want to try it?" I asked.

"Is that really how it goes? The pudding ran away?"

"That's what it says."

"Let me look at that." He swiped the sheet music off of the stand. He held it close and read the words for himself. "This is awful."

"I'm afraid I agree with you. But, we'd best learn it, right?"

I played the tune again for him, and pointed out that the same melody repeated each verse. "You only need to learn this one tune, and then read off the words from each new verse. Let's try the next one."

After a few attempts to change the subject, Gordon finally agreed to sing. He managed to carry the tune all right for a kid his age. It wasn't much of a tune to carry. He got to the line about the songs coming out all wrong, and he giggled.

"This song sure came out all wrong," he said and snickered some more.

"So, you think it's funny after all?" I said.

"I think it's stupid!" he replied. He was seized by a fit of giggling so acute, he almost fell off the bench.

"Are you all right?" I asked him.

"I'm just trying to picture it," he said and then burst into another round of laughter. "Imagine hearing the choir sing this . . . in church!" And then a blasting chortle that hurt my ear a bit. Gordon stood up and began running down the aisle in fits.

"Gordon, you've got to get control of yourself. We'll never get through this."

"What did you say your name is again?" he asked, through his wide, wild grin.

"Mannie."

Another spasm of screeching laughter. "Mannie! That's a good one!"

"It's just a name."

"Right, but it's funny. You're a boy called Mannie! See?"

"No." And that answer struck him just as hilarious as everything else.

"Okay, let's *try* to sing through it," I said, and I struck up the piano again. "Just sing the next verse."

Once he had calmed down, he began the fourth verse.

> *You filled my Christmas stocking*
> *With candied fruit so sweet*
> *But when I tried to take a bite*
> *It smelled like stinky feet . . .*

Of course, Gordon collapsed into a helpless heap once he got to the end of that fourth line. I stopped playing and waited patiently for the storm to pass. It began to seem as though it never would.

The door opened, and Martin stepped through.

"Is he all right?"

"It's this song. It's . . . too much for him."

"Will he be ready to perform it?"

I looked at Gordon, who was too far gone to even notice that Martin was there. "I don't think he'll *ever* be ready to sing this one," I said. "But he knows it all right."

"Well, there's no more time. Come along, both of you. We've got so much to do."

I took Gordon's hand and led him to the chapel door, then through it.

Martin gave a stern look to the boy. "Young man, this giggling must stop. We can't move on until you calm yourself."

Gordon looked at Martin, with his feathered hat and pointed beard, and then turned away, giggling some more.

Martin gave him a severe look. "What is it, young man?"

"You're name is Martin," the boy said. "Like a magpie! Martin! See?"

"They're both birds," I said. "He's so giddy, simply everything will set him off."

"I see," said Martin. "Well, we do want merriment, I suppose." He flashed a brief smile at Gordon and said, "Well done, lad." His face immediately returned to a worried frown. "I hope he'll be all right," he said quietly.

He led us to another hallway, this one narrow, with only two doors at the end of it.

The door to the left was carved with a relief representation of a small palace partly covered in snow. A banner flew from its turrets—VN.

"We are about to enter the main chambers of the fortress. I will take you first to the Den of Friendship. There you will meet the other candidates."

"I've already been there," said Gordon. "I ate three biscuits. The fireplace is awfully nice. Do you have a fireplace? We don't." Gordon continued to chatter. Martin gave me a look of bemusement. I shrugged my shoulders in sympathy.

"Anyway, welcome," he said. He pushed a latch and opened the door.

The den was cozy and inviting. The fireplace was at the center of a round room, and there were soft chairs, blankets and cushions set about it. Four other children were lounging or crawling near the central pit.

A Yule log extended from the fireplace, one end burning in a heap of coal and ash, the other end propped up on a metal stand. Red ribbons were tied to that end, along with sprigs of mistletoe and holly.

"Here's Gordon," shouted a small boy, through a mouthful of cake. A girl almost my age sat next to him, and quickly admonished him not to shout with his mouth full.

Another girl with black hair, cut in bangs over her green eyes, ran straight to Gordon. "Did you learn the song?"

Gordon laughed and then gave me a short punch in the arm. "Ask my music teacher about that!"

"Are you a musician?" the girl asked, having just noticed me at all.

"I can play a little."

"Tell her about the song," Gordon said, and he began giggling again.

"The song is very silly, it turns out."

"Very silly! That's not the half of it. It's the stupidest song ever written!"

The other two had come to meet us. I decided that introductions would be helpful.

"My name is Mannie. I'm not a candidate. I sort of stumbled into all of this."

"I'm Samantha," said the dark-haired girl. "How do you do." She gave an impassive curtsy.

"You're not from New Zealand, are you," I said, noticing she had an accent that didn't sound Kiwi.

"I'm from Atlantic City, in America."

"Oh! That's nice," I said.

"I'm from Auckland," Gordon added. This is the coldest place I've ever been."

"It's the coldest place anyone's ever been, except maybe the North Pole," Samantha said, and she took Gordon by the hand and whisked him away. "So tell me more about your song." He seemed surprised, but one look at Samantha made it clear that a crush had taken hold of her.

The other girl, about eleven years old, spoke next. "Hullo. I'm Tabitha Boyd." She smiled, revealing braces. She nodded toward a younger boy standing by her side. Both had long, dirty-blond hair, and wore clothes made of bleached sackcloth, cheap though finely sewn. "This is my brother Jeremy. He's five. I don't think he knows what's going on."

"I don't think I do, either," I said.

"It is something, isn't it?" said Tabitha. "I've never even dreamed anything like this."

Her younger brother tugged at her skirt. "When are we going to meet Trimble?"

"I don't know. I think we're supposed to eat first."

"I've already eaten cake."

"We're going to have a proper dinner soon," Tabitha said, as much to me as to her brother.

"Where is Trimble!" young Jeremy demanded. "You said we could see Trimble!" He said this to me, despite the fact I couldn't have told him any such thing.

"Jeremy, be polite. We've never met this boy before." She smiled at me, but kept her gaze down, not quite meeting my eyes. "I'm sorry. He's anxious."

"I would be too. This doesn't happen every day."

"Or ever," Tabitha said. "So, do you know what comes next?"

"I don't know anything at all."

She sat down on a cushioned chair not far from the ribboned end of the Yule log. "It's been quite a night, hasn't it, Jeremy?" she asked her brother. He fidgeted his way up onto her lap.

"I'd like to see Trimble soon."

"Aren't you excited to meet Father Christmas?" she asked.

"He's very nice," I said. "Kris, I mean, but I think Kris is . . ."

". . . is Father Christmas! Yes, everybody knows that." Samantha gave me a look. "You sound as though you've met him."

"I have met him. Trimble, too." I stopped short. "You know, I do think I was supposed to keep that secret."

"Where is Trimble!" Jeremy shouted.

"If you've seen Trimble and Father Christmas," Tabitha said, "you must be important."

"No. It just happened that way, I guess."

"Then you're the luckiest person I've ever known. When did you see Trimble?"

"I'm not supposed to . . ."

"I know, not supposed to tell," Tabitha finished for me.

"How did you two get here?" I asked.

"That's a secret, too," she said, and smiled.

"Of course," I said. And we sat near the fire without saying much else.

A woman with elfin ears entered the den and waved to us. "Hello. Candidates, please." She glanced at a hand-written note and then announced, "I need to see Jeremy Boyd and Gordon Gibney."

"Who is that?" Jeremy asked his sister, pointing to this newcomer.

"My name is Della," the woman said. "I have something very nice for you. New clothes to wear. They will keep you warm, and make you feel cheerful. There are knitted sweaters and hats for you candidates."

Della first took the two boys to an adjacent room, and returned with them a few minutes later. They came back decked in the most brightly colored garments I had ever seen. Everything was candy-striped or decorated with reindeer, snowflakes, evergreen trees and Christmas star designs. Jeremy was grinning, but Gordon wore his disdain on his glowering face.

Samantha shrieked and ran to him. "Gordon, it's adorable!" Her approval didn't change his expression much.

Della then announced that it was time for the girls to get their new clothes. She referred again to her list. "Now, I will see Tabitha Boyd, Samantha Krupp and Olivia Murney." She looked around for three girls, and found only two.

"Olivia won't be here," I said. "Her little brother took her place."

"Are you sure?" Della looked at her note. "I don't see any mention of it here." She stared at the paper, as if waiting for an update to materialize there.

"I'm certain," I said. "But I don't know where Clive is."

"And who are you?" Della said. "If you don't mind my asking." As soon as I answered, she squinted at her list again.

"I won't be on your list," I said. "I'm an unexpected guest."

"Oh! I didn't know we had those. I haven't got anything for you."

"That's all right. Clement gave me these I'm wearing."

"Clement, eh? No one tells me anything." She took the two girls away while shaking her head.

Martin arrived and praised the newly clad candidates. "Who could fail to be merry in such fine apparel, eh?"

Della conferred with him about the discrepancies between her own list and the actual arrivals. "There's no Olivia Murney," she said, "and what am I supposed to do with this boy?"

"Leave all that to me," Martin told her, and then turned to the children. "When Father Christmas arrives, we will greet him with singing and dance. If you candidates would follow me to the Great Hall, we will teach you a quadrille that Kris especially likes."

As he led the group out into a long corridor, I approached Martin and asked him, "Should I follow? I'm not a candidate."

"Indeed, Mr. Candler. There is someone *else* in the hall waiting to speak with you." He didn't sound especially cheerful saying it.

The narrow corridors gave way to a broader hallway. Here, the real splendor of the palace showed itself. The walls were hung with gorgeous tapestries. Tall candles burned in golden sconces. Wrought iron chandeliers hung above the promenade. It was as richly arrayed as any royal castle, but the atmosphere was welcoming, not formal or forbidding. We followed a long red carpet, embroidered with green and gold. We reached a bay with three doorways side by side, marked by elegant gothic arches. These doors stood wide open, and we could see into the Great Hall.

Stepping into the ballroom, the young candidates gave voice to their delight with cries of 'oh look!' and clapping of hands. They hollered 'Hallo' into the vast space to hear their words bounced about the giant room. I'm pretty sure I gasped a bit myself. After so many narrow passages and split corridors, walking into the Great Hall was like leaving a shuttered cabin and emerging onto the open plains.

The floors were polished wood of differing types, inlaid into elegant patterns. The surface of it shone, and reflected the lights of the crystal chandeliers overhead. Three men in gray frocks lit candles and lanterns. A small contingent in aprons were setting trays along two banquet tables. Long mirrors hung on the walls to the east and west of the hall, so that the whole room looked even longer than it was. Along the southern wall, tall windows looked out onto a snowy yard below, but the outside landscape lay mostly in darkness. The low howl of wind could still be heard in this bright and gladdening chamber.

By the east wall stood a table on which rested an elaborately sculpted model of a snowbound castle. Martin gathered everyone around it.

"This is a sculpted depiction of Very North," he said. "In another season, you might ski or sled along the snowy banks and look back at our palace. This is what you would see."

The candidates seemed impressed. Gordon reached a hand out and stroked it against one of the thick stone towers. "Is it all right if I touch it?" he asked as he did so.

"Carefully, yes. Now, everyone look at these windows. You presently stand in the Great Hall, here, at this end of the palace. If you look inside, you will see an exquisite miniature of this very ballroom." One by one, the candidates looked into the model.

"This fortress is very old, but the Great Hall is most recent. Kris had it built some forty years ago. The windows are gothic in style, while much of the original structure is practically medieval. You are free to wander this end of the palace as you will. The towers are not safe."

"Are we to live here?" asked Gordon. "I lived with my Grannie once for a while. She used to be a teacher. My granny hasn't got much hair."

"You're gibbering," Samantha told him.

"Oh, I know! I always do that! Last year, we went to Weka Pass. I told everyone I saw a Moa bird, but I didn't really . . ."

Martin cleared his throat. "No, Master Gibney. You won't be living here. You are simply guests for the evening. Honored guests."

Next Martin pointed to the miniature yard just outside of the model's Great Hall. "See on this model, there are seven lanterns just outside." He turned to the three tall windows that looked out into the dark sunless terrain. "They are just beyond these panes of glass. The lanterns are dark right now. We must light them. We can't do it by going out into the cold with a match. The seven lanterns must be ignited by our own merry-making."

Martin clapped his hands, and Della entered the hall pushing a gramophone, with a rose-colored bell and silver turntable, on a wheeled cabinet. "All right, candidates!" Martin called out. "Della is going to instruct you all in the dance. Please give her your full attention and cooperation. We'll light that yard so that Kris can find his way, all right?"

Della gathered the children into the center of the long dance floor. I knew I was not a candidate, and so I made no move to join and learn the dance. Instead, I went to Martin Piper. I wondered what he meant when he said that someone in the hall was waiting to speak to me. He anticipated my question, and pointed me to the west wall.

A mirrored panel opened out and two men stepped in from a hidden hallway. They were fair-haired and muscular. Both wore bright blue jackets, with tightly knit patterns of red, green and yellow about the sleeves and collar. Each wore a tall hat, woven of the same jagged tri-colored patterns.

"These are the men I mentioned to you. They are caretakers for the reindeer," said Martin. "And they have asked to speak to you."

Martin and I went across the room to meet them. "Andras, Ariast, this is Mannie Candler. Mannie, these men are Sami deer herders, and longtime friends of Very North."

"How do you do," I said. Neither responded. Their blue-gray eyes conveyed no pleasure in making my acquaintance.

"It's true," the first said to Martin. "We felt it ever since he arrived. It practically sings around him."

Martin looked at me closely. "Mannie, are you carrying something? Perhaps a medallion?"

I nodded.

"You had best follow us," said the second herder, Ariast. I followed the three of them through the mirrored panel. On the other side, a narrow staircase spiraled up to a hidden floor. The four of us huddled at the foot of it. Martin stepped up one step, bringing himself nearly up to the height of the two men.

"Andras and Ariast have a keen sense for certain magics,' Martin said. "Especially those involving Trimble."

"Yes," I said. "I have Trimble's medallion." I produced it and showed it to them.

"It's a crime even to hold that without permission," said Andras.

"Kris knows I have it," I said. "He told me to keep it. Ask him. He'll tell you."

"If only we could ask," said Ariast. "Kris' two reindeer, Banner and Lina, just arrived minutes ago. They appeared at the stable drawing an empty sleigh."

"No driver," said Andras. "And no Kris."

Chapter Twelve
A Gilded Gaol

"What did Kris say to you?" Martin asked urgently.

"He said he'd meet me here," I answered. "Was Trimble . . . on the sleigh?"

"No," said Ariast. "Should he have been?"

"Kris loaded his body there."

All three of the men were silent. The eyes of Andras and Ariast might as well have been razors, so cutting were the looks on their faces.

"I thought I felt it," said Andras. "Then Trimble is . . ."

"Is dead, yes . . ." I said. "I saw it happen."

The two Sami men conferred with each other in their own language, then talked to Martin.

"He's got to be arrested!" they told him. "We will need a full statement. What does he know? How did he get that medallion?"

"Lemuel stole it,' I said. "Do any of you know Lemuel Greenleaf?" The other three exchanged meaningful looks.

"That, at least, I can believe," said Andras.

"All the same, Martin, we've got to follow protocols." Ariast jerked his head toward the stairs, and the floor above. "Take him into custody. At least until we know what's happened to Kris."

Martin faced me solemnly. "I don't have the authority to place you under arrest. All the same, until Kris arrives, I am responsible for this place. There are holding cells at the next landing. I ask that you remain in one of them, voluntarily, until such time as I can make inquiries."

"Won't one of you just take this medallion?" I said. "I don't want it. I never wanted it."

"We can't," said Andras. "She would curse us."

"Mother Solstice, you mean?" I said.

"You seem to know an awful lot, for an *accidental* visitor," said Ariast. I suddenly felt like an enemy.

Martin proceeded up the winding steps, and I went along. Andras and Ariast followed after, with grim expressions.

At the next floor, we walked a dark hallway. Black iron lanterns hung from primitive sconces on both sides. Martin stopped at a door with a golden plate, on which was etched Cell Number Six. Beneath this was a lock, and Martin removed a key from his own long coat.

As soon as the door opened, I felt a waft of chilled air. The cell was a spare stone room, with bare floors and no windows. A tiny pot-bellied stove sat in the corner, by a wooden bench, alongside a cot so short, I could tell that my legs would hang off the end of it if I tried to lie down. A small door, sized for gnomes, was installed on the right hand wall.

"I will see to a fire for the stove," said Martin. "In the meantime, please wait patiently. Oh, and if you wish to visit Cell Number Seven, that door leads right to it. That's assuming the prisoner in Seven hasn't locked it from his side." He gestured toward it with his head, as if making certain that I had heard about it.

Martin and the two Sami herders backed away without another word, and the cell door shut. I heard the sound of tumblers rolling and locking into place.

I have heard people speak of a sense of unreality, even in mundane everyday pursuits. Who hasn't occasionally been overcome by that strange feeling that whoever one is, and whatever one is doing, it is so very odd, once you think about all the other people you could be. When you find yourself in a snowbound palace, imprisoned in a cold room, worrying about the disappearance of Father Christmas, that unreal feeling is, I can report, highly intensified.

The cell was as miserable as my own mood. My sense of guilt, that I had somehow earned this punishment, made war with a new stirring of anger. I had gone from guest to prisoner so quickly, with so little sympathetic inquiry. There was no place to sit down, not comfortably. No fire, no food. How long would I be kept here?

It didn't take me long to decide I'd better investigate Cell Number Seven. I knocked on the small door. I didn't hear any response, but I pushed against it, and it swung open. I crawled through.

Number Seven was a sumptuous suite. There was a corner fireplace, complete with kettle and chestnut roaster. A modest Christmas tree sat nearby, alongside a grand table and a writing desk, with tall chairs, upholstered at the seat in rich red. The place was furnished with a plush day bed, accompanied by two dressers, and a sideboard stacked with tea service, biscuits, cakes and tiny sandwiches. In the opposite corner, I saw a game table with chessboard and two chairs. Darts, skittles and other amusements were dotted about the place.

At the large table sat Clive Murney, scribbling away in his notebook, using a quill and ink. He paused long enough to give me a glance, then lowered his head and continued to write, now very quickly.

"Hello, Clive. It's a relief to see you."

"Just a minute, Candlewax. I've got to finish this." He wrote for another few moments, then set the quill down. He blew across the page and blotted it, then turned his attention to me.

"Are you here to get me out, Candlewax?" His voice was quiet.

"No, Clive, and please call me Mannie."

"All right. Why are you here?" He was almost whispering.

"I'm in the next cell over. Thanks to Lemuel."

"We're prisoners," said Clive. It was troubling to hear him speak without his usual insolent tone.

"Have you seen my cell?" I asked him. "It's nothing like this one."

"I don't deserve this." Clive turned to another page. It was the last leaf in his little book.

"What did they put you here for?" I said.

"You know very well. I stole Olivia's letter, and I took her place."

"So, you've got to stay here? With all this? It's not much of a punishment."

"I know!" he said, and I saw that his eyes were tearing. "I deserve so much worse."

He put his head down on the table, and I went to him, and put a hand on his shoulder. He was shaking. "Clive, please don't . . ." I started, but then his arms were around me, and his head was on my shoulder. I had never seen him cry before. I had scarcely seen any emotion but his usual smug self-satisfaction. That and the brief, beatific expression he wore as he sang in the cathedral last Sunday.

"I ruined everything, and look how they treat me . . ." he said at last.

"Then, they can't be *too* upset with you, right?"

Clive let go, and sat back in his chair. His nose was running pretty freely. I grabbed a napkin from the nearby table and handed it to him. He turned away from me and took a few moments to compose himself. As affected as I was by this show of honest remorse, I was still secretly amused by the loud, musical honking sound he made as he blew his nose.

"Are you all right, Clive?"

"Sorry about that, old man," he said quietly. I had to take a swipe at my own eyes, now dewy at the corners.

"Think nothing of it," I said.

"I think something terrible has happened." He looked at me again. "To Trimble, I mean."

I nodded. "He was shot. Kris said they were agents of someone called the Grim Frost. And now, Kris is gone."

We talked for a while. I persuaded Clive to eat a few bites of cake. This made him feel better. We each recounted our own stories of how we ended up at Very North.

"I wanted that key, the good one," Clive admitted. "When I saw Drillmast had snitched it, I thought he'd be more fun to follow. I really thought it was all just a game."

He had been persuaded that bringing Trimble to Very North was the safest route, but the F.A.B. knew it was a trap from the Grim Frost. I was glad to learn that Clive had not seen the shooting. He had been found by Andras, and brought to Very North, before that occurred.

I told him my story, and Clive laughed a little when I described how the bent key had opened the rock doorways only a fraction.

"They were all wide open for me," he said. "I guess it really should have been you going through."

"It *really* should have been Olivia," I reminded him.

"I wish Olivia was here," he said.

"So do I."

"I'm sure you do," he said, and a little of his usual smirk showed. "What I mean is, she's good at making me feel better. You're a bit of a drip, Mannie."

Then I remembered what Kris had told me just before he left me at the entry to the ice labyrinth.

"Clive. Kris said something I didn't really understand. He said that the candidates, the other children here, he said they might still meet Trimble."

"Didn't you say Trimble is dead?"

"Yeah. But Kris said it might be possible. Not easy, but possible."

"Did he say how?"

"The last thing he told me was that I should . . . be merry. Cultivate a jolly mood, that's how he put it."

"I have never felt less merry in my life," Clive said.

"I know. But, perhaps there is some kind of magic, maybe a spell that . . ."

"That will bring Trimble back? Did he say that?"

"No. He didn't say much. But, we have to be hopeful. Hey, have you seen *my* cell?"

I took Clive back through the center door to my unadorned prison. As soon as he saw it, he smiled.

"You must have done something really awful, Candlewax!"

"No. It's all a matter of me having this medallion. It seems to be a curse."

"You really going to stay in here?" Clive said. "You'll freeze!"

"Someone's supposed to bring a fire."

"Well, until they do, you better stay over on my end, don't you think?"

"Yes. I suppose I'd best. Thank you, Clive."

He grimaced. "Don't thank me! You make it sound like I'm doing you a favor."

At the sound of a key in the lock, the door to Number Six opened. In stepped a familiar figure. It was Lemuel. He was wearing a gray tunic and a crooked work hat. It didn't complement his russet beard nearly as well as his usual leafy green clothes. Martin came in behind him.

"Gentlemen," the gnome said.

"Lemuel!" I answered, astonished.

"I'm caught." Lemuel's expression was contrite. "And rightly so. This night, I have misled you both, and a great many others. In my own defense, I will only say, I thought I was protecting that reindeer. I made a deal with an icy devil, and I will regret it all my days."

"So you know what's happened," I said.

"Exactly what I was trying to prevent." Lemuel removed his hat and looked down. "It's all on my head."

"How did you get here?" I asked.

"I escaped from . . ." He hemmed and hawed a bit.

"Mother Solstice," I said.

"Yes! Shhh! Are you trying to bring her here?" Lemuel looked around nervously.

"It might not be such a bad thing," I said. "Maybe she could take this medallion from me."

"Oh. Right. Guess that got you into some trouble." Lemuel chuckled nervously. "Sorry about that. You couldn't bribe *me* to take it back from you, though."

Martin interrupted. "Lemuel made his way here by another passage. I am sure he will be placed under official arrest, so we have inducted him into our service."

"Gave me these nice gray duds," added Lemuel.

"Fortunately for you, Lemuel has been able to corroborate much of your story," Martin said. "I am giving Lemuel this cell, Number Six. As for the two of you, I have decided to place you both under my own supervision. We can use your help downstairs."

"Am I not a prisoner anymore?" Clive said. "Those other two men, they said I'd be kept here for at least a year!"

"It's not up to me," Martin said. "Now, Mr. Candler, Mr. Murney, please come with me. There is merriment that needs making. And keeping you locked away here isn't going to help Kris."

Martin instructed Lemuel to wait in the cell, until further instruction. Clive and I accompanied Martin back down the stairs.

"Mr. Piper," I said, "I don't want to sound impertinent, but why are those two cells so, well, different?"

"It's a bit of a test, Mr. Candler. We place a door between a room of paucity and a room of plenty. Two convict guests can demonstrate much about their characters, if they will reach an equitable means of sharing what is good and improving what is woeful."

"So, if we return, we might share with Lemuel."

"That's right."

I leaned in to Martin and spoke very quietly. "You should know, Mr. Piper. When Clive saw my cell, he offered to let me stay on his side."

"That's good to hear," Martin said. Very good indeed." He pushed open the mirrored panel, and we reentered the Great Hall. There, four children danced an elegant quadrille, to sweet, melancholy music scratching and thumping its way out of a spinning disc on an antique gramophone. Della stood by, giving occasional reminders of the next steps. Gordon, Samantha, Tabitha and Jeremy had made good on their practice time. Their steps were sure, their faces bright. With Martin and Clive, I stood to the side and watched. The four children stepped around each other, formed into pairs, changed partners, joined hands in a circle, spun around. Outside, seven lanterns began to flicker and glow.

Martin shut his eyes, and I saw tears begin to fall as his lids closed together. He turned away so I could no longer see his face.

Chapter Thirteen
The Chamber of Good Cheer

W hen the dance had finished, Martin led us back to the hallway with the many different-sized doors. We each found the one that matched our height, knocked and passed through. Then we were taken around another few corners, to a solid oak door, on which was carved the VN symbol.

Martin stood before this entrance and gathered us around him.

"Candidates, guests, you are not the first young people to grace these halls with your company. Each year, for countless seasons, a lucky few have enjoyed the honor that you share tonight. That you are here at all means that you are especially sensitive to the strange magics. And the magics are sensitive to you."

"Are we going to eat soon?" asked Gordon.

"Yes, young man. Very soon. But for now, you are going to enter *my* true domain. At Very North, Father Christmas is sovereign, but in this chamber, I make my own contribution. Inside are countless amusements and diversions. Here, I am curator, custodian, sometimes even inventor. I welcome you to the Chamber of Good Cheer."

He opened the door, and the children immediately cheered and scrambled in. The sheer number of objects was astounding. There were toys, hundreds of them, but also machines: ornate clocks, automatons, mechanical trains, and music boxes. The room was two stories high, with twin staircases leading to a balconied loft. There, even more curios beckoned.

Martin shepherded us to an open, circular space in the center of the room. From there, we could get a sense of the impossible scope of the hall and it's many features. By the entrance was a miniature fortress large enough for a child to enter, surrounded by a plaster hillside, and boxes with countless toy soldiers, cavalry and artillery. At the opposite side, an exquisite three-story doll's house with a Mansard style roof, and cabinets nearby, offered hundreds of different dolls and furnishings. Centered against the far wall, I spied an elaborate toy theatre.

"This is the heartbeat of Very North," said Martin. "Here, the strange magics respond to the simple pleasures of human amusement. Your experience, your feelings, your happiness and surprise, all of that energy remains here. It is the lifeblood of Very North. It's our greatest secret."

Everyone stood in the center of the hall, spinning in slow circles, taking in the view of endless games, toy trains and more. Martin called out, "Go! Play! Enjoy!"

Jeremy went to the fortress first, and began an invasion of the toy countryside by Napoleon and an army of Huns, against a team of mountain climbers and jungle animals. Tabitha followed him, picking up vanquished wooden figures from the floor and returning them to their shelves. Samantha found the controls for the cranes and tractors, and dug a trench through an elevated sandbox. Gordon ran the miniature railroad.

Clive stood off to the side, and gawped at the entire spectacle. I encouraged him to take part.

"I don't know any of these people," he objected.

"It doesn't matter," I said. "You're meant to have fun." Clive gave me a doubtful frown. "You have heard of fun, right?"

I led Clive over to Gordon at the controls and switches of the toy trains. "Gordon, this is my friend Clive. He might like the trains."

"I'm glad you're here." Gordon sided up to Clive instantly. "This engine looks just like the one that goes to Auckland, except this one's a steam train, and ours has a diesel engine. Do you like currants? I don't. I always pick them out. We have two privies in our house."

I left Clive to Gordon's friendly onslaught, and wandered to the upstairs loft. There, I found shelves of antique toys and inventions. Martin sat at a small desk, topped with a thick ledger and a few smaller notebooks. He held a quill, which he tapped against the cover of a leather-bound folio, nervously.

"Is everything all right, Mr. Piper?"

"To be honest, I am nervous, Mr. Candler. This is the first time I have ever brought a group of candidates into this chamber without Kris. The whole purpose of this room is to create joy. Without Father Christmas, maybe we are only distracting them."

"They look like they're enjoying it."

"That's good." Martin sighed, then made a clear effort to shake his momentary lapse into doubt. "Now, why aren't you enjoying it with them?"

"I wasn't certain that I should."

"Oh course you should! We all should."

"It's just that, I know by now my parents must be miserable. And Kris could be in danger. And I've got this awful medallion. Everyone says it's magical, but I don't care. I just want to be rid of it."

"Those are all good reasons to fret," said Martin. "But we must not! Go. Explore. The seven lanterns are not fully lit."

"Then, Mr. Piper, shouldn't you be having a bit of fun as well?"

Martin gave a surprised look. "My boy, you're right. I've no business brooding." He stood and went to the railing. "I'll be back shortly. Keep an eye on everyone until I return." He peered down to the floor below. "And help your friend Clive. He looks miserable."

That was true. Clive had his hand on a control dial for a locomotive. He watched as the model engine rhythmically zipped across a bridge. His face showed no pleasure in it. He was grimacing, while Gordon continued his monologue, uninterrupted. I would have expected Clive to tell the boy to put a sock in it, but here he was enduring it stoically.

I asked Martin a single question, to which he gave an unqualified 'yes.' Then I followed him down the steps. As he left the chamber, I made my way to Samantha. She was busy controlling toy cranes and bulldozers. By pulling levers and pushing buttons, she raised up and then demolished a series of wooden skyscrapers. I asked what she was doing.

"Knocking things down, mostly," she said. "I like knocking things down."

"You see Gordon over by the trains there?" I said.

"Yes?"

"He was asking about you," I lied.

Her face brightened to full beam. "He was?"

"I think so," I said, giving myself a shred of wiggle room for my shameless fib.

Samantha wasted no time, but went to Gordon's side. Without missing a syllable, he kept talking, shifting his focus away from indifferent Clive and on to the far more eager audience of Samantha Krupp.

I tapped Clive on the shoulder. "Follow me," I said. He did so, in a daze.

"Are you all right?" I asked.

"I'm not sure,' he started, then his gaze locked on mine. "Mannie! How am I supposed to respond to all this? I can't even take it in."

"The other children seem to be enjoying it," I said.

"I'm not a bit like the other children," he said, in an almost manic whisper.

"You've never said a truer word," I answered. I led Clive upstairs, and to the little desk. He immediately noticed the notebooks and quills, and he jumped at them. He opened a pretty green journal and found it contained blank pages. "Will it be all right?" he said.

"I've already asked Martin. He said you may write whatever you like in it."

Clive smiled. "I'm glad someone around here understands me." He moved the chair to the edge of the balcony and looked down, then began scratching out his own observations, as fast as his wrist would allow.

I returned downstairs, satisfied that Clive was as merry as present circumstances would permit. I wanted to investigate the toy theatre I had seen when we first entered the Chamber of Good Cheer. Tabitha and Jeremy were now redecorating the ornate doll's house. She was trying to impose a Georgian motif, while her younger brother had decided that what the house most needed was more giraffes. Gordon had not finished talking, but Samantha appeared content to let him ramble while she poured sand into the freight cars.

The theatre had two rows of bench-like seats in front of it. Miniature boxes and balconies, a painted audience of well-dressed patrons within, surrounded the proscenium. A lever beneath the orchestra pit bore the label START. I flipped it down, and the show was underway.

Music box tones played an overture. The curtain lifted mechanically. The first scene was a three-ring circus. Carved wooden figures of horses and riders, tigers and tamers, moved and spun along a grooved track. Two trapeze artistes swung from above. The sound of the sprightly march caught the attention of the other children, and soon, all four candidates were gathered around.

To their great delight, each candidate soon saw him or herself on stage, represented as a tiny wooden doll. A fifth figure, a girl clearly meant to be Olivia, appeared with them. *She was meant to see this. I should call down Clive.* I looked back up at the second level, and Clive was fully absorbed, wandering from shelf to shelf, taking notes with uncommon intensity.

The circus backdrop was lifted away, and with a whirring of gears, another took its place. This time, the setting was a snowy countryside. The figures now appeared to ice skate across a frozen pond. The music changed to fit the new spectacle. Presently, a Christmas tree emerged from below the center of the stage.

All of the figures crept off to the wings, and out of view. The curtain lowered, but the music continued. This time, the melody that came forth was familiar to me. It was the tune Rex Palmer had composed for the Christchurch Cathedral pageant. I had heard it so many times, it did not occur to me, at first, to think how strange it was to hear it in this setting. The curtain lifted again, and the cathedral sanctuary was now the setting. It was a perfect representation, lovingly crafted of painted plywood, with stained glass windows made of semi-transparent tissue paper.

My astonishment was multiplied when I saw figures emerge from the sides dressed for a Christmas pageant. The figure of Olivia was there, in costume as Mary. Every element was alike with that event, so recent, and yet so long ago. It was uncanny to see a scene from my own recent experience recreated in this fanciful way. There was, however, no little effigy of myself on that stage.

Rex's song continued to chime forth. Suddenly, there was singing. Clive, still upstairs examining the shelves of antiques and making notes, had begun to perform his solo along with the gentle music box tones. He did not cast a single glance down at the theatre or us. As before, his voice was clear, his tone pure. The moment seemed to me uncanny, as unreal as any miracle.

So breathed a new life
Into the cold night air
So breathed a new life

The cathedral scene shifted away. The curtain closed and opened again, this time to a dance set in the Great Hall of Very North.

A trap door in the stage floor opened, and a new puppet came into view. It was a reindeer, with antlers decked in shining tinsel. On its head, unmistakably, was the mark of VN, and hanging just above it, a tiny medallion. It was a perfect miniature of the one in my pocket. *So that's where it belongs. As a crown on Trimble's head.*

"It's Trimble!" Jeremy shouted. Soon, new figures of Jeremy, Tabitha, Gordon and Samantha appeared, dressed in little copies of the same knitted apparel each had received earlier. *This theatre is showing us what should have happened*, I thought. *Olivia should be here. Trimble ought to be alive. He ought to be wearing his jeweled emblem.* The little Trimble puppet bowed its head as the little candidates assembled around it, and the curtain came down.

The notes from the music box slowed and came to a stop. Martin spoke, startling us, as we had not noticed his return.

"Your merriment is having an effect. The seven lanterns have a nice glimmer. Perhaps Kris will find his way now."

As soon as he said this, we all shook from a blast of sound, as of trumpets and pipe organs playing at fortissimo. The entrance to the chamber flew open, and for a moment, we were flooded with blinding white light. Mother Solstice had arrived.

Chapter Fourteen
The Grim Frost

The bright lights seemed to emanate from every corner of the room. I looked away at first, but the intensity soon tapered off. I saw Mother Solstice for the first time. She was beautiful, her raven black hair touched with a few strands of pure white. She moved with the grace of royalty, in a gown of pale orange and light blue. A crown of ivy rested on her head. In her left hand, she held a silver scepter with a head of tessellated crystal. With bright green eyes, she surveyed the room.

Her gaze commanded silence and deference. Many of the candidates bowed their heads or averted their eyes. I found myself staring. So was Clive, from the upstairs loft.

"Where is Kris?" she asked, her voice calm, but not a soul in the room was put at ease. Martin came forward to speak with her.

"We don't know." Martin could not meet her eyes.

"Why so nervous, Martin?" There was no guile in her voice, no threat or accusation, and yet, I felt a chill when she spoke.

"I wasn't expecting you, good lady. You risk much by coming here."

"So, is there to be a feast?" There was some impatience in her question.

"Yes." Martin's voice shook.

Mother Solstice gasped. She looked back to the door. "I feel his presence."

"Kris?" said Martin.

"Trimble. He's near. He's got to be."

She closed her eyes and held out the crystal-topped scepter. "Yes, I feel his life force. Unless . . ."

She swung around in a flare of light, and instantly, she was face to face with me. "You! Why do I feel Trimble's light coming from you!"

My legs wobbled, nearly buckled, from the rush of shame and guilt. I didn't say a word, but neither did I look away.

"Do you have something?" she asked gently "Something that doesn't belong to you?"

I held out the medallion. There was nothing else that could be done.

Her eyes widened. She seized the jeweled object and held it in her fist. Bright lights flared, and there was another shriek of noise. Her face tensed and she moaned. Her hand opened. The medallion was gone, as if it had somehow seeped into her skin. Only the chain was left, and it slipped from her fingers and fell to the floor.

Mother Solstice put one hand on my cheek. Her face returned to its prior state of preternatural calm. "Thank you, young man. You are safe now." With dignified step, she rose and left the chamber.

The uneasy stillness was broken by a call from the loft. "Scotched Eggs! What was that all about!" Clive had dropped the book and pen from his hands, and now gawped at us from the bannister.

Martin waved to him. "Come down. I declare our feast officially begun. To the Great Hall. Everyone!" He knelt and picked the chain up off the floor, then hurried to the door. "Now!" he shouted to the rest of us, and we followed.

When we reached the Great Hall, the view from the tall windows had changed. Out in the darkened courtyard, seven globes were dimly lit. Little spheres of light flitted and drifted around them like fireflies. Some of the tiny orbs were red, some green, some icy blue. They faded in and out, they danced around. The young candidates ran to the windows, fascinated by the display.

Mother Solstice stood at the center of the hall, facing the windows. "So, you *have* been making merry."

"Yes," Martin said. "We've made it our task."

"And yet, without Kris . . ." She rapped her scepter against the floor, and everyone turned from the windows and faced her. "I have a question for you all. You must answer, and you must answer honestly."

Some of the young guests nodded an assent, but both Clive and I froze.

"Where is Trimble?" She said it plainly. Then she turned to Samantha.

"Do you know," she asked.

"I . . . I came here to *see* Trimble," Samantha said. "I think we all did."

"And?"

"We haven't seen him yet."

Gordon piped up. "Maybe Father Christmas has gone to get him."

Mother Solstice scanned the faces of each child in the party. When her eyes met Clive's, he glanced away.

"Do you know anything about Trimble? Do *you* know where he is?"

"No, I don't know where he is," Clive said, which was technically true.

She did not even have to look at me. She stood beside me.

"What is your name?"

"Mannie Candler," I said.

"How did you come by Trimble's medallion?"

"A gnome called Lemuel stole it. He handed it to me when you arrived at his home."

She touched the top of my head. "Good. That was a true answer. Is there anything else you can tell me?"

"Yes," I said. "But I think it might be best if I tell you in secret."

"What is it?" Tabitha said, and Samantha followed with "Is something wrong with Trimble?"

"You had better tell us all," the woman said, and now my eyes met hers. I wanted to look away, to run, but I fought the impulse.

"Trimble was taken by the F.A.B."

"I know that. And weren't you with them, at the tavern, just before I arrived?"

"Yes, ma'am," I said. "I had a key, and Flutterbold said I should open the passage, the one that led me here."

There was a laugh from my right. It was Gordon. "Flutterbold!" He giggled, and then, catching a look from the lady, quieted down. "Sorry. It's a funny name."

"Go on, please," she said to me, as gently as ever, but I don't know if I had ever been so terrified by a presence so understated and mild.

"When I got here, I saw men in the shadows. They hunted Trimble. He was shot."

I heard cries and gasps from the children. The terrible moment had come. "He was killed, my lady. I'm sorry."

Mother Solstice bowed her head. "Thank you for your honesty," she said, and she turned to Martin Piper.

"Martin, the seven lanterns are barely glowing."

"Yes, m'lady."

"Surely they can burn brighter than this?"

Martin looked at the rest of us, and his expression was terrible to behold. "I didn't want to upset anyone."

"Light them. Use Kris's scepter if you must. We need more light."

Martin practically ran from the room. Mother Solstice looked at us and smiled, but it was not a happy smile. She addressed me again.

"Did Father Christmas ask you to keep this sad news a secret?"

"Yes, my lady."

"I am sure he meant well. He had everyone's good cheer and happiness in mind."

"Yes," I said, "he was very clear about that."

"He spoke to you about it?"

"Yes. He said it was important that we remain, well, jolly is what he said."

Suddenly, a light flared from the other side of the windows. The first lantern had been lit, but it was not the amber flame of a gaslight. It was a soft white glow. Martin held a long stick that burned bright white at one end, and as he touched it to each of seven lanterns, the entire courtyard was made clearly visible. What we saw in that expansive, snow-covered yard turned our sadness to fear and alarm.

In the middle of the yard, Kris was sitting in the snow, next to a mound covered in green tarp. I knew right away that it was the body of Trimble. Without needing to be told, everyone else quickly grasped this terrible fact.

Kris was hunched over Trimble, and his own coat was covered in frost. After Martin lit the seventh lantern, he walked over to Kris and held the lighting scepter out to him. Kris shook his head, and the light on the scepter faded and died. Kris looked at us. His face and beard were covered in ice. He looked pale and sick. He turned to the mound beneath the green tarp again and hunched over. *Has Kris been out there all this time, in the frigid cold, ever since I last saw him?*

"Kris, my love," I heard Mother Solstice say under her breath. She turned and ran out of the Great Hall.

"Is that Father Christmas?" Jeremy said. His tone revealed less fear than honest curiosity, but Tabitha turned his face away from the windows.

"Don't look, Jeremy," she said, and he responded, "Why?"

"What's he doing?" Gordon asked, and Samantha moved closer to him. "I think he's praying," she said.

"He's freezing," Tabitha cried. By now, Martin was trudging through the snow back toward the palace. He saw that we were watching. He used both hands to motion for us to stay put, then hurried along to reenter the palace.

"What's he saying?" said Gordon.

"Martin wants us to stay here," I said.

"But we could help him." Samantha took Gordon's hand in her own.

Jeremy squirmed his way out of his sister's embrace and was now pressing his nose up against the window. "Come inside!" he shouted. "Father Christmas! Come inside!" He slapped his palms against the glass several times.

Martin reentered the hall a moment later. "Everyone, please, come here. I've got to talk to you." The children clustered very close to him, but Clive and I kept a slight distance.

"I am sorry you had to see this awful plight. It is not how Father Christmas would have chosen to greet you. But I am happy you are here. I need your help."

"What should we do?" I said.

"I know this will sound absurd. And it is. I want you to be merry."

"You want what?!" Tabitha sounded indignant.

"Did you see those little globs of light that were dancing around outside? Those were yours. You created them, with your own surprise and delight. It wasn't much, and we need more."

"We're supposed to ignore what's happening out there and, what, laugh?!" Tabitha pulled her brother a few steps away from Martin.

"I'm not saying we should ignore our fear. In fact, we must face it."

"Why doesn't he just come inside?" Samantha said, now clasping Gordon's hand with both her own.

"It's what I want him to do," Martin said, "and I know he won't." Saying this, he looked back out the windows. "The light's going out." We all watched as the seven lanterns sputtered and faded, barely even glowing anymore.

There was a low rumble, a deep booming sound that we felt in our bodies before any of us heard it with our ears.

"The Grim Frost is coming." Martin said. "Somebody sing a tune, tell a joke, anything."

After a few moments' silence, Jeremy began to sing Jingle Bells, very quietly. No one joined him.

"Louder," said Martin. "That's the idea."

Jeremy started over, loud but out of tune. I sang along, and soon, Samantha and Tabitha lent their voices. Martin kept looking to the yard, and found no new lights there.

"Keep going, but smile as you sing. It will feel wrong, but you've got to try."

Our little group now assembled into the world's saddest smiling choir, singing Jingle Bells through gritted teeth. The deep rumbling only got louder.

Then there was another sound, a wheezy musical noise. It was Lemuel. He stood nearby, in his gray work clothes, holding a small squeezebox concertina. "This whole situation may be partly my fault," he said. "Least I can do is lend some musical expertise."

I looked to Martin. "Will this really help?"

"Nothing else can."

"All right," I said to Lemuel. "Let's give it a try."

He began to play, a moderate oom-pah-pah-pah, and we all resumed singing.

"All right, keep it happy," Lemuel admonished us.

The world outside the windows was now darker than ever, with not even a single orb of light.

"Let's move it along. Faster," said Lemuel, and he accelerated the tempo. Before another chorus was up, we were barely able to get the words out.

"Jinglebellsjinglebells jinglealltheway . . ."

Then Lemuel went even faster, far beyond our ability to follow along. With stunning dexterity, he turned the song into a fast, complicated mini-concerto.

"Don't say I haven't learned a thing or two," he said, and grinned as he took a little bow. Most of us were smiling, at least, and the girls even applauded.

"Well done," Martin said, and now there were two dozen little lights dancing around the pitch-black courtyard. "That's the idea."

Jeremy began singing Jingle Bells again, but Lemuel shouted, "Something else!"

"*Silent Night* . . ." began Samantha, but Lemuel interrupted her. "Not jolly enough," he snapped.

Then the low tone grew so intense, we could no longer ignore it.

A bright, blue-white light shone at the edge of the yard, by a frozen iron gate I had not yet known was even there.

"Look at that light! Did we do that?" Gordon said.

"No. That's not us," Martin replied.

The white light faded from the gate, then reappeared, as if beaming from overhead, like a spotlight, right on Kris, now prone on top of the green mound. He lifted his head for a moment, then buried it beneath his hood. The harsh light faded again.

"If it isn't us, what is it?" I asked.

Martin didn't reply, but closed his eyes and bowed his head. I heard a roar, like a giant beast. All seven lanterns were alight again, but this time, with the same bright, icy blue light, shining an intense brightness. We could see the entire snow-covered yard, cold and forbidding.

The Grim Frost stood just a few yards beyond Kris and Trimble. It looked like a bearded man, nine feet tall. The beastly figure wore a white fur coat, and the heads of wolves and small deer still hung from its sides. The antlers of a great stag grew from the creatures' head. His face was savage anger. His eyes seemed to glow with the same cold blue light that now shone all around the yard.

The Grim Frost reared its head back and opened its mouth, baring long, sharp fangs. It gave a roar of brutish ferocity, like the sound of crashing waves and scraping metal all at once. The force of it pushed the long glass doors inward. They swung in on their hinges. Now the ballroom was open to the bitter cold.

Instinctively, we all ran from the windows. Jeremy let out a screeching cry and bolted to the hallway. Tabitha ran after him. Samantha and Gordon fled to the walls on the west end of the room. Clive and Lemuel followed me to the left, near to the serving tables. Only Martin remained where he was, in the center of the floor.

"You mustn't run away," he shouted. "But keep some distance if you will. Kris needs us!"

I saw the Grim Frost lean forward, and a pure white cloud bellowed from the giant's maw as he roared again. Our view of Kris was obliterated in the misty blast. When it subsided, Kris was half buried in the snow.

Clive looked at me. "We should go out there."

"No one goes out in that yard!" Martin ordered.

Samantha ran to Martin, and Gordon followed. She pointed to the window. "Look! She's outside now!"

Mother Solstice stood in the yard, in her gossamer-thin gown. She pushed her way through the snow, deeper as she went, until she was halfway between the hall and the spot where Kris lay by Trimble's side. She raised her scepter, and the end of it lit up in a blaze of red fire.

Then Mother Solstice raised both arms, and swiftly dropped out of sight, under the snow, as if she had fallen through the earth. Where she had been standing, there was now only a glow of red light. The light pulsed and faded, then shifted to green. This green light began to spread, glowing from beneath the drifts.

She can move through ice and snow. That's what Lemuel told me.

"Can she make it go away?" I asked him. He gave no answer.

Kris strained to move. Slowly, he sat up, and held his own scepter aloft. I stepped much closer to the window. In this light, I could see Kris's face more clearly. It was encrusted with ice, his eyes surrounded in bruised purple frost.

"He's not going to live if he doesn't come in," I said. I went to the very rim of the window. Kris shook his head, and motioned me to step back. I did so, and I suddenly felt a little sick to my stomach.

The lights beneath the snow grew larger and swirled about, shifting colors. The Grim Frost looked around at the strange light show, then reared its head back again. Kris was straining and struggling his way up to a standing position, all the while holding the glowing scepter aloft. The ice monster locked its eyes on the light. Kris pointed at the tarp with his right hand, and the Grim Frost looked at the mound. Then the creature did something truly horrible. It smiled.

Kris's scepter erupted in flame. He tossed the burning scepter onto the tarp-covered mound, and the tarp caught fire.

"No!" Clive shouted.

Martin corralled us. "Everyone, please, keep together." We'll be safer that way."

"Why is he burning Trimble?" Samantha asked.

"I don't know. But we can't let it frighten us. In fact, we've got find a way to laugh in the face of it."

We looked at each other hopelessly. Samantha bravely let out a sound that resembled a laugh, a truly sorry croak of a laugh. Then she frowned as she realized how far short her noble try had turned out.

The flames grew higher. *At least Kris will be warmer now.* I scowled at myself for entertaining such a ghoulish thought.

"No one feels like laughing, Mr. Piper."

"Well, think! When was the last time any of you had a good laugh?"

I had an idea, sudden and welcome. "Mr. Piper, how fast can you run to the chapel?"

"As fast as you need me to."

"Please, go and fetch the sheet music from the piano."

He nodded and then moved with impressive speed across the floor, not running, but moving his legs with precision and motivation.

"Lemuel!" I called out. "You still here?"

Lemuel's face appeared from beneath one of the long tables, peering from under a decorative cloth.

"Right here, old friend!"

"Come out of there! We're going to have a song."

Lemuel crawled out from beneath the table, then bent down and pulled the little accordion after him. Soon, he was standing alongside me. He glanced out the windows and winced.

"I'm going to pay a steep price for this!" Then he sighed.

"Never mind that. Do you know The Magpie's Christmas?"

Lemuel's face fell. "You've got to be joking."

"I'm not," I said. "Gordon and I are going to sing it together."

"Oh, Gordon!" Samantha cried, and she threw her arms around him.

"Wait just a minute!" Gordon protested.

"It's what we practiced."

Right away, Martin was back with the music. "Give it here," I said, and once it was in my hands, I pulled Gordon closer and held it where we could both see.

"It sure got you laughing before,"I said to Gordon. "But this time, we'll just sing it and see what happens." I turned to Lemuel. "Are you ready?"

Lemuel frowned. "This is truly desperate!" he sneered, and then he began to play.

I was singing by myself at first.

"I have a little magpie, I don't know what to do . . ."

The edges of Gordon's mouth curled up. He turned to Samantha. "It's the stupidest song ever!" She smiled. I kept singing.

"She tells me that this Christmas Day has left her feeling blue,
Oh, speak, Magpie, what has made you blue?"

Lemuel briefly stopped his accompaniment and helpfully shouted out loud: "And the magpie said."

"Here we go," I said to Gordon, and he began to sing along.

"You brought me Christmas pudding, to bless the holiday
But just before I took a bite, the pudding ran away
Oh, who made my pudding run away?"

The seven lanterns in the yard dimmed. The Grim Frost made several short huffing noises. Colorful lights continued to swirl in waves beneath the snow, but they no longer spanned the entire space. They rolled in ever-smaller circles around the fire. Kris gave a nod and a slight bow in our direction, and made a beckoning motion with his arms. Then he knelt and shivered before the flames.

"He's heard us." Martin said. "Well chosen. He likes that tune."

"He does?" I heard Gordon whisper.

We launched into the next verse.

"You sang me Christmas carols, you chose my favorite song"

Tabitha and Jeremy reappeared, peeking past a door at the far end of the dance floor. I motioned them over as we continued singing.

Jeremy stayed near the back wall, thumb firmly tucked into his mouth. Tabitha rejoined our group just before the next verse. By now, Samantha had her arms around Gordon. She read the words over his shoulder and gave full voice to the notorious fourth verse.

> *"You filled my Christmas stocking with candied fruit so sweet*
> *But when I tried to take a bite it smelled like stinky feet*
> *Oh, who made my sweets smell just like feet?"*

"Didn't I tell you?" Gordon said.

"Let's do that verse again, everyone." I said. "As loud as you can. Make it ridiculous."

"It's already ridiculous," Lemuel said, and he resumed his accompaniment.

We all but shouted the silly verse, not looking out at the horrors beyond the window, but at one another. And we laughed, not for a long time, but we had a brief, true laugh, looking at each other's faces as we sang those terrible lyrics.

Martin called for our attention. "Look, everyone! I think we've helped.

All of the lanterns had gone out. Now, there was only the glow of the flames, and a few wispy flashes of light here and there. The Grim Frost looked completely demonic in the firelight.

The flames burned lower and less intensely, and in another few moments, the fire had gone out.

"Did we do that?" Tabitha said.

"Everyone be silent, please," said Martin. "Look at the place where the fire has just gone out. Look nowhere else. And think of that laughter, those few precious smiles."

Martin knelt down on the floor and bowed his head. We stared at the dim light where the fire had so recently been. Then that dim light was gone. All was darkness. There was no light from the lanterns, none from the fire, and none within the banquet hall. For just a few seconds, there was nothing to see. Nothing to hear.

The seven lanterns began to glow again, faintly. I could hear a low, growly breathing from the Grim Frost. The light grew just a bit brighter, until we could see that the giant was no longer standing. The creature was kneeling as if in pain. Kris was nowhere to be seen. Perhaps he had fallen into the snow. I couldn't tell.

A high-pitched note, like a flute, sounded from somewhere. The note held for a long time, growing louder, until a second pitch joined it and then a third, making a shrill musical chord. The Grim Frost gave a half-hearted roar and bent its head forward.

The chord stopped, then played again, an octave lower this time, sounding more like trumpets. The lights went out again.

With a sound like hushed whispers, and a smoldering fume of ash and sulphur, the globes of the seven lanterns caught fire. The yard was calm and still. Kris was gone. The Grim Frost was collapsed, his arms over his head, and his head nearly on the ground. The great beast was trembling.

"Is he all right?" said a voice. It was Jeremy. He was once again with us, holding Tabitha's hand.

"He looks frightened," said Tabitha.

"That's good, isn't it?" said Samantha.

"I think so," Tabitha returned.

Another chord sounded in the air. I recognized it at once. It was the sound I had heard in the forest, whenever Mother Solstice approached. It grew louder, and white light beamed from high above.

In a burst of snow and ice from the ground, the burned remnants of the tarp flew up into the air. With an explosive flash, Trimble stepped up, alive and whole. Riding on his back was Mother Solstice. She held her scepter, and cool blue light shone from the end of it. Trimble climbed away from the pit and stepped up onto the back of the collapsed Grim Frost. For a moment, Mother Solstice looked our way, holding the scepter high, and she smiled. It was a pose of triumph.

I wish I could remember exactly what words we shouted or how loudly we cheered. There was never another moment to compare to it. Trimble was alive, and the Grim Frost defeated. We raced for the windows and shouted and waved.

Mother Solstice stepped down from Trimble's back and gently led him forward, toward us, then disappeared as she neared the story below our own. She was soon out of our sight.

Martin closed the windows, and turned to face us. A trace of tears showed on his face, but I had never seen such radiant happiness.

"My friends," he said, "now the Secret Feast is truly begun!"

Chapter Fifteen
The Secret Feast

In the aftermath of that strange battle, many things happened in a short time. Della appeared, eager to make sure we were all right, and hurried all the candidates back to the Hall of Good Cheer.

Everyone had questions. Was Father Christmas all right? Where was Trimble now? Was the Grim Frost dead or just sleeping? Della didn't know the answers to any of them.

Back among the myriad toys and diversions, no one was prone to continue playing. Instead, we all chattered at once about what we had just witnessed. Even Clive stayed with the group, rather than going back to his note taking.

A few minutes later, Martin asked us to follow him to the den. "There is someone who wants to meet you," he said, smiling.

I knew it was Trimble before we got there. To be blunt, Trimble had a conspicuous odor. This did nothing to diminish everyone's delight in seeing him. Andras and Ariast stood beside him, one brushing his coat, the other feeding him an oatcake. The jeweled medallion hung on Trimble's forehead, attached by chain to both antlers, perched just above the VN marking in his fur.

"Hello, stranger," said Andras to Clive. "We've met before."

Clive gave a worried nod in return.

"Is that true?" I asked.

"They're the ones who arrested me," said Clive.

"What's he talking about?" asked Gordon.

"I'm pretty sure it's a secret," I said.

"Lot of that going around." Gordon turned his attention to Trimble. "Is it all right if I touch him?"

"Be my guest," said Ariast. "But gentle. He's been through a lot."

The deer lowered his head and Gordon reached up to place his hand on Trimble's forehead. The two girls went to either side and scratched behind Trimble's ears. Jeremy kept a safe distance, while Clive stood near Trimble's right flank and tentatively stroked his fur.

"*Várrugas*," Andras said softly. "Be very careful. He's sensitive, and he's bigger than any of us."

Everyone had words to say to Trimble, about how worried they had been or how pretty he was. Gordon regaled the noble reindeer with a detailed account of his trips to the dentist.

Martin returned with an announcement. "Your host waits for you in the Great Hall! The night's terrors have ended. It is time for celebration!"

With that, he spun around and shouted, "Follow me!" So we did.

Kris, now truly Father Christmas, stood at the center of the dance floor. He wore a long hooded velvet cape, deep red, with a smaller matching capelet around his shoulders. Beneath this, he sported a forest green tunic. Everything was trimmed with ornate stitching in golden thread. He held a long wooden staff topped with a gold ornament on which the letters VN were boldly visible.

"Friends! At last, I can welcome you to my home at Very North!"

The children stood in the doorway and stared, shy of moving any closer.

"Please, come in," Father Christmas said, "Run to my side if you wish!" The candidates all sprinted, suddenly shouting, clamoring to be first to take his hand or steal a hug. He bore it patiently for a while, then gently guided the herd toward the banquet tables.

"All right, all right. I will talk to each of you in turn. But first, we all need something hearty to eat."

We gorged on roast goose, turkey, ham, and cranberry tarts. Each candidate had a small pudding exclusively marked with his or her name. Clive and I split the pudding that had been made for Olivia.

Each pudding held a colored stone. "I wish it was money," said Jeremy.

"Those are rare elf stones," said Lemuel. "They're worth a lot more than money in our world."

"It's true," said Father Christmas. "If you need to barter with the forest folk, cash will get you nowhere. Those stones are highly valued by forest gnomes." He paused and then looked at Lemuel. "Of course, if you have Kramer's soups on hand."

"Heard about that, did you?" Lemuel smiled sheepishly.

"Are you really Father Christmas?" Gordon asked.

"Yes, but I'm more than that."

"What else are you?" countered Gordon.

"I'm a man named Kris."

"Kringle?" shouted Jeremy.

"If you like."

Clive spoke next. "Are you all right?"

"Hmm? Oh, certainly, I'm fine."

"It's just that, it looked like you were freezing to death." Clive's head nodded toward the windows.

"Oh, that. It already seems like a long time ago."

"It wasn't a quarter hour ago," Tabitha said.

"I know," said Father Christmas. "And you are right, Clive. It was an unpleasant ordeal. But I'm well and warm now. I'm happy that you asked after my well being."

"Is it still there, that big monster?" said Samantha.

"The Grim Frost? Oh, no. He is gone. There's nothing to worry about. I am only very sorry that it happened this night, with all of you here. I never meant for you to encounter such a fright. But it's over, and all is well."

"Is it dead?"

"No. Just defeated. The Grim Frost always returns."

I looked through the windows. Where the Grim Frost had stood, there was now only a few mounds of unsettled snow, and a set of tracks that led to the gate beyond.

They couldn't have been the tracks of the monster, though. They were too small.

Lemuel appeared at the doorway and cleared his throat.

"Your honor, assembled guests, it is my privilege to announce the arrival of my lady, Mother Solstice."

She walked softly into the Great Hall. This time there were no bright lights and blasting tones. She wore a small fur coat over her shoulders, and she looked a little weary as she stepped across the floor.

"Welcome, my dear," said Father Christmas. "Welcome to the Secret Feast. How long I hoped we might one day share it together."

She gave a weary smile, and said, "I need something to eat."

"Of course. Young man," he said, looking at me, "Would you bring my wife a plate of cheeses and barley bread?"

"Your wife?" said Tabitha.

"Yes. She is my beloved, and I hope I am still hers."

"Always, my love," she said. Then she looked to the door. "Lemuel, where are the others? This banquet needs some music."

Lemuel gave a loud whistle down the hallway. Presently, three little men arrived, chained together at the ankles. Each carried an instrument, and they clanked and clattered into the room. I recognized them at once. It was Wheatbrew, Copper and Branchstaff, members of the Forest Abduction Brigade.

"My captives," said Mother Solstice. "I caught them in a forest tavern on the island of Aotearoa." She looked at me briefly as she said it. "I have asked them to play for us. It's just a small part of their punishment."

The three began to play. Copper's violin squeaked and scratched out a tune. Wheatbrew's trumpet was shrill and harsh. Branchstaff strummed on a lute, out of time with the others.

"Is it their punishment, or ours?" said Father Christmas.

"Hold on," said Lemuel. "A little holly beer, and they'll be fine."

The improving mead was given to the musicians, and the benefit was near instantaneous. Their sound was now coordinated and sweet. After she had enjoyed a few bites of bread and fine cheese, Mother Solstice stepped to Father Christmas. The two joined hands and began to dance, slowly, across the floor. Before long, Samantha dragged Gordon out as well, and deftly pulled and shoved the young man in a semblance of romantic waltz.

Even as Mother Solstice danced, questions rained down on her.

"Are you a witch?" asked Jeremy, with the innocent tactlessness of a five year old.

"Not quite. Though if you ask the fellows in the band, I know they call me so," and she pointed to the F.A.B. as she said it.

"But, you do magic," said Samantha, "right?"

"There are powers that live in the very earth itself. Sometimes, I am able to command them."

"How did you move through the snow like that?"

"Did you bring Trimble back to life?"

She stopped dancing and gave Father Christmas a small kiss, then turned to the candidates.

"Any spells I used, I could never have managed by myself. You all helped me, you know."

"What, by singing that dreadful song?" said Gordon.

"Yes, it did help. Not because of the song so much. It helped because it let the strange magics know where we all stood. I don't suppose that will make much sense to you."

"What are the strange magics?" said Tabitha.

"Father Christmas, do you care to take this one?"

Father Christmas drew a chair and sat down. "I tire easily these days. Everyone, sit near so I won't have to shout. You have so many questions, and you deserve some answers."

When everyone had gathered around him, he shouted out to Lemuel. "Let's have the band take a break, shall we?"

"Don't you like us?" shouted Copper from across the room.

"I am very grateful for your playing, Copper. Go and enjoy some food."

"Can we get out of the chains, then?"

Father Christmas looked to his wife for an answer. She shook her head.

"I'm sorry," he shouted back. "You'll have to make your way to the banquet table together. The chains stay on, for now."

The three of them shuffled in tandem to the table, and Father Christmas began his address.

"Now, everyone, you have heard us call this the Secret Feast. Let me tell you why. Everything that we say to one another here, everything you have seen and heard in Very North, must be kept secret. You have all kept secrets before. In fact, most of you have kept secrets for me, at my own request. When this night is over, and you go back to your homes, and your day-to-day lives, you will be tempted to speak about the evening's events. Be sure that if you tell your story to anyone in your world, they are not likely to believe you. They will say that you are inventing a tale, or that you were dreaming. But be sure of this. You are not dreaming."

"The strange magics are embedded in the earth. They are all around, but you seldom hear about them. Most people, as they get older, lose their ability to sense them. The folk of the forests begin to fade from view. One day, the secret passageways are beyond your reach. Even lucky young people like you, when you grow older, may start to doubt that these things ever happened to you. And that is a good thing. It protects us. It keeps the busy outside world from trying to find us."

The children continued to hang on his every word. Clive looked restless, and I knew why. He was nowhere near his notebook.

"Write it down tonight, Clive," I whispered. "You'll remember, I'm sure."

Father Christmas took a drink of mulled cider and continued.

"I live the happiest of lives here at Very North. I've been here a long time. I'm quite old, much older than I look."

"You look about a hundred," said Jeremy, and Tabitha, horrified, apologized for him.

"I take no offense. I am older even than that."

"How old?" demanded Gordon, then instantly regretted it "Sorry, that was rude."

"I lost count after 170 winters, and even that is going far back."

"I know exactly how many years," said Mother Solstice, "even if *you* can't remember."

"How many?" said Gordon, re-emboldened by the candor of our two hosts.

"I will not say," said Mother Solstice. "A lady never reveals her age, and I am a few years older than my husband."

"You don't look it," said Gordon, and he was rewarded with a kiss on the forehead.

"Aren't you sweet," said Mother Solstice. Gordon didn't look especially pleased at the boon.

"My wife and I, we met before either of us knew anything about the strange magics. We fell in love, but we could not marry."

"Why not," asked Samantha.

"It's hard to explain to young people," he said, and looked over at Mother Solstice.

"He was a priest, and in his church, priests do not marry."

"So you're Catholic, then? Me too." Samantha looked rather happy at this coincidence.

"It's true. I was once, long ago, a priest, and for a while, a bishop, in a very small diocese."

"He brought me gifts," said Mother Solstice. "He brought food for my family, and to others in the village."

"That's so sweet!" Samantha gushed.

"It was my calling to help the poor. But, after I met . . . , well, she had a different name then, and so did I."

"What was your name?" Tabitha asked Mother Solstice.

"It was a plain, forgettable name, and it doesn't matter anymore," she said. She gave a sideward nod to Father Christmas, one that seemed to say please continue but leave the names out of it.

Father Christmas nodded in reply. "I fell in love at first sight of her. I made any excuse I could find to see her. That village got twice the provisions of any other."

Father Christmas stood up and began pacing as he continued, circling Mother Solstice.

"She was in my every thought. At vespers, I tried to keep my mind on our Heavenly Father, but it was she who haunted my dreams."

He held his hands out to his wife, and she took them. They both smiled. Soon, they were dancing again, without music, in slow circles.

"For months, I kept my love secret. One December evening, her father called me to her house. She was ill. Gravely ill. I went to her side, and there, I pledged my devotion. I remember now what she said when I finally confessed my love."

"I told him he was a reckless fool."

"Yes, her very words. And true enough."

The two stopped their dance, and Father Christmas returned to his chair.

"Well, the village doctors had abandoned hope. She couldn't eat. She shook with fever. On a cold night, I ran to the forest, in search of curative plants. And that is when I met him."

"Met who?"

"Father Christmas, of course. Oh, I'm not the first. I am only the latest. But more on that anon."

I thought I saw movement along the periphery of my vision. A shadow seemed to pass by one of the doorways of the nearest corridor. I was troubled, but not sure of what I had seen. I returned my attention to Father Christmas.

"I found the old man cutting roots by moonlight. I didn't know exactly who he was, at first, but I sensed something about him, something mystical. He spoke a blessing when he saw me. He asked what was troubling me. I poured my heart out, about the dying woman I sought to rescue. And that Father Christmas, who would soon be my mentor, smiled. He said that if I would bring my love to Very North, her life could be spared."

"I asked him, where is this place? He said it was several days journey, but that he knew a secret way. He summoned an animal to carry her. Can anyone tell me what animal that was?"

"Was it Trimble?" said Clive.

"Yes, young master, it was indeed Trimble. For that deer is much older than I, older than Mother Solstice, older than any other creature you might meet."

"Is it all right if I have a raspberry tart now?" said Jeremy. Tabitha narrowed her eyes and said, "He's trying to tell a story!"

"I'm listening," replied Jeremy.

"You are welcome to as many treats as you like. Go on, help yourself. You'll be more attentive if you do."

Jeremy was not the only one to take this advice. Everyone soon had second or third helpings in front of them. As foretold, their attention became more focused.

"I hurried to her side, and stole her from her bed. I hoisted her onto the back of Trimble, thinking myself mad for following such strange suggestions. Trimble carried her away, out of my sight. He took her through one of the mystic passages, such as all of you have now traversed. At the time, I knew nothing of them. I thought she was lost to me. Indeed, her father, her brothers, the entire village demanded to know what I had done with her. When I told them my story, you can imagine their anger.

"I was chased into the forest, and threatened with my very life. But soon enough, I made acquaintance with the forest folk."

"But what about you," Samantha said to Mother Solstice. "What happened to you?"

"I found myself here, at Very North. It was different then, not as grand as you find it tonight. I was very confused. Father Christmas, at that time, was an old man named Ambrose. He was a doctor. When I awoke and saw him standing over me, I thought perhaps I had already died."

"The forest elves brought me to her side," Kris interrupted. "I was taught the ritual. I pledged myself to the strange magics, and to Very North. It's the same ritual we perform tonight. The Secret Feast."

"Our first in many years." Mother Solstice signaled to the band that their mealtime was done. They dragged themselves together back to their platform.

The dance resumed. This time, it was ceremonial, almost pagan. Copper played a flute and Wheatbrew beat on an elk skin drum. Father Christmas and Mother Solstice stepped in patterns to the beguiling minor key melody.

Martin sat nearby, treating himself to a fig pie with brandy butter. I took a chair next to him.

"Why has it been many years?" I asked.

"A spell has kept them apart. A spell of jealousy. She abides in the cold climes of the southern hemisphere. He must remain here. For the winter, at least."

"So, they can see each other the rest of the year?"

"They can, and often do."

"So why is it different this time?"

"Trimble," said Martin, his voice now quite serious. "Her ladyship has paid a price. Her powers are gone now. She gave them over, permanently."

"To Trimble?"

"Yes."

"What will happen to her?"

"She will live at her home in the Southern cold. Every day she spends away from her own fortress is a day she will age."

"And Father Christmas?"

"It has always been that way for Kris. It's why he remains here most of his time. A venture into the other world costs him. Any place that isn't Very North . . ."

"That's so sad." It was Tabitha. She and Samantha had overheard Martin's remarks to me. "So any time they are together, one of them has to get older?"

"Yes. Unless the spell is broken."

As the melancholy tune slowed to a close, Father Christmas and Mother Solstice shared a long, tender kiss. Tabitha and Samantha sighed loudly, and Gordon rolled his eyes.

Father Christmas clapped his hands. "Now, our ritual requires the Dance of Secrets." He turned to the children. "You have learned the dance, yes?"

They gave the expected bashful demurrals and shuffling of feet, but after a little prompting, the four of them assembled in a circle and began their dance. The movements were simple, walking in circles, waving arms and turning in place. As they did so, the seven lanterns on the other side of the window began to glow and brighten again.

Our two hosts watched, and encouraged with clapping and laughter. As the music ended, Father Christmas yelled out, "Let's bring more light to this long night."

Mother Solstice handed out tapirs to all of us, and asked us to be silent. "The next part of our ritual is the spreading of light throughout Very North. As we light candles, we will sing a simple tune. Listen now."

She and Father Christmas sang it softly to us in the calm silence:

May all who come to this enchanted place
Forever any grievances erase
And from this night until the dusk of time
Impart to all new hope and love sublime

We sang it together a few times, and then Father Christmas prompted us to sing it as a round. We continued to do so as we walked the corridors, lighting candles set in every place; on mantles, in grottoes, on shelves, surrounded by pine branches or holly. We passed empty corridors, arrived at hidden rooms, turned around, and found the once bare walls suddenly trimmed with holly boughs and lanterns. The halls of Very North grew magically more splendid before our eyes.

The labyrinth of stone corridors was soon aglow with light, resounding with our cascade of song. Every inch of the place was suffused in a soft amber haze. Delicate shadows of branch and berry danced along the walls. And yet, around every corner, I detected the passing of dark-cloaked figures, silently racing to stay out of our sight.

We ended our song in a courtyard, surrounded on all four sides with rough-hewn stone walls. Above us, stars showed through the haze. I recognized Polaris, almost directly above. My eyes followed the trail of stars in Ursa Minor. The hazy sky hung low, and the starlight piercing through the mist seemed almost near enough to touch.

Two sculpted ice figures stood on pedestals in the courtyard. One depicted Trimble, the other a long-horned goat. Father Christmas lit fires in tall stone altars before each of them. He uttered a few words in an ancient language. Then he turned and looked to his right.

"Where is Mother Solstice?" he said.

Through the windows that surrounded the courtyard, I saw a dozen figures in black move quickly to surround us. They held fiery torches, and each wore a black mask depicting an animal. Where Silbersee had been a disquieting presence, a dozen such were terrifying.

Just as Father Christmas saw them, two hooded men stepped into the doorway holding Mother Solstice between them. One wore the mask of a gryphon, the other a boar.

"We are placing this witch under our custody," came a voice from the boar, coarse and deep, much like that of Silbersee.

"Our master demands a spell," said the gryphon.

"Take your hands off of her," said Father Christmas. There was no fear in his voice, but anger.

"Follow us," said the other hooded man, and then Mother Solstice was led away, and Father Christmas ran after, leaving us alone.

Chapter Sixteen
The Ritual of Treasures

Clive, Gordon, Tabitha, Jeremy and I stood in the snowy courtyard for a few heartbeats, shivering, not wanting to go back inside after what had just happened. Della soon arrived.

"I hope you haven't been too badly frightened," she said. "Very North has been invaded. But I do not think any of us are in any danger."

"Who is it?" asked Tabitha. She held Jeremy protectively by her side.

"They are servants of the Grim Frost. Until I know why they are here, I think we would do well to avoid them. But I must get you back inside, out of the cold."

We followed her back into the hall. Martin appeared around the corner.

"Take them up through the escape corridor," he said. "I don't think they mean any harm, but we would do well to avoid them."

Della and Martin led us around several more corners, and to a paneled section of wall.

"Behind these panels, we can disappear into the north tower. We'll wait there until this business is done." Martin leaned against one of the panels and pushed.

"Can't you open it?" Jeremy asked.

"I haven't had to make use of it very often," Martin said. He pushed and pressed again.

Without warning, the panel opened out, not in. Five black-cloaked figures filed out of the secret passage and into the hall. Martin spun round and motioned us away.

"Never mind that! Let's go to the Great Hall!"

All of us, candidates, guests and hosts, half-ran the way we had come. The cloaked servants followed at a slow pace. They didn't appear to be giving chase. One of them wore a deer mask. He looked exactly like the coach driver back in the forest at Christchurch. Perhaps it was the same man.

"I don't like them," said Samantha.

"Everything is fine," he said. "They won't cause trouble."

"I wish they didn't have to look so frightening," Della said. "And they sound terrible!"

"They are just people, Della. People under a spell."

"How soon can we send these children home?"

"Not yet, Della. Father Christmas needs them to complete the ritual."

"Even now?"

"Especially now." Martin gestured to the right hand corridor and led us away.

"I've seen one of them before," I said to Martin as we walked. "Back in Christchurch. One of those hooded figures was driving a coach with two reindeer. A fellow named Drillmast was with them."

"Drillmast is an old friend."

"He's turned," I said. "Just like Lemuel."

"Nothing but spies and turncoats around here," said Clive. I looked at him and cleared my throat.

"*You* joined the F.A.B."

"And I'm doing my time," he said. "I'll have to stay here for at least a year to work it off, don't you think?" Clive was smiling as he said it, not in a cynical way, but with delight.

"We'll get that sorted later. Father Christmas needs your help, one more time, and so does my lady."

"We aren't going to have to sing The Magpie's Christmas again, are we?" said Gordon.

We reached the Great Hall, and there was Mother Solstice, surrounded by about a dozen black-robed intruders. Each was wearing a different animal mask. I saw the faces of a tiger, a bear, a bird and a dragon sitting near to the lady. She looked untroubled by her uninvited guests.

"Are you all right?" Martin called out to her.

"They are honest men and women, Martin. They are under a spell. Don't forget that I was once nearly deceived by the same force."

All of the hooded people stood suddenly, then got down on one knee and bowed their heads. Someone else had entered the Great Hall.

The man was bearded and broad-shouldered. He was tall, over six feet, and wore a white fur coat. His head was crowned with antlers. He strode toward Mother Solstice, but stopped to look at the rest of us, just long enough for all to see that he was the very likeness of the Grim Frost.

"It's him," Samantha whispered, but no one else said a word.

"Rise and step to the hallway," the man said. His servants all obeyed his command. Then he faced Mother Solstice, and she looked at him, without fear, not rising from her chair.

"Iris," he whispered.

"I'm happy to know that you were not harmed," she said.

"I am not killed, Iris. That doesn't mean I'm unharmed."

The man walked to Mother Solstice and knelt before her. "I seek your mercy," he said. She stood immediately.

"You seek a spell you know I cannot grant you."

"I seek what is mine!" he shouted forcefully.

Mother Solstice walked away from him, and all but barked out at us, "Children, to the chapel. Go now!" Then she turned down the corridor on the right and disappeared from view.

The man stayed kneeling on the floor, but he faced us and shouted, "You heard the lady, get to the chapel!"

We all but sprinted out of the room, except Jeremy. He ran to the man and shouted up to him. "I know who you are! You're the grim monster!"

"I am not the Grim Frost," said the man, his irritation easy to hear.

"You are so! You tried to kill Father Christmas!"

Jeremy began kicking at the tall man's boots. Della raced to his side, picked him up and whisked him out of the hall.

"I'm not afraid of him!" Jeremy shouted. "Let me kick him some more!"

Jeremy was still in fighting spirit when we arrived at the chapel. We each took a hat, placed it on our heads, then removed them at once, and the door opened. Inside, the chapel was brighter than when I visited earlier. More light shone through the windows, and the colors on the stained glass images appeared to burst with incandescence.

Father Christmas sat on a bishop's throne at the near end of the center aisle. Now he was gowned in rich green, and wore a tall bishop's miter.

"Welcome, faithful friends, to this sacred chapel." He stood and raised his arms upward.

> *"In this place of riches and comfort, let me transcend my need*
> *for wealth*
> *And sacrifice those things I hold most dear*
> *Let me shed these trappings, and unleash manifold blessings*
> *That they may find others less fortunate, but no less worthy,*
> *than I. Amen"*

I repeated his 'Amen,' and a few others echoed it too, perhaps as much out of church habit as anything.

"Father Christmas,' I said, "the Grim Frost is back. But now, he's a man."

"Yes, I had a feeling he would return."

"So, it *is* him," said Jeremy, with the hint of a gloat.

"Yes, and no. In human form, he is not the Grim Frost. He is free of that curse, for now."

"So, he turns into a monster sometimes?" said Samantha.

"Yes. And it falls to me to release him from that state every now and again. It's a task that grows more difficult every time I attempt it. If Mother Solstice had not been here this year, I would surely have failed."

"Is her name really Iris?" said Tabitha.

"Yes," said Father Christmas. "Did she tell you that?"

"No. The man called her Iris," Samantha observed. "He seems very angry."

"He's frightened. He wants more power, and right now, she hasn't got any."

"Can you make him go away?" said Samantha.

"I have no intention of doing so. He is my welcome guest."

"I don't like him," Jeremy said.

"And I love him," said Father Christmas, "even if it's not always easy to do so. Even if he refuses to return that love."

"Who is he," I said.

"He's my brother," came the reply. As soon as he said it, a ferocious pounding knock came to the door of the chapel.

"We have guests," said Father Christmas. "I must open the door for them. They don't know about the hats."

He opened the great door, and the robed people stepped in, marching in two lines. They proceeded down either side of the chapel. Kris's brother followed them. He walked up across the transept, to the nativity, and then stood facing Kris's throne.

"Don't you look holy, Father Christmas."

"I welcome you, dear brother, to Very North. Here you are always at home."

"Here I *ought* to be at home," said the man.

Kris sat down, and he motioned for the children to draw nearer to him. I stayed back, not sure if he meant for me to join them.

"You are just in time for our final ritual, Evan. You are all welcome to bear witness to it."

"Will it generate the spell I want?"

"It will surely generate some kind of magic. I doubt that it will be the power you seek. I'm not that strong."

"You're not much more than a parlor magician, old man."

"Old man?" Kris chuckled. "Do I have to remind you that I am, in fact, your younger brother?"

"You don't look it."

"Time has been kind to you, Evan."

"Nothing has been kind to me!" shouted the man.

"Temper, Evan. Always such a temper."

"Get on with your silly ritual, then" said Evan, and he assumed a defiant stance, arms crossed, chest high, glowering. "Impress me with your kindly magics."

A weary expression passed across Kris's face, but then he summoned up a warm smile, and he gave each of the five children a quick embrace.

"Please, my friends, help me with this last, most important exercise. You have created mirth, and joy. Now, we must create understanding. Be sure that all danger has passed, and we are all among friends."

Kris slipped off the throne, and sat on the floor, making a circle with the others.

"This is the Ritual of Treasures, and it is very simple. Each of you carries secrets in your heart. Right now, I ask you to reveal one secret, each of you in turn. As it happens, many of you hold secrets at my own request. Isn't that right, Gordon?"

Gordon looked astonished. "You mean me?"

"Is there another Gordon here that I don't know about?"

"Sorry. No, not that I know of."

"Is it true that you have been keeping a secret for me?"

"Yes, sir," said Gordon.

"Good. Please tell us all what that secret is."

"I've seen you before."

"That's right," said Father Christmas, his face animated with excitement. "Please tell everyone. When was it?"

"Last summer. I was out walking with my Mum and my older brother. Oh, and our dog. His name is Lamb Chaser. Because he's good at chasing lambs around, you know, at our farm. We have a sheep farm, you know."

"Yes, I know," said Father Christmas.

"I didn't know that," said Samantha. Her look of astonishment made me laugh.

"You should come see it sometime!' he said. "It's better than the Gaveston's farm. We've got more farmhands, for one, and we've won more prizes. Oh, I'm not supposed to boast about that, actually."

"Is there a point to this?" Evan barked from the other end of the chapel.

"Please, no interruption during the ritual, Evan," said Father Christmas. "Now, Gordon, what about that day last summer?"

"Oh, sorry. So, Lamb Chaser ran off, and I was running after him, and next thing I know, there you are, giving him a scratch behind the ears."

"It's true. I was there, very briefly. Flutterbold and I were looking at a new path that had opened in the forests. So, what happened then?"

"I called you Santa Claus, and you told me you were Father Christmas, and then you asked me if I lived nearby, and I said yes, and I think I told you about our farm."

"You did. At length."

"And you asked me if I could keep a secret, and I said I'm really not that good at it."

"But you have kept it, after all."

"Yes. You asked me to walk into the forest once a week, and look at this one tree, and see if there were any deer tracks. And if I ever saw any deer tracks, I was to shout out the name Flutterbold very loudly."

"And so you did," said Father Christmas. "For it was near your farm that Trimble emerged into your island country. Well done, Gordon."

"What was he doing there?" said Jeremy.

"I sent him there, as protection from the agents of the Grim Frost."

"You mean me?" said Evan.

"I mean the creature that sometimes possesses you. Be glad I don't hold you accountable for its actions." He returned his attention to Gordon. "Thank you, Gordon. You were very brave."

Evan made a grunting noise, and then grabbed a chair and sat down, looking impatient for this part of the ritual to end.

Father Christmas continued. "Now, Samantha. Have you got a secret to tell us?"

"I saw you too. In Atlantic City."

"Yes. But you didn't speak to me."

"No. I talked to a little man."

"Woodthorpe," said Father Christmas.

"That's him! My father was helping to build a hotel, and this little man Woodthorpe showed up one day, when I was visiting Dad at the construction site."

"Your father builds hotels?" said Father Christmas.

"He used to. He was in charge of the men who build these big hotels on the boardwalk. But this one, it was in another part of the city. My mom brought me out that day to see it. She and my dad went off together somewhere, and this little man came out from behind a tree."

"Were you surprised?"

"I was. He said most people couldn't see him. That includes the men who were building the hotel. Woodthorpe said they had cut down his home. He was trying to find another."

"Yes, it's true. If it's any comfort to you, Woodthorpe settled in a lovely forest near Montclair."

"Oh, okay."

"Anyhow, Woodthorpe spoke to you again, did he not?"

"Yes. A week later, I went back to the hotel. He said he wanted my help. And that's when I saw *you*."

"Yes. I was there for a brief visit. I gave him a key."

"Yes. I saw you give it to him, and you looked at me and waved. Then you disappeared."

"As you might imagine, it's not safe for me to linger in such places for very long. Woodthorpe may be invisible, but I'm quite conspicuous."

"Woodthorpe gave the key to me," Samantha said. "He told me to protect it for him. He said that someday I might meet another elf like him . . ."

"Forest gnome, not elf," said Father Christmas.

"Oh, right. But, it was true. I met another . . . um, another gnome, and I gave him the key."

"But by then, you were far from home."

"Yes. My father lost his job in Atlantic City. We had to move."

"Yes, very good," said Father Christmas. "You moved to a place where my agents could easily get the key from you. And one of those agents is sitting here in this very circle. Isn't that right, Jeremy?"

"Oh! She's the one who gave me the key!" said Jeremy.

"Yes!" said Father Christmas. "For you carried out one of our most difficult missions. The Forest Abduction Brigade was on to our plans to move Trimble to the southern lands. They knew that keys would be changing hands. And so, young Jeremy, what were you asked to do?"

"I had to dress up like a gnome."

"And so you did, right?"

"Yes. It looked very silly."

"It looked adorable," said Tabitha.

"That was you?!" said Samantha. "I had no idea."

"Yes," said Tabitha. "I made the costume. I got the instructions from Flutterbold."

"So, Samantha gave the key to Jeremy, and he gave it to Flutterbold. The whole exchange utterly confused the F.A.B." Father Christmas clapped his hands, and the other children joined him in a quick round of applause. Tabitha gave her younger brother a hug, and he squirmed.

"Now, there were complications. But that key opened the passage by which most of you arrived here. Each one of you met Flutterbold. All of you were promised a chance to meet Trimble here at Very North.

You each received written communications from me. You were asked to keep your part in the proceedings a secret. I commend your integrity, every one of you."

The four children smiled, and then Father Christmas looked at Clive.

"Now, we must turn to a young man who has a very different kind of secret to share."

Clive cast a nervous glance at Father Christmas, and another, even more unnerved, at Evan.

"I guess my secret is that I stole my sister's letter." He glanced at the others. "I think it might be my fault, that Trimble got shot."

"Now, now, you followed the advice of people you assumed were in the right. There is no reason to feel remorse. Trimble is alive."

"Is he?" said Evan, standing up.

"No thanks to you," Kris answered, then to Clive he said, "If your sister had been able to meet with Flutterbold, she and Trimble would have taken a different passage. Trimble would have been hidden, in South America, or in Asia, perhaps. Until the way was safe."

"Is that how you work all your magic now?" Evan said with contempt. "You find children to do all your meddling for you? You really are powerless."

Father Christmas leaned closer to Clive. "You've proven your heart. You helped us to conquer the Grim Frost. I hereby rescind your sentence. You may vacate your prison cell."

"He put you in prison?" said Evan. "I would have treated you better than that."

"It's an awfully nice prison," Clive said.

Father Christmas looked at me. "Mannie, we have met. Earlier this very night. I gave you a secret to keep as well."

"Yes sir. I didn't keep it, though."

"Please, tell the others."

"I wasn't supposed to be involved in this business at all. Lemuel showed up with Trimble behind the house I was staying at. When Clive showed up, I had no choice but to get mixed up in the whole thing."

"You bravely followed Clive and Trimble all the way here to Very North."

"Yes. When I got here, I saw Trimble hunted and killed. I think it was these men in black hoods." I glanced at Evan.

"Don't look at me," said Evan. "I have no memory of it."

"I met Father Christmas," I continued. "He asked me to keep Trimble's death a secret."

"Without knowing it, you also carried a medallion that held the greater part of Trimble's powers. That too was a secret. But it was impossible to keep."

"Yes. I was put in jail too."

"I am sorry about that. But then, that powerful treasure ended up with Mother Solstice. When she asked you for the truth, you did the only thing you could do. It's nearly impossible to lie to her, or even to remain silent."

"Yes, I noticed that."

"So, one by one, each of you helped in my conspiracy to protect Trimble. It took a fight, but we are all safe now."

Father Christmas stood and stepped into the center aisle.

"So, it's only fair that I share a secret with all of you."

He looked up at the stained glass rosette, and then he bowed his head and gave a little genuflection toward the East end of the sanctuary. He might have been showing deference to the infant Jesus in the nativity manger, or to his brother Evan.

"You have all learned that I have a brother. No doubt you sense the disharmony between us. It's a sorrow we've borne for ages. In this sacred place, I confess my role in this unhappiness. Evan believes that I stole his love away from him. And I suppose it's true. He and I were rivals for the love of Iris."

Evan said nothing, but he stood. His face took an expression so hateful I could not look at it. His presence seemed to charge the air in the chapel with palpable hatred. All the same, Father Christmas continued.

"When I told you about my younger days, I did not tell you about Evan. For long months, Evan helped me to care for Iris. While I saw to my duties as priest, and then as bishop, he and Iris became great friends. One day, he came to me and confided that he sought her hand in marriage. He even asked me to perform the ceremony. How could he know of the secret love that had grown between Iris and myself?

"I was blinded to his pain by my own youthful passion. And it has been a kind of war between us ever since. If it weren't for the strange magics, we might have lived our lives in silent resentment. But now all three of us are bound up in these spells."

"Am I supposed to be grateful, hearing you admit your duplicity?" Evan said.

"No, my brother."

"Your confession means nothing. You made a promise."

"Yes. I promised to wed you to Iris, but then everything changed."

"And you live here in comfort and warmth, while I am abandoned to eternal cold."

"My home has always been open to you."

"But it ought to be mine!" Despair colored Evan's shouting.

Father Christmas went to his brother and tried to place a hand on his shoulder, but Evan swatted it away.

"There will be no reconciliation between us. There's not a thing you can do for me, *Father* Christmas."

The servants in black began to walk in through the rows of chairs, and they surrounded Evan. Father Christmas backed away.

"My friends," said Father Christmas, "I must complete the ritual. Time is running out, and I may cast only a few minor spells. Please, feel free to stay and observe. Once I am finished, we can attend to my brother's grievances."

Now, Father Christmas smiled at the group of children he had appointed as his trusted agents.

"This is the gladdest part of our ritual, the giving of treasures. Each of you has earned a reward. I will try to work a little magic for each of you. I will need your help to do it. Samantha, I call upon you first." With this, he sat on his throne again, and adjusted the miter on his head. Samantha stood and approached him.

"I begin by asking, is there anything you have right now, some toy or some nice thing to wear, which you could give up, with glad heart, for someone else?"

"I guess so," she said.

"It should be something that you really think would bring a bit of joy, especially to a person in need."

"Gosh, I've got about ten fancy dresses I've worn to parties and to Sunday school. I don't really need them."

"Will you promise me to find someone to give them to?"

"Yes."

"Good. I think you will discover that the giving of these things will bring you as much happiness as having them ever did. Now, my second question. Is there something you have been wishing for in your heart?"

Samantha's eyes widened. "How did you know?"

"Everyone has a secret wish. What is yours?"

Samantha gave a bashful glance at the other children. "I don't want to say it out loud."

"It's all right. You can whisper it to me."

Samantha leaned to Kris's ear, and soon a broad smile bloomed on his face.

"Very well then. Let us consider this wish. Look at the stained glass window above my throne. Do you recognize the child there?"

"Of course. It's the baby Jesus."

"Yes. Officially, it is the *Christkind*. In some parts of the world, it is believed that this holy child is the bringer of gifts. Now, turn around and walk to the crèche at the altar. Look in the manger."

The hooded people stepped aside, and Samantha walked to the sanctuary. Just as she approached the elaborate stable, we all heard the sound of a crying infant.

"There's a real baby in here!" she exclaimed.

"It's a spell, my dear," said Father Christmas. "Just an illusion. But please, see if you can touch him."

Samantha reached into the manger, and she brushed her hand against the baby's face.

"He's real!"

"Perhaps he will let you pick him up."

"I don't dare," she said, but she scooped the bundled infant up into her arms at the same time she was saying it.

The baby stopped crying and soon made the kind of happy noises anyone holding a baby wants to hear.

"He's beautiful," she said. "Who is he?"

"From that manger? It could be the Christ child, I suppose. Except that, if you look very carefully, you'll see his eyes are the same color as yours. Why do you think that might be?"

"Is he . . . ?" Samantha's eyes met Kris's. "Is he who I think he is?"

"Set him back in the manger, dear child. And then look up again at the *Christkind* in the stained glass." He pointed upward as he instructed her.

Turning to face the throne, and raising her head to the window above it, Samantha said, "All right. I'm looking."

"I want you to speak your wish out loud this time," said Father Christmas. "Let us all hear it."

Samantha's voice stammered as she spoke her heart's desire. "I want . . . I want a . . . baby brother." A tear ran down her right cheek.

"I have held the spell as long as I can," said Father Christmas. "Check in the manger again."

Samantha got there in three leaping steps. The baby within was once again a plaster figure of the Christ child. "Where is he?"

"What you saw was a shadow. It's faded. But, my dear Samantha, this very night, in your home, a baby brother has arrived, and your mother with him."

"Is that true?" she gasped.

"I think so. I'm usually right about these spells," he said. "I can see that your heart is anxious to return. I will hold you here no longer. Lemuel and his brethren can see to your speedy passage home."

There was a flurry of movement among the robed figures. From the mingling chaos, Lemuel stepped into view. I had not seen him enter the chapel, but then, my attention had been well drawn elsewhere.

"Lemuel, you are released from your sentence."

"That's very merciful," said the little man.

"Yes, it certainly is. I want you to find passage for this young lady. I will send Della and a contingent of these servants with you."

Evan held out a hand. "Not one of you will move," he commanded. "Fall back!"

"I'm sorry. They are no longer under your control, Evan," said Father Christmas. "And as soon as they leave Very North, they will be free of all magical influence."

"Is there anything else you mean to take from me tonight?" Evan said.

Father Christmas paid no attention. He turned to Samantha. "You needn't fear these servants. They are under my command for now. They will protect you. I promise. I am only sorry that your visit must end so soon. I hope I might see you again. Perhaps one day, in the company of your new brother. I will hold it as a wish."

Della came and took Samantha's hand. She and Lemuel led the girl away from the throne, but she turned and jumped to Father Christmas, throwing her arms around his neck. She smiled at him through reddened face and teary eyes. Then, on her way to the door, she turned, ran to Gordon, and kissed his cheek. Following Della, Lemuel and two of the mysterious servants, she dashed through the door and disappeared down the hall.

Gordon smiled on one side of his mouth, and wiped his cheek with his sleeve. "That wasn't completely necessary," he said.

"Gordon Gibney," said Father Christmas. "Please approach. There is very little time left."

Gordon stood before the throne.

"Tell me something. Did you enjoy the song I selected for you to learn?"

Gordon screwed up his face and made a 'hmmm' sound.

"Now, please notice, I didn't ask you if you think it's a good song. I asked if you enjoyed it."

"It made me laugh," he said.

"It made him giggle uncontrollably," I added.

"It has that effect on a lot of young boys," said our regal host. "So, do you think it's a good song?"

"Heavens, no!" Gordon said.

"I'm afraid you're right. It's terrible. I ought to know. I wrote the silly thing."

"You?" Gordon looked truly shocked.

"Yes, I know, it knocks me right off the pedestal. Now, that verse about the stinky feet, that's not mine."

"That's my favorite part!" Gordon said.

"You can thank Martin Piper for that choice addition. Now, follow me to the front of the sanctuary. There is something hidden beneath that cloth that covers the altar.

The two of them stepped past the nativity and each grabbed one end of the altar cloth. At the count of three, they tossed it away. Beneath it was just the altar, nothing else.

"My apologies, Gordon. I didn't invoke the spell properly. Let's throw the cloth back on."

They re-covered the altar by tossing the cloth in the air. As it settled, there was now something beneath it. It looked as if a multi-towered castle was hiddden under the cloth now.

"That's more like it. Now, Gordon, keep your mind on a treasure you might wish to have for your own. Got it?"

"Yes sir."

"Now, let's remove the cloth again."

This time, when the cloth fell away, there sat on the altar an antique chemistry lab. An old wooden box, decorated with symbols, stood open at a central hinge. Its contents were clearly visible; vials, burners, spiral glass tubes, metal racks filled with bottles, topped with corks, their contents carefully labeled. A tall, impressive microscope stood in front of the whole array.

"There you are, Gordon. A treasure from our extensive collection. This once belonged to the son of a rajah. The giving spirits of Very North have selected this treasure for you to keep. It is yours now, and nobody else's."

I was glad I happened to be looking at Clive, because his mouth was agape. He looked like he had just been jolted by an electric shock. Gordon, on the other hand, was forcing a smile, trying to look pleased at his gift.

"Thank you, Father Christmas." Gordon said. He didn't manage to make it convincing.

"It's my great pleasure, young man. Now, I have one more question for you. This one is important. Is there anything that you own, anything of great value, that you would willingly give to someone else, to increase their happiness?

Gordon cringed a bit. "Yes. I can think of something."

"What is it?"

"Well, sir. I could give away . . . I don't want to say it."

"We have no secrets here, my son. Perhaps you have recently acquired something that might be better suited to someone else."

Gordon looked at Clive, whose hands were clasped in a gesture of pleading supplication. He looked as though he might well explode.

Gordon read the cue with complete understanding, and no small measure of compassion.

"Not that I don't like it, Sir, but I think it might be all right if I let *that* fellow have my chemistry lab."

"Thank you!" shouted Clive, and he rushed over to Gordon and hugged him. "Thank you thank you thank you!"

Father Christmas smiled.

"You have revealed a wise and giving heart, Master Gibney. You must know that this is what I had intended all along. Clive Murney, the chemistry lab is yours. But, we must cover it back up. Come along with me. This one is just an illusion, you know."

He and Clive threw the cover back onto the chemistry lab, but as the cloth settled, the shape beneath was now something entirely different. When the cloth was removed again, a beautiful wooden skittles table was in its place.

"Here, I believe, is the treasure you had in *your* heart, young Gordon.

"Yes sir!" the young man said, "Is it really mine?"

"It is. With the assistance of my network of agents, it will find its way to your home by Christmas morning. You will have to wait. For now, I will cover it again. It is just a shadow, after all."

Father Christmas placed a hand on Clive's shoulder.

"Now, my young spy. You have your reward, but I require your help." Clive nodded and stepped back to the throne.

"Jeremy and Tabitha Boyd, please come forward." The brother and sister obeyed the command, and Clive stepped out of their way as they approached the bishop's chair.

"My friends, I will not ask you if you have anything to give. I know that you have almost nothing to call your own."

"Yes sir," said Tabitha. "My father says we're very poor. We live with some other families."

"Are they kind people?"

"Yes. Most of them."

"That is some consolation, then. It is my wish, however, to see if we can't find a home for you, a place that your family can really belong to."

"Can we live here?" Jeremy said.

"I would be honored if you would visit me again sometime. But Very North is no place for children to live day to day." Then he turned to Clive.

"Master Murney, my weak and superficial powers have all but drained away. This wish I have for the Boyd children, it isn't possible for me. But, your sister and I, we exchanged a few letters. There is something she mentioned to me. I wonder if you can guess what it is."

"Yes," said Clive, very serious now. "Our house, we're moving out of it. And it's not just one house. We have two guesthouses as well. So, I don't know, but maybe one of them . . ."

"Exactly what I was thinking. It isn't up to me, but when you return, will you take the matter up with your family? Be an advocate for these two, and a friend. That is what I ask. I feel nearly sure that you will find success in this endeavor."

"Then, we'll have a house?" said Tabitha.

"A house, a school, and a new start for your family. It's a tall order, but I believe it will happen."

Tabitha hugged Jeremy as she thanked Father Christmas.

"And with that, I must call this ritual of treasures to an end." He removed the bishop's miter from his head. He sighed and slumped a bit in his throne.

Evan stepped forward and clapped his hands. "What a performance," said Evan. "And what trivial patches you apply to these troubled young lives."

"Mannie," said Father Christmas, "I am sorry if I've kept you waiting. You deserve a reward as well. I am not yet able to provide one."

"Just being here has been enough," I said.

"Yes. I am glad you got mixed up in this. Now, I must speak with my brother in private. I will speak to you one more time before you return home." He nodded, and I understood that it was time to leave.

Martin Piper stood by the door, and I walked through it with the other children. I looked back at the two brothers, standing face to face in the chapel. Martin urged me along, but I was uneasy.

"Let them be," said Martin. "There is nothing we can do to heal this rift."

Seconds later, Martin pushed the heavy door to the chapel shut. The creak and thud of it echoed down the hall with many doors.

Chapter Seventeen
Coronation

The feast continued in a quiet way back at the Great Hall. Gordon and Jeremy were picking morsels off of different trays. Tabitha drank hot cider from a ceramic German stein. Clive had found a scrap of paper on which to write some important notes. A few of the robed servants danced to tunes coming from Wheatbrew's lute. Mother Solstice stood in the middle of the room. As soon as she saw me, she beckoned me over.

"I haven't had a chance to thank you," she said. "You were entrusted with a powerful item. Within it was the key to bringing back Trimble's life force."

"I'm glad it worked," I said.

"You live much closer to my palace than to this one."

"Where is that?" I asked.

"It is called Far South. Only the Amundsen expedition has happened past it."

"So it's just as cold as here?"

"Colder. But inside, it's warm, and its magics are strong. It contains worlds within worlds. You could spend a lifetime there."

"I don't suppose I could see it someday?"

"It's much harder to reach than Very North." She touched my face. "Very soon, you will be too old to see it."

A few minutes later, Evan walked into the hall. He wore a sneering smile of triumph.

"Iris," he said. "Come to me. I would embrace you in the spirit of the season."

She did not move. "Where is Kris?"

"He will be here. He has surrendered."

"What do you mean?" she said.

"I mean that I have won. Kris and his pathetic sideshow tricks cannot match me. What is more, he has confessed, in a sacred place, to his own moral failings. I have right on my side, and I have access to far greater magics than he."

"I will not go through with it," said Mother Solstice.

"With what?" I asked.

"He wants a coronation," she answered. "I will not give it to him."

"Good," I said.

"What is your name, lad?" Evan's voice was steady, neither threatening nor friendly.

"Mannie."

"Mannie, you will see my coronation, no matter what Iris may say now. I will be Father Christmas, and you will swear your loyalty to me."

"No sir," I said matter-of-factly.

"So be it!" he shouted. "My first act will be to rescind all of the gifts Kris has arranged for this pack of brats!"

This sent a flurry of gasps and frightened whispers among the candidates. Mother Solstice gave Evan an unbelieving look, then moved quickly to the corridor.

"Do not walk away from me!" he thundered.

"I have a gift to bring to you," she said, and then she quietly walked away.

"You know there is only one gift I will accept! I demand that you yield your power!"

"I have no power," she said quietly just before she disappeared out the doorway and into the hall.

The children beckoned her to stay, and shouted imprecations at Evan. Jeremy would have resumed kicking his feet if Tabitha were not holding on to him.

"Shut them up!" Evan shouted at me.

"No sir," I replied, happy to defy this raging man.

"Silence, everyone!" came another voice. It was Kris. He walked into the hall, followed by four of the hidden servants. "Let us at last find peace together," he said, his voice tired. "First, Evan, I will let these servants go free."

"I call to the Servants of the Grim Frost!" said Evan. "Am I to believe you truly respond to this man's shallow charisma? He is a pretender. And he is no longer Father Christmas. He has pledged to turn that honor over to me! Now, stand away from him."

But the servants did not move. They formed a protective circle around Kris.

"It is true. I have promised Evan that he will have the throne and the bishop's miter. But these servants are no longer his. They will be freed."

"We'll just see about that." Evan looked to the entrance of the Great Hall. "I want Iris to be here for this. Where has she gone?"

Nobody answered, because nobody knew. But then, there came the sound of trumpets blowing a triumphant chord, and a bright white light shone into the ballroom.

Mother Solstice led Trimble to the center of the Great Hall. She stopped and bowed to Evan.

"I greet the noble brother of my husband. What Kris has pledged, I must honor. Evan, I come to present you with a gift."

Evan looked as surprised as the rest of us. "Are you saying what I think you're saying?"

"The power you seek, indeed, all the power that was ever at my command, is guided and centered in Trimble's spirit. This gift I now bestow, with Trimble's consent."

I heard Samantha whisper 'No!' Tabitha gave Mother Solstice a pleading look.

"Place your hand upon his head," she said to Evan. "You must ask Trimble to be your companion and guide."

Evan smiled and stood taller. He wore his triumph in an unsettling, smug grin that he showed to all present.

"My lady, I accept this generous gift. And you may be sure that I will show you all the mercy you require."

Mother Solstice stepped aside, and Evan approached Trimble. He took hold of the harness and lifted, so that he could look directly into Trimble's face. "I am your new master," Evan said firmly. Mother Solstice gave a quiet cough.

"You have to show *some* humility, Evan," she said. He gave her an annoyed glance, then sighed.

"Forgive my audacity," he said, with no change in his arrogant tone. He placed his right hand on Trimble's brow, directly over the medallion. More softly, he said, "Be my companion and guide."

Trimble and Evan were caught in the beam of white light. For a moment, there was perfect silence, broken by gentle, flute-like sounds. Evan's expression changed. All of the pride, all of the anger and hard feeling fell from his face. He collapsed to his knees, buried his face in his hands and began to weep. Outside the windows, flurries of snow and ice began to blow, and a low rumble shook the floor beneath us. There was a roar, so loud I covered my ears. It was nearly identical to the sound that had been made by the vanquished Grim Frost. The awful cry grew in intensity, then faded away. As the noise disappeared, the flurries of snow in the yard settled. The quiet flute-like melody lingered for a short time. The bright lights faded, until the ballroom looked as it had before. All of the robed servants were gone.

Kris went to Evan and took his hand. Evan stood and held Kris in a tight embrace, still weeping.

"It's gone, Evan. Trimble has lifted your curse," said Kris.

"Forgive me," Evan's voice sounded, muffled by the vestments on Kris's shoulder.

"We all forgive, for the many sorrows we have long brought one another."

Kris held Evan's face in his hands. "My brother, how I've longed for this moment." Then Kris placed his right hand on Evan's chest. "Bitterness has released its hold on you. May your heart remain as innocent and guileless as that of the child you once were." He moved his hand to Evan's brow. "May your mind stay always on alleviating the sorrow of the less fortunate."

Kris took the bishop's miter off of his own head, and Evan removed the antlered crown from his. Kris placed the miter on Evan's brow, and then extended his hand. Evan kissed it.

"In the sight of these good souls, I pass along the miter of St. Nicholas, and I proclaim you, from this day forward, Father Christmas."

Evan's face shone with newfound joy. "I promise to carry on this work, as long as it pleases the strange magics."

"This palace is yours. The spirits of glad tidings which quicken it are now at your command."

"Will you stay here with me?" Evan asked.

"For a little while. But when the Yule log is fully burnt, I will go to the palace of Far South and join my wife there for the rest of my days."

Evan went to Iris. "If we live another hundred years, I will never be able to atone for the hardship I've caused you."

Iris embraced him and kissed his cheek. "I owe you everything."

The forgiven members of the F.A.B. struck up a tune. The solemnity of the coronation gave way to happy celebration. Kris went around and embraced each of his young guests. Evan, now Father Christmas, asked each of the candidates' names, and apologized for the terrible first impression he must have made.

Eventually, Della came to announce that the servants had found a safe passage, and that the children must soon make use of it. The candidates were sent to the Den of Friendship. I started after them, but Kris tapped my shoulder and leaned next to my ear.

"Master Candler, if I could keep you here just a while longer. I require your help, on a small matter. I hope you don't mind."

"Will I be able to get home?"

"I'll see to it. Please excuse me. Wait here for Martin Piper. In the meantime, make yourself at home."

With that, Kris left us, and soon, everyone else was gone too. Evan and Mother Solstice walked out together down one corridor, and Della went off with the children in the direction of the den. An eerie silence fell on the entire place. There was no music, no howl of wind, no brassy horns or gentle flutes. Candles still burned all around, and there was warmth and beauty, but also an unsettling stillness. The seven lanterns outside the windows had gone dark. When Martin returned, I was sitting in a chair, looking out into the blackness beyond the windows.

"Please follow me, Master Candler. And let me thank you for your kind and helpful manner."

"Of course," I said.

Beyond the chapel and the Chamber of Good Cheer, Martin opened a door, beyond which was a set of stairs, carpeted in red, with oak bannisters. We ascended two stories, and then came to a hallway less sumptuously appointed.

"Take the second door on the right," said Martin. "Kris is waiting."

Chapter Eighteen
The Changing Room

K ris sat at a small table. He was once again wearing his red cape and hood. Behind him was a three-paneled wooden screen, the sort that people step behind to change clothes. There was a wooden chair opposite his own, and he motioned to it.

"Please have a seat, Mannie Candler."

The little tabletop was set with a mat of green felt, a deck of cards, three small brass cups, a magician's wand, and other items. I recognized them at once as the contents of a child's magic kit. I sat down, and Kris smiled.

"When I was your age, I once attended a performance by a traveling magician. I was fascinated, even though my mother had told me that the fellow was simply doing tricks. It wasn't until I came to Very North that I was able to learn a few of my own. Oh, by that time, I had already been chosen by the strange magics, and had even cast protective spells against the Grim Frost. But, I thought I'd better teach myself a few conjuring tricks. You know, to amuse young visitors."

He picked up the deck of cards, fanned them out. He presented them, backside up, to me.

"Select a card," he said, and I did. It was the Eight of Diamonds. "Would you be impressed if I told you that it is the Eight of Diamonds?" he said.

"Well, it depends. Are they all the same?"

He flipped over the deck, revealing all fifty-two cards were, in fact, identical.

"It didn't fool me, either. Let me show you a better one."

He reached below the table and brought out a wooden platform that he set up top. There were four shallow, circular indentations on the platform, and a narrow wooden groove that ran horizontally along the center, separating the two front circles from the two in the back. Kris set a small cake in the front left circle.

"This is an enchanted dessert tray. I have only this one cake, and it's very small."

He picked up a mirrored panel and slid it along the center groove. Now the cake at the front of the platform was reflected in the mirror.

"By sliding this into place, it looks as though there are now two cakes, one in the front row and one in the back. Of course, you and I both know that the second cake is just a reflection of the first. But keep looking."

He slid the mirror away, and now there was a second cake in the second row, no longer a reflection but a tangible reality.

"Happily, we now have two cakes. One for each of us. But I am feeling greedy. Let us tempt the enchanted tray again." He took the cake from the back and set it beside the first cake in the front row. He then slid the mirror through the groove once again.

"With the mirror's reflection, it now appears as if there are four cakes. Perhaps there are." He slid the mirror away, and now, four cakes indeed graced the tray.

"Whatever happens in front of the mirror becomes real behind it." He slid the mirror into place once more.

"I am keeping my hands visible at all times. Now, I want you to take one of those cakes up front. Pick it up and take a nibble out of it. Go on."

I took the right hand cake, and bit just a little off. It was slightly stale. My face probably showed my disappointment.

"I know. Magic these cakes may be, but I didn't say they would be tasty, now did I."

I smiled.

"Now, put the cake back," he said, and I placed the now partly eaten cake in the shallow indentation. Kris slid the mirror away, and the cake on the right hand side of the back row now had a nibble taken out of it as well.

"What happens in front comes true on the other side. If only all mirrors could do this. What do you think?"

"It's very good."

"This illusion was handmade, very expensive. Martin found it for me."

I nodded and gave a mild laugh. It was a nice trick, but next to the wonders I had seen that night, it was a comparative also-ran.

Kris leaned forward from his side of the table, and motioned me to move closer.

"May I ask you a question?"

"Of course."

"Right now, where do you believe you are?"

"In my bed, asleep and dreaming," I said.

"Many who visit here think that. But this isn't like any dream you've had before. In your heart, you must know that you aren't asleep at all, right?"

"Yes. I do know I'm not asleep."

"But it's easier to think so, isn't it. Because saying what seems to be true is sometimes confounding."

"Yes," I answered, and knew what he would ask next.

"So, where do you truly think you are, right now?"

"Someplace called Very North, which seems to be in a forest. I think maybe I'm in Finland."

Kris's smile showed that this was the answer he was hoping for. "A thousand blessings, young friend, on your pure, trusting soul."

He stood up and with his right arm, indicated the chair he had just been sitting in. "Would you please take my place in this seat?"

"I can if you want," I said.

"Good, but first, I should mention something. I have found that there are two kinds of people. Some of them, when they see this trick, want to know how it's done. They want to see the secret mechanisms that make it possible. Others, well, they simply want to believe that several cakes magically appeared, and be content with that. Which of the two are you?"

"I'm the sort that wants to know how it works."

"Yes, I thought you might be. Now, why do you want to know? To satisfy your curiosity? To add to all the other things you know?"

"All of that, I guess. But really, I suppose I would want to know so that I could do the same trick for others."

Kris held his arms aloft and looked upward. "Yes! That is a perfect answer! How happy it makes me to hear you say it."

He indicated again his chair. "Please, come over and look for yourself." I stood and stepped past Kris. As soon as I sat down, I saw that the entire table was really a narrow, hollow box. There were levers and gears hidden within it.

"The table is cleverly designed to assist in all sorts of conjuring tricks. It was built and used by Professor Carabello, a conjuror who traveled the world in the eighteen-nineties. Examine the whole works closely, but be careful. It's all very delicate."

Kris flipped the hood back from his head, revealing his bald pate and the ring of white hair that surrounded it. He began to wriggle his way out of the coat. "I hope you don't mind. It's warmer here on this upper floor. Heat rises, you know." He turned and set the coat on a hook mounted to the wall. I leaned over a bit, and saw that there were two more hooks to the left of it. His green bishop's vestments were on the next over, and the rugged brown fur coat was set on the hook next to that.

"Please pardon me. I must change," he said, and he stepped behind the hinged screen, directly behind the chair I was sitting in. He continued speaking, though he was now out of my sight.

"Take all the cakes off of the platform, and line them up on the markers you see at the back of the hollow shelf." I had no trouble finding the marks he was talking about. "When you start the trick, you've got one cake with a nibble already taken out of it. There are six cakes in all, and they get moved around and lifted into place by moving plates and levers. All you've got to do is slide the mirror in and out of the groove in the platform. Try it. Always slide the mirror from your left to your right. You will feel it catch halfway across, and then you will see what happens."

I did as he said. I was fascinated to see the intricate movement of sliding and rotating parts. With impressive precision, the shallow circles along the back row would lower down, receive their cargo, and lift back up into place, locking in just as the mirror slid out of sight.

"It's amazing," I said. "It's more amazing from here than when I was watching you do it from the other side."

"That is exactly how I felt about it!" I heard him say. "The secret is more remarkable than the illusion." From the other side of the divider, there was the sound of a faucet turning on, and water running. I hadn't thought about it, but I supposed that even a place like Very North would need such amenities.

"Slide the mirror a few more times, and you'll see how the whole mechanism cycles through. There are many ways to make use of this, in dozens of different tricks. The cake platform is just one of many illusions the Carabello table makes possible. There are other traps and secret compartments as well. Switches and tiny mirrors and all manner of gimmicks made to deceive. But it is a friendly deception."

I had started to wonder what was behind this demonstration, but I was getting an idea. "Excuse me, sir," I said. "If you don't mind my asking, are you really Father Christmas?"

"Not any longer," came the reply.

"What I mean is, were you ever?"

"Come over here, my boy. To this side of the room."

I got out of the chair and stepped around the divider. On the other side, I saw that I was in a dressing room, the kind found backstage at a theatre. Kris sat before a mirror, surrounded by small incandescent light bulbs. There were trays and tables on either side of him, wet cloths and towels. He was wearing an undershirt, and suspenders. He turned in his chair, and I saw right away that his beard was gone. But it hadn't gone far. It was sitting on the counter just in front of him.

"You have guessed why I spoke of deceit. I am a fraud. An imposter. Or, to put it another way . . ." and he began to pull at his scalp, just above his brow. It looked as though he was lifting the top of his head right off of his skull. His baldness peeled away, and revealed a head of long brown hair beneath. "I am an actor," he said.

When he had removed the false top, he ran a towel over his face and head, and then he leaned forward, and put his hands to his eyes. I watched as first one then another tiny glass lens fell into his palm. He held them out to me.

"The twinkling blue eyes of Father Christmas," he said. "Mine are a more mundane brown, you see. These are the finest lenses ever made for such a disguise. Very expensive, too. They used to hurt like the devil when I put them in, but now, I'm very used to them."

He set the lenses carefully into a small tray with a cover that closed over them. Then he looked back up at me, and I recognized him at once. He was the man with the long hair and the sad face, the one I had seen visiting my father alongside Mr. Prassler, just days ago.

"My name is Michael Brams. I am delighted to finally meet you, Mannie Candler."

I stared at him, disbelieving. But for the remnants of face paint and latex skin still clinging to a few spots on his face, I would have found it impossible to accept that this was the same man who had shown me the enchanted cake trick just minutes ago. I finally remembered to answer him.

"I . . . I'm pleased to meet you . . ." I said, and he gave a salutary nod.

"I would shake your hand, Mannie, but I'm a mess. Give me a moment to apply a little more cold cream, and to scrub my face into better shape. Oh, and if you go back out the door, the next to the right is a bathroom, in case you need it."

The moment he mentioned it, I discovered I needed it very badly.

A few minutes later, I emerged from the loo, and Michael Brams was standing by a door further down the hall. He was talking to somebody else, but when he saw me, he motioned me over. He had changed into a flannel shirt and dungarees. He was as tall as Father Christmas had been, but skinnier. His hair was mussed.

"You must have a thousand questions, and I promise to answer them all. But let's start with the biggest question."

"Where am I?" I said.

"Yes, that's the one. Follow me." We walked to the end of that rather plain corridor, and around a corner, where the walls were bare concrete. Just in front of me was a steel door with an iron push bar. The words EMERGENCY EXIT were stenciled in red across it.

"Go ahead and push it open," said Michael. When I did, I felt a surge of warm air. I stepped out onto a balcony of metal grating, from which steel steps extended and continued on down. I looked up into the expanse of night sky. The smell of the air, the sounds of the natural world beyond were immediately familiar to me. This was a clear, warm December night in New Zealand.

"If you turn around and look toward the roof, you'll see where you've actually been the last several hours," the man told me, and so I spun around and looked up. There was one more story above us. In the dim moonlight, I could make out the words painted on the upper corner of the giant warehouse. *MARBURY MEATS*

Chapter Nineteen
Audra's Gift

Michael held open the door, and I walked back inside. I felt a strange kind of shock, a feeling of rocking reality. It was an uncanny sensation, stranger than any I had felt along the whole night's journey.

"So, Very North is in this building . . ." I muttered.

"Yes, along with a snow-covered forest and much else. Outside the property at our east end you'll find the forests where your adventure began, just a few hours ago."

"How . . ."

"You will soon learn many secrets. For now, it's enough to say that you have just played a central role in a glorious theatrical production entitled "The Secret Feast of Father Christmas." You and the other candidates were both audience and stars. This elaborate drama is presented only a few times every year. Only a few *very* lucky young people have had the privilege."

"So, everyone else . . ."

"The other children were as innocent as you. By now, they are all reunited with their families. No doubt, they are trying to decide if it was all a dream or not. But please, come back to the Great Hall with me. You played your role so well, I think it's time for you to collect a bit of applause."

Michael led me down the carpeted stairs, and back to the Great Hall. Now, it was brightly lit, and alive with people, some in overalls, some in evening dress, not one of them looking like a gnome or a fairy queen. There must have been thirty or forty gathered there, assembled near the tables, eating the leftovers of our recent feast, drinking red punch out of clear glasses. As we arrived, Michael shouted to all of them, "Bravo, everyone! An exceptional show tonight!" There were cheers, shouts and applause. Then Michael drew everyone's attention to me. "Let's hear it for Mannie Candler! He's just now found out how close to home he really is."

There was a hearty cheer, and I scanned the faces surrounding me. In short order, I recognized several. I saw Tabitha, standing next to a woman who by appearance could only be her mother. I saw Martin Piper, but he was now in casual clothes, with moustache but no pointed beard, and suddenly a stranger. I saw the man who had played Evan, well cast because the beard was actually his own. And then I saw my own mother and father.

"Mannie!' my mother called out. She ran at me and gathered me in the closest embrace I think I had ever received. "Mannie, my darling, are you all right!"

"I'm very confused," I said. Michael appeared by my mother's side.

"They are part of the grand conspiracy, Mannie. Your mother and father both. They were in on it the whole time."

"How long?" I said.

"We've known about this for months," said Mother. Now my father took my hand. He pulled me close and gave me a short embrace.

"Your mother thought it was a good idea, just as soon as Audra suggested it. *I'm* the one who needed convincing."

"Audra? What did she . . ." I began, but then Tabitha approached.

"Hello, Mannie. Are you surprised?"

"Surprise isn't the word. There's *no* good word for it."

"You're not cross, are you?" she said.

"No. Did you just find out too?"

"I knew all along. My brother Jeremy was the one we did it for. I was asked to come alongside him, because he's so young. I got to run through a rehearsal of the whole thing during the day. They told me every bit that was going to happen. They asked me to play along. So, I led my little brother through the whole night."

"You fooled me," I said, and we talked for another minute or two.

A little man approached, dressed in a jacket and tie. So recently, I would have called him Lemuel.

"Nice to meet you, Mannie. My name is Kevin Liftin," he said, and he shook my hand.

"It's going to be hard to think of you as someone other than Lemuel."

"Sure. Even my wife forgets sometimes. You met her tonight. Sara, at the little house in the tree. We really are married, and that really is our little girl, Elvira."

"So, you didn't drink anything with actual holly in it."

"No, and we didn't steal any soup or chocolate from anyone." He winked at me.

My mother greeted him. "Mr. Liftin! I was hoping I'd get to see you again!"

"Hello, Mrs. Candler. May I say, you gave a remarkable performance tonight!"

"Thank you," she said. Only then did I realize that I had earlier watched the two of them standing face to face. I had believed that my mother not only couldn't see the little man, but that she was yelling at me while unaware of his risible song and dance.

"Mother, you had to pretend not to see him!"

"Yes, and it was the hardest thing I've ever had to do! When he started dancing around, well . . ." she broke out into the grandest laugh I had ever heard. "Oh, Mr. Liftin, I had to yell louder at Mannie to keep from falling to pieces. The instant I got back inside, I fell to the floor! You can ask Sissy."

"Wait, was Sissy in on this too?"

"Yes, Mannie. Oh, my poor dear, it will take a year for you to sort out what's real and what isn't."

"Precisely what I'm worried about, boy," said my father. "You're dreamy enough already, without all this to occupy your mind." He gave a half stern, half smiling look. My mother gave him a gentle shove to the shoulder.

"Stephan, let's not bother him with lectures now. Let him enjoy."

Now Michael had moved to the great glass windows and he called for everyone's attention.

"Ladies and gentlemen, for you guests who wanted to know how we did it, may I present to you the real genius behind this production. Please give a rousing cheer to our designer, Martin Milberg."

The man I had known as Martin Piper stepped up next to Michael. Even out of costume, his wiry frame and the bounce in his step gave him a fantastical kind of air. He bowed to everyone's rigorous applause, then held his own hands up to quiet it.

"Thank you, everyone. I am happy so many of you could join us at this after-show reception. Our season is nearly at an end. We've had a great many wonderful nights this year, but I believe tonight was our best."

Enthusiastic applause rippled through the room. Martin continued.

"We have tonight many of the parents for this year's candidates, and many volunteers who have done so much to make the show run smoothly. It's a significant undertaking, with a thousand logistical challenges each night. So, as promised, I want to reveal for you a glimpse into our most spectacular scene, the attack of the Grim Frost."

There was another round of applause from the crowd, and then Martin waved a hand at the windows. The darkness beyond suddenly burst to light. Not only were the seven lanterns lit, overhead lamps came on from scaffolding on the opposite side of the wall. The yard was now clearly visible, flatly lit. For the first time, I saw it for what it truly was; theatrical scenery in a vast warehouse.

"The chamber beyond these windows is the largest set in our facility. It used to comprise the ice plant next to which Marbury Meats once operated. The refrigeration system was upgraded, and allows us to keep that entire section of our stage at a chilling nine degrees Fahrenheit. Those of you who may have helped us backstage will know that we try to keep everybody dressed as warm as possible when they are working that side."

There were whispers and muttered comments from those who had spent more time in that cold than they had wanted to.

"Some of the snow drifts you see out there are hollow structures hiding our apparatus for lighting and staging. But most of the snow is real, chipped and flaked by machine. There are several miles of wiring for the various lighting effects. These must be carefully insulated. We've got four sets of lifts and trap doors. And best of all, there is our star attraction. Let's bring him up now."

The Grim Frost loomed up from beneath the drifts, immobile but for the platform that raised him into view.

"Here he is, the villain of our story. He doesn't seem so ferocious right now, but if you saw his performance earlier, you know he's a fearsome brute, all right."

The giant figure began to move. His arms flailed and his head reared back, but he made no sound.

"We call him Grimms. He's over nine feet tall, eleven if you count the antlers. He's actually a highly sophisticated puppet, controlled from underneath by cables and levers. There is also a brave puppeteer situated in his chest. That performer allows old Grimms to open and close his eyes, and move his eyebrows. The brave fellow also presses the button that does this . . ."

With a hiss, white mist shot from the figure's mouth. Grimms moved through a few more gyrations, and then stood still again. A man dressed all in black appeared from behind the figure, stepped around him and took a bow.

"Let's hear it for Jacob Fineman, our lead puppeteer!" And there was an enthusiastic ovation.

Michael took the floor once again, and thanked everyone for their patronage and their help. He invited all to have one final drink, and bid us a safe journey home. The attendees thinned out pretty quickly after that. My mother told me to get ready to leave, and then Michael joined us once more.

"Mannie," he said, "before you go, let me say good night. And also, well, one other thing." He looked at my mother, and she nodded.

"What is it?" I asked.

"I don't know if your mother has told you yet. This entire night, your participation in it, that was a gift. It was bought and paid for by someone very special."

I knew immediately who it must have been. "Audra," I said.

"Yes," Michael replied, "and she meant to be here tonight." He took both my hands and met my eyes. "I can't begin to tell you how sorry I am."

My mother was wiping her eyes when I glanced at her. "There's something else he has to tell you," she said.

"If it's all right with you," Michael continued, "I would like for you to return here tomorrow and help us out behind the scenes. There will be another show, another group of children."

I turned to my parents. "Did he really just ask me if I would help out tomorrow?"

"Yes, Mannie," said my father. "And you'd better agree to it."

I grabbed Michael in an embrace. "Thank you," I said. "Of course I will."

"Then you'd better be off. It's very late, and you'll need the sleep. I want you back by ten o'clock in the morning."

I agreed, and next thing I knew, we were following a group of volunteers down a very plain hallway, down some stairs, and out a door onto a perfectly ordinary parking lot.

Once in the back seat of my father's car, exhaustion took over my body. I don't remember the drive back to Sissy's house, or anything about getting ready for bed, but I do remember my mother coming to see me just before I fell asleep.

"You're going to be out like a log," she said.

"Mum, you and Audra planned this all out for me?"

"Yes, Mannie. She told me about it years ago. She always wanted it for you, but she couldn't say anything."

"So, you had this secret between the two of you, for all that time."

"Yes."

"And even when I yelled at you, and acted so horribly."

"You don't have to say another word, Mannie."

I sat up, drew my mother in, and I held her close. "What I mean it, the two of you didn't always quarrel," I said.

"No, of course not." She took my face in her hands and kissed me. "Mannie, listen to me. Try to forget how we disagreed. We fought, yes. But we shared so many things. Anyway, there was one subject we could agree on for hours and hours."

She held me tight and whispered, "You Mannie, dearest love. Always we could talk about you."

Chapter Twenty

The Retrieval
of Clive

December 24th
Christmas Eve

My deep sleep ended when the downstairs phone rang. My eyes opened the instant the jangling bell sounded. I felt the brief surprise of waking up in an unfamiliar house. My mind soon came out of its slumbered haze and remembered where I was.

By the faint dim of the morning light, I knew that it was still very early. I decided it would be wise to get some more sleep. I closed my eyes, but within minutes, I heard footsteps, and a gentle knock at my door.

"Mannie?" a voice said quietly. It was Sissy, and she opened the door just a crack.

"Hullo," I said. "I'm awake."

"Did you sleep all right?"

"Yes, ma'am."

"I've just got a call from Michael. He wanted to know if we could bring you over a bit earlier than planned."

My mind rushed into awareness. Today I would return to Very North. I had not yet fully processed the previous day's adventure. Sleep had taken me over before I could begin to sort through the experience. I had lived through a remarkable story, in a world in which gnomes and magical deer were commonplace. Then I had discovered that this world was in fact a theatrical contrivance. And that, I found, was harder to grasp than the fantasy had been. Still, true or not, Very North was a real place, and I was about to go back. I felt an intense excitement, like every Christmas morning of my life taken together.

"Yes!" I said. "I can go now!" I was already climbing out of the bed, as keen as if the house was on fire.

"I'm going to fix you a breakfast first," she said. "And we'll let your mother sleep a bit longer. She needs the rest. Your father will drive you over to the stage."

"The stage?"

"Very North. It's our stage, you know."

"Right," I said. "Like a stage in a theatre."

"Only much moreso," Sissy added. She advised me to wash and to choose comfortable clothes. Downstairs, she served hot porridge and sliced fruit. I devoured mine in less than two minutes.

"Careful, Mannie. Don't give yourself indigestion," said my father. "Tonight, we've got to get back to Clarketon. It will be very late by then."

"I would let you stay here another night, if I could," said Sissy. "But we've got the new candidates arriving soon."

"Candidates," I said. "I guess I was one of them after all?"

"That's right. Yesterday, you were a candidate. We did everything we could to make it feel like an accident. You got to be the unsuspecting outsider. That role always begins here, at this house. A boy and girl from Wellington will arrive tonight. They will meet Trimble and Lemuel out by the well, just like you did."

"That's amazing," I said. "So, you're an actress, then?"

"That's right. Lettie, as well."

"And your house is part of the show each night?"

"Three times a week, for four weeks each year. But tomorrow is the last round."

"Do you live here the rest of the time?"

"No, dear. Lettie and I have perfectly modern lodgings in the city. This house belongs to Michael. It was one of his childhood homes."

"So, when my Mum said that you were a friend of Audra's . . ."

"She wasn't making that up. It's quite true. We were on stage together when we were much younger. Perhaps I can tell you more about it someday. But I think you two had better be on your way."

My own happiness in this was acute, but as my father drove me back to Marbury Meats, I knew he harbored misgivings about Audra's gift. He already thought my toy theatre an unfortunate frivolity. He must have thought the Secret Feast a scandalous distraction indeed. So neither of us spoke on the short drive. When we arrived at the concrete parking lot by the warehouse, I broke the silence by thanking him, and by assuring him that I would not let the excitement affect my studies.

"That's what I like to hear," he said, and he gave a curt nod and a smile. "I'll be back tonight. You'll have to say your goodbyes and be ready to leave the instant the show is finished."

"All right," I said. "Thanks again." I left the car and saw that Michael was standing nearby, waving from a dozen yards away. My father waved back, then rolled out of the lot.

I gave the warehouse a look. It was remarkable to think that such a great lummox of a building could house something so exquisite as Very North.

"Good morning, Mannie," Michael called out. "Thank you for coming so early. We've got an unexpected crisis that I think you can help us with."

"What is it?"

"Clive Murney. He's still here."

"He is?"

"He refused to leave. He didn't feel he had paid due penance for his role in Trimble's capture."

"Really?"

"He insisted on staying in his gilded prison cell for the night. And he seems very serious about staying out his year's sentence." Michael laughed.

"I'm not too surprised," I said. "I've learned Clive takes things very seriously."

Michael opened a door into the warehouse. "Before we start your orientation this morning, I thought you might pay him a visit. He still believes everything that happened last night really happened. I don't want to spoil that impression. So, if you will tell him that you, too, have been here all night. Guide him to the Den of Friendship. There will be a surprise for him there."

I was given a sweater and cap, similar to those the other children had worn. Michael led me into the palace halls. It was strange to see the transition. From the concrete lot, just a few steps down a grey corridor, open a door and here is this stunning other world. I thought of the geode rocks that Anaru kept in his room. On the outside, craggy and rough, and on the inside, filled with crystalline beauty.

Michael guided me up some stairs to the door of Cell Number Seven. He handed me a key.

"You were never locked in. If you or Clive had tried to open the door at any time, you would have succeeded. But mimic your unlocking the cell with this key."

"All right," I said, "So I'm acting already." I was delighted by this carefully managed detail. How many more hundreds there must be in this manmade dreamscape.

"One other thing. When you walk Clive to the den, don't take him through the Great Hall. The work lights are on in the snow yard, and my crew are making repairs on Grimms. Let's prevent Clive from seeing the mundane reality behind all this." He instructed me on an alternate route. Then he left me to my task.

I knocked on the door first, just to alert Clive that someone was here. Then I put the key into the lock and turned it. I pushed the door open, and found Clive sitting at the desk. He looked up.

"Oh, it's you . . ." he said. "I thought you had gone home."

"No, I stayed to help Kris," I said.

"You don't intent to hang about all year, do you?"

"No," I replied. "I've got to get home soon. And you?"

"I'm staying, a year at least."

"Father Christmas released you last night."

"It's a matter of personal honor," he said, and then yawned.

"Have you slept at all?"

"I have to write it all down. That will *take* a year."

He had filled a dozen pages of a hardbound journal with notes. At a glance, I could see that his normally careful handwriting had turned into a lazy scrawl, no doubt owing to lack of sleep. Clive picked up a hefty leather-bound book.

"Look at this! Martin brought it to me. It's manual that goes with my chemistry lab! I need all year to learn this, too."

"So, you plan to spend your year's sentence in here, playing with your chemistry lab?"

"Maybe I'll invent something useful. Then I could split the profits with Father Christmas."

I couldn't help but laugh. "There's only one of you, Clive Murney," I said.

"Of course there's only one of me. What kind of a crack is that?!"

"I've been ordered to bring you to the Den of Friendship."

"What's in the den?"

"I don't know. We're both overstaying our welcome. They might put us to work. I bet there are floors that need scrubbing."

"Oh. I hadn't thought of that. Are we likely to be scrubbing every day?"

"Yes. I expect there will be lots."

"I don't enjoy scrubbing much," he said. "But I don't suppose I have a choice."

He stood up and walked. He weaved and swerved a bit.

"My gosh, Mannie. I'm a little wobbly."

"Well of course you are," I said. "You haven't slept."

I opened the door to the hallway, and Clive stumbled out. "Here, you better lean on me," I said. He grabbed hold of my left arm, and together we made our way around the corner to the right, and then bore left until I saw the doorway to the den.

Martin was there, in costume. "Masters Candler and Master Murney," he said, and for a moment, it was as though yesterday's story was still going on. I could nearly hope that last night's reveal of the reality of Very North was itself the dream.

"Good morning Martin Piper," I said. "We're here to report for duty."

"Mmm . . . Morning," Clive muttered. It was clear that fatigue was overtaking him fast.

"Eyes open and face front," said Martin. Clive made an effort to come to attention. Martin swung open the door, and there, sitting near the fireplace, was the Murney family; Cyrus and Joan hand in hand, and Annabella seated in a chair.

"Merry Christmas, Clive!" they all sang out.

Clive blinked and shook his head lightly. "What?" he said, and Annabella laughed.

"Clive, it's us. You know, your family?"

"I know who you are," he said sleepily. "What are you doing here?"

"He stayed up all night," I said. Anna came to Clive's side and embraced him.

"My darling, you're about to collapse!"

"I'll be all right. I'm supposed to scrub floors now." Then he yawned. Anna tried to pick him up, something she hadn't done in a long while.

"Oh, my heavens. I can't carry you anymore, Clive."

"Why . . . why would you?" he said, and then he collapsed into a chair and went promptly to sleep.

Joan wedged herself into the chair and heaped Clive onto her lap. "He'll sleep all day now."

"He's been through a lot,' I said. "I don't know if he'll tell you about it. We've all been sworn to secrecy."

Cyrus laughed. "We know all about it. We were never far away. You remember that menacing coach driver?"

"Couldn't forget him."

"That was me!"

This was astonishing news. "You?"

"Michael often arranges it that way. If you or Clive had not willingly got on board that coach, the rest of the story couldn't have happened. In an emergency, I would have unmasked myself and told you I was in on the whole gnome conspiracy."

"I never would have guessed," I said.

"I was sure Clive would see through my disguise. But he never did."

"So, he was meant to find Olivia's letters, then?"

"Oh yes. We took a gamble that Clive would fall for this scheme more easily if he thought he was getting the better of someone. He fell for the whole business."

"I think he took it more seriously than you might have expected. When I visited his prison cell, he was . . . well, I think he was heartbroken."

Joan looked at her husband with a frown. "I worried it might be too much for him."

"He's come through fine," said Cyrus. "I wanted this to build his character a bit. And he's got the chemistry lab. That was a pretty penny, I have to say!"

Michael walked into the den. Everyone greeted him by name.

"I'm told you need a strong shoulder to hoist young Clive away," he said. Anna laughed and warned Michael that Clive was heavier than he looked. Michael lifted the boy and propped him against his left shoulder without struggle. Clive barely seemed to notice.

I walked along with the Murneys all the way out to the concrete lot. Joan walked alongside me. "I think you were a very good friend to my son,' she said. "I don't mind telling you. I'm anxious as hell about that chemistry lab. Who knows what evil things Clive might do with it."

"I think he just wants to know."

"Know what?" Joan asked.

"Everything," I said.

As Michael arranged Clive into the backseat of Cyrus's car, Clive's eyes opened briefly. "Who are you?" he said, and then he saw that he was under a New Zealand sky once again. "How did I get here?"

"You're almost back home, son," said Cyrus.

"Oh," Clive muttered, and then slumped back on the car seat and resumed his long-delayed sleep.

"Say hello to Olivia," I said as Cyrus got behind the wheel.

"When I see her. She's keeping company with Nate Garrick right now. She'll be home this afternoon." He said this in such a carefree way, he couldn't have known how sorry I would be to hear it. He revved the engine and engaged the clutch. "You've quite a day ahead of you. The merriest of Christmases, Mannie."

"Thank you, Mr. Murney," I said.

He smiled and waved as he pulled away. Anna blew me a kiss, and then the Murney family was gone. It was time for me to uncover the real secrets of Very North.

Chapter Twenty-One

A Second Look

"Are you ready to start?" Michael said. "I can only give you an hour or so, but I'd like to show you around."

My orientation began with a tour of the grounds. Michael and I walked around the lower perimeter of the great warehouse. Rounding the first corner, we followed a narrow dirt trail into a copse of trees.

"Any idea where we are now?" said Michael.

"This must be the forest where Lemuel's house is, and the tavern," I said.

"Right you are. It won't look nearly so enchanted in the bright light of day."

We came to a steep hill. The trail went on a gentle incline along the side of it.

"This is an artificial berm," said Michael. You passed underneath it when you entered the tunnels from the tavern. It's here to keep the warehouse hidden during the early acts of our drama. We planted these nice, tall trees along the top to act as a screen. It's been here ten years now, and it's grown in rather nicely."

We reached the top of the berm, some ten feet above the ground, and began the descent on the other side. "In daylight, you can see the warehouse through the trees, but at night, you'd really have to be looking for it."

"I didn't see it at all," I said. Of course, I hadn't been looking.

Soon, we stood at the door of the tavern.

"You were selected for the role of accidental keeper. You got to hold the medallion. We endow our older candidates with that track. It's a more involved story. We can add one or two more to that narrative.

Your friend Clive was included through one of our most elaborate plots yet!"

"You guessed right that Clive would steal Olivia's letters."

"It was satisfying to see it all come together. Tonight's story will be slightly less involved. Every night is a little different."

"Is it always as frightening?"

'We do add a few unnerving touches to the drama. Seems to make things more believable. It gets a bit scary, and that's on purpose."

"I noticed,' I said.

"Our play has darkness and light. Each brings out the essence of the other. Of course, the younger children are sometimes overwhelmed by it. Our younger candidates take a somewhat gentler course. But then, everyone faces the Grim Frost. We always win, though. Here, take a look at this."

He swung open the door of sculpted gnarled roots. He pointed to several indentations hidden behind the grooves and curves of the twisting body of the tree. Curves of glass peeked from within the knotted cover.

"There are lights hidden all over this tree, inside and out. Some of them are bright white floods, for when Mother Solstice shows up. There are soft yellow and blue lights, quite dim, to give the tree a spectral quality. It's subtle, but I quite like it. There is a real tree just behind this false front, though it's off a bit to the left, and this entryway swerves over to the right, and down to our show structure. The branches above us are real. The tavern is not. Take a look behind the tree. The shed is more obvious in this light."

Two corrugated metal sheds stood behind the tree, and butted up against the berm. I tried to picture how this had looked the night before, but my memory was still richly colored by the dreamlike feeling that I had been moving in.

"It's hard to believe this is the same place," I said.

"I hope it isn't a disappointment."

"No, not at all." I looked at the detail of carved concrete tree bark along the false sections of the tavern entrance. It was intricate work, designed to fool the eye. I ran my hands along the painted surface. "It's fantastic," I said.

"Let's go in." Michael pushed open the door and stood aside to make room for me.

A few of the interior lights were still on, but it was harder to see having come in from the sunlight.

"You met the F.A.B. here. So did Clive. Just so you know, nobody was drinking anything like actual beer, holly or otherwise. In fact, my actors tell me they find the sugared punch in those barrels utterly repulsive. Try some for yourself."

He grabbed a mug and drew some liquid from the barrel marked Wish Number Three. I drank it. It was tepid and bland. "I've had worse," I said, and laughed. "The F.A.B. sure looked like they were enjoying it."

"They are some of the best actors in the world. Most of them have been with me for all twelve years we have been in operation."

"Twelve years!" I said.

"Yes indeed. This production has been staged twelve times a year, for twelve years. So, that's something like a hundred forty-four performances, once tonight is done. And that means nearly a thousand young people have lived through our story."

"Have they all kept it secret?" I thought that if a thousand children in New Zealand had been through the experience I had just had, the news would have traveled.

"Nothing so strange could stay secret for long," said Michael. "I hear from parents, and even from former candidates. Their stories have leaked into playground conversations and holiday party gossip. But remember, those odd stories about Father Christmas must compete with many more thousands of tales about Santa Claus. So far, I am a very distant second in the popular consciousness."

"Still, more than a thousand candidates . . ."

"That's not really so many, over a dozen years. Ours is the most exclusive show I know of. And the ticket price is so high, it would make your head spin. I wish it weren't so. I wish that thousands more could be a part of it. I never meant this to be so exclusive. It's been a luxury for children of wealth."

"*We're* not wealthy," I said. "Tabitha and Jeremy. Surely they're not either."

"No. You and the Boyd children were here thanks to a charitable fund that Martin and I created. Half of our candidates each year are now drawn from less privileged homes. Of course, you had an advocate. Audra campaigned for your inclusion. I'm so glad she did."

"The Boyds, are they really going to move into the Murney's old house?"

"Yes. Their father will be working for the ranch after the handover to the new owners. They will be in one of the smaller ranch homes. That really is how they were selected. Mr. Murney told us about them, and I put them onto the candidate list. I wish all stories could have such nice endings. Here, let me show you another secret."

He went past the counter, and the painting that hid the door to the secret distillery. He pressed on the wall and opened a well-hidden panel.

"There is a narrow hallway parallel to the one which you traveled. Go on in. Watch your step. It's dark."

Once I was inside the tunnel, I could see, through a small glass window, back into the tavern.

"From inside the set, it simply looks like a mirror. From this side, it is a window from which the scene can be observed. More than half of the mirrors that decorate all of out sets are actually viewing ports. You were being watched much of the time."

"By who?" I said.

"By our staff, for your safety. And on occasion, by your parents."

"They were along the whole time?"

"Much of it."

This revelation was difficult to fit into my re-weaving of reality. "So all that time I worried about being missed, they were watching?"

"Your mother was very pleased when you tried to get word to her by way of Flutterbold," Michael said. "Let's go carefully," and we continued down the narrow hall.

In a few steps, we were looking into the distillery. The vats were empty and the mechanisms were immobile.

"Any moment now, the compressors inside the main building will be turned back on. We have to run them, to keep the temperature low enough. But, it always bothered me that the machine noise leaked over into our forest set. So, I came up with the notion of this distillery, and its chugging machines. Now candidates believe that it is the source of all that factory noise."

"That's what I thought when I saw this. I was amazed at how much noise it made."

"I'm happy to know that the ruse worked." He was smiling, an impish smile, like a boy whose practical joke has gone off perfectly.

As if on cue, the machinery of refrigeration kicked up in the warehouse with a thunk and a whirr.

"There it goes," said Michael. "It's off and on throughout the day. We must keep the ice from melting, without driving up costs too much. And keeping fresh layers of snow is a constant messy business"

We walked along the edge of the room, circling around until we came to a simple door on a hinge, that pushed open and into the first tunnel behind the VN portal.

"I'm sure you remember the start of your journey here. You put a key into this door from the other side. One of our crew stood in this spot, reached into this crevice, and pulled it through so that the key was yanked out of your hand."

"Yes, I remember."

"Then our stage hand opened the door, just partway, and ducked back into the parallel corridor by pushing here." He motioned for me to follow him back into the hidden walkway, and then we were alongside the second passage, behind another door.

"The same key was set up for you, along with the jacket and boots. I'm sure you remember all the mirrors along the walls. Much of what seems like decoration is born of the need for viewing ports. Here, let's go all the way through to Very North. We won't stay long. The fans aren't yet blowing, but it's still cold."

We emerged into the taller of the two warehouses. Not only were the work lights on, but a large sliding door was opened to the east side, letting considerable sunlight into the cavernous room. A crew was running crates out onto a truck parked nearby.

"What are they doing?" I asked.

"Believe it or not, picking up deliveries. There is a section of this warehouse where we still store fresh cuts of meat. They're taking it to the local market."

"So, Marbury Meats . . ."

"Is still a going concern. A modest one."

In this light, I could see that the largest drifts and mounds of snow were actually structures of wire mesh and concrete. There were a dozen trees to the right of the largest hill, and near these was an entrance I recognized. It was the cottage where Kris first took me in. There I had sat by a fireplace and believed myself to have traveled thousands of miles, across oceans by way of some earthen tunnels.

"If you look to the left, you can see where our other passageway comes into this space. That is where our younger visitors enter Very North. Their journey is much less complicated. Of course, those children are spared the site of poor Trimble being hunted and shot."

As soon as he mentioned it, I had to know how that had worked.

"Here, walk around this embankment. Stay on the plywood planks. Careful, they can be slippery."

On the other side of the modest white drift was an apparatus of lights, fans and air blowers.

"During the show, we blow a mist throughout this chamber. It adds to the atmosphere, and makes it easier for our guests to believe that they are outdoors. I could only create the outside world of Very North in a state of darkness and storm. Those lights are aimed upward, and in the mist, they create a beam against which Trimble and the hunters are seen in shadow."

In front of one bank of light cans, there was a platform, on top of which was a puppet, about two feet long, carved of wood, with articulated joints. It was finely crafted in the form of a reindeer.

"This puppet cast the shadows of the dying Trimble. Those lights nearer the crest cast the shadows of three of our crew, in hoods and masks. It's a simple trick, but dramatic. More than once, I have seen brave young visitors try to rush to Trimble's aid. Of course, Father Christmas is always nearby, waiting to intervene."

"Has anyone ever made their way around and seen the whole works?"

"Oh yes. Every illusion in our show has been discovered by one clever child or another. The real trick is to come up with some explanation that will keep the candidate in our story. I once told a young lady that this was an illusion set up to frighten away any real hunters."

"Did it work?"

"Oh yes. She was convinced, and as far as I know, still believes that she spent an evening in a magical place."

I saw the sleigh on which I had made a brief journey.

"This is the trickiest part of our story. I try to make sure that everyone keeps their heads down for the duration. It's on a track, you see."

Michael showed me the track used to guide the sleigh on its short ride. The groove led through a tunnel, with blowing fans designed to keep young eyes tucked into coats and hoods. Small projections of moving lights were installed, so those who peeked would see little flashes whoosh by. The sound of howling wind was amplified by speakers to drown out the compressor and fans that kept the place cold. The double-grooved track ran through a wide round tunnel, sloping gently to the entrance of the labyrinth, which was actually in the basement.

"We work hard to convince our candidates that they have actually been outside, riding in a storm. Once we establish that, then our play is truly something that can only have happened by magic. Everything that follows is twice as enchanted."

Michael took me to the back of the set for the snow-covered yard. From this angle, opposite the Great Hall, I could see the floor above the three long windows. The show control booth was situated above. I saw the many lights that hung from scaffolding. I saw speaker cabinets, air ducts and catwalks. From inside the ballroom, this endlessly complicated apparatus was invisible. From this side of the scene, it was staggering, even intimidating.

Michael showed me the amazing apparatus that animated the Grim Frost. I saw the lifts that raised and lowered Mother Solstice, and the endless cables that powered the dancing lights. Michael was perhaps proudest of the simple mechanism that allowed the fluttering, flittery orbs to circle around the seven lanterns. It was a simple and clever design.

"Martin is a genius," he said. "Every idea I've had, he's found a way to bring it to practical life. Of course, it's all just clever tricks if I can't arrest the emotions. So I focus on the story. Together, we've really got something, I think."

The hour raced by. Michael announced he could show me only one more place. He walked me to the interior of the Very North palace, and into the chapel.

The stained glass window shone at full electric brightness. Michael opened a panel near the door and dimmed them to half power.

"It's all real stained glass," he said, "and it cost me a fortune." He sat on the throne, leaned against its back and sighed. "The rest of these rooms are just sets, a stage for me to put on the show. But this place, it's as sacred to me as any could ever be."

He closed his eyes and folded his hands. "I can forget myself here." A contented smile spread across his face.

It didn't seem like the time to say anything, so I went to the railing at the transept. I knelt, facing the nativity by the altar. Just by habit, I put my hands together and lowered my head. The two of us were silent for at least a minute.

"Praying?" Michael asked.

"No," I said. "I don't think so."

"Meditating then."

"Just letting myself be here," I answered.

"Wise beyond your years," Michael said, approaching the rail. "You sound like a Buddha."

"I don't think so. I don't even know what that means."

Michael pointed to the window that depicted the robed monk. "Like the Bodhisattva. You are a student of Zen without even knowing it."

"At least I'm not like this one," I said, pointing to the trickster figure, Hans Heilig-Teufel. "He doesn't seem so nice."

"He's cunning. He can choose to be kind or cruel. I thought it might be best to remind myself that we have the potential for either. The choice is ours."

I looked at the plaster baby in the rough-hewn wooden manger.

"How did you get that statue to change into a baby?"

"That was clever, if you can forgive my boasting. Maybe the finest little miracle I've pulled off yet. But when I tell you, you may be disappointed to learn how simple it was."

"All right, I don't mind," I said. "Is there a lift or a trap door?"

"No, nothing that complicated. I had so little time to plan for it. The child was born last week. Samantha's been away from her mother for six months. She had some inkling that she might one day have a brother. That's why it was so much on her mind. I daresay, that may be why she found herself so drawn to Mr. Gibney. There is something younger-brotherish about him."

"Yes, I thought so too."

"Samantha moved to New Zealand with her father, all the way from Atlantic City, New Jersey. Her mother arrived just days ago. I couldn't resist the opportunity."

"So, that really was her baby brother!" I'd had to remind myself that, after all, Samantha had been in Christchurch last night, not in the remote North.

"Yes. Now, perhaps you've sorted out the truth behind the robed servants."

"One of them was Clive's dad." I said.

"They were your parents, nearly all of them."

"What? My Mum and Dad as well?"

"Yes, alongside parents, friends and relatives for all the other children."

"They made me nervous."

"By design. More tension to the story. It makes for a happier resolution at the end. Anyway, Mrs. Krupp entered the chapel through this panel," he said, pressing on a section of the wall. "She had the baby child bundled in her arms, and she was surrounded by the others. They gathered around the manger, just as I directed Samantha to look up at the rosette glass, way up there on the opposite wall."

"Misdirection!" I said.

"Spoken like a true magician," said Michael. "Mr. Krupp lifted out the fake baby, and his wife placed the real baby, just in time for us to turn around and look."

"Then you made Samantha look at the window again when they switched it back. We all looked up."

"It's hard to resist following someone's hand when they face and point upward," Michael said. He looked up at the rosette and pointed. And sure enough, I looked too.

"I thought it wise to reunite Samantha with her family as quickly as possible. The instant they go to the den, her parents dropped the whole charade and took her home. I doubt she's thought about us since."

"She didn't get to see the end of the story, with Evan and all."

"She'll have a visit this very afternoon by Gordon and his family. No doubt, he will fill her in on all the details. Who knows what they will make of the whole business? They may figure it out, and that's fine."

"Do you mind if they find out it's fake?"

"I'm always impressed when skeptical minds figure it out. But I love it even more when they don't. It doesn't matter to me if my candidates continue to believe or not. What matters is that it's miraculous to them while it's happening."

"I believed every moment of it."

"That's what I live to hear. Now, today is your turn. You will help us make the grand miracle for others, for a few splendid hours."

"Mr. Brams," I said. "What will I be doing?"

"To the children, you will appear to be someone who works on the staff, alongside Della and Martin. You will help us keep an eye on our charges. Oh, and one other thing." A sly smile crept into his expression.

"What is it?"

"You did such an excellent job last time, so, you will teach another young man how to sing The Magpie's Christmas."

Chapter Twenty-Two

Souvenirs

Before he left to meet his many obligations, Michael instructed me to go to the third floor, and find the faculty green room. ("It's the room that isn't green.") I was told to wait there for a stage manager who had been appointed to train me.

The walls of the green room were painted light beige, and it was furnished with plain tables and folding chairs. Newspapers were stacked near a percolator and a tray of biscuits. A few serious-faced people drank coffee and scanned headlines in silence. No one looked twice at me.

On the wall, I found a bulletin board busy with notes, schedules and reminders. My eye went to the largest sheet, a chart listing each performer, and a box in which to indicate by check mark that they had arrived, presumably on time.

Secret Feast Call Sheet
Call Time 4:30 PM—Friday, Dec. 24
(Happy Christmas Eve!)

Principal Players
Father Christmas/ Kris—Michael Brams
Mother Solstice/ Iris—Charlotte Remy
Martin Piper—Martin Milberg
Grim Frost/ Evan—James Pym

Forest Players
Flutterbold—Nigel Storm
Drillmast—Ivan Holst
Lemuel Greenleaf—Kevin Liftin
Sara Greenleaf—Sara Niley-Liftin

Forest Abduction Brigade
Wheatbrew—Kenneth Kilser
Copper—Brenda Schoene
Branchstaff—Heinrich Schoene

I studied the list with fascination. Putting names to characters I had met, had believed in, less than twenty-four hours ago was new in my experience. I wanted to meet each of them before they put on these fanciful personas. As I stared at the typewritten sheet, I heard my name.

"Mannie Candler! Good to see you again."

A young man with sandy blonde hair approached. It was Nate Garrick. "Recognize me?" he said. "Captain Magnificent, in person."

Very North was full of surprises. This one turned my face red, with a combination of embarrassment and defensiveness.

"I never called you that," I said, lying on an impulse.

Nate chuckled. "Not what I've heard. Hey, you look surprised. Didn't anyone tell ya I'd be your stage manager?"

"No," I said, and it came out impetuous.

"Figures. Everyone's so busy." Then he held out his hand. "Welcome aboard," he said.

I didn't put out a hand, but stood fixed to the spot, overthinking my next words, and so, saying nothing.

"All right, we better get it out of the way," said Nate. "Everyone says you're jealous about me an' Olivia. So, all I got to say to that is, I know how you feel."

"You do?"

"She talks about *you* so much, I can't tell if she cares a crap for me." Next came the ingratiating smile. He mussed my hair with his hand. I glared.

"Right, we'll leave it be. Ya ready to get to work?"

"Fine," I said, very quietly.

Nate ignored my terrible manners, and spoke to me affably.

"We've got to sign you in, first," he said. He pointed out a second sheet on the board. It was labeled Faculty Sign In. Near the end of the list, I saw my own name.

Mannie Candler—Apprentice

I knew instant delight in seeing myself acknowledged as an official part of this operation. My name on that sheet meant I belonged, even in modest capacity, to something wondrous in the world.

"All right,' said Nate, "We've got a lot to cover. Let's start in the frock shop."

The costume department was just down the hall. Amid the riot of clothes racks, sewing stations and walls hung with scraps and samples, half a dozen women in aprons busied themselves with repairs. Even on this upper floor, the temperature was cool enough that most of them wore sweaters. From the middle of the shop floor, a voice shouted "Hello Mannie!"

It was Olivia. She was sorting through the candidate's colorful knitted sweaters. She wore a pair of wire rim glasses. I hadn't known she ever needed them, but then, I saw her so seldom. Her hair was tied in a loose ponytail with candy-striped ribbon, and she sported a black turtleneck sweater. The overall effect was that she looked a few years older than she had at the party last Sunday. And I felt so much younger still when I answered 'hello' back, and my voice cracked.

"Another surprise, eh?" Nate clapped my back again. You couldn't fault him for lack of exuberance.

"You work here?" I asked Olivia.

"I'm just volunteering for today. Nate actually gets paid to be here. Isn't that great?"

"Yeah," I said. "It must to be the best job world."

"Got that right," Nate said.

"He'll talk your ear off about it later. Let me show you the frock shop!"

Olivia took my hand and led me to the back of the wide room, past racks of clothes and bags of laundry.

"I want to show you the master wall first. It's got everything."

Before me, the entire story of the Secret Feast was laid out in costumes, mounted on pegs and displayed for optimal visibility. I could run the events of last night through my head as I scanned the display. They were nearly in order; the forest clothes of Lemuel and Flutterbold, the different coats and hats worn by Martin and Kris, Iris's gowns and Evan's antlered crown.

"These are the prototypes," Nate said. "The crew here make sure that every costume matches the concept perfectly. My mum's in charge of it."

"That's how Nate got the job," said Olivia with a wry smile.

"Let's show him the masks." Nate pulled me to a nearby corner. I saw three faces of Kris hanging on the wall. These were carefully crafted masks of Father Christmas, in two different phases of frostbite. I was stunned and unsettled by the realistic depictions of Kris's frozen expressions of agony.

"Michael is only on stage at the beginning of the Grim Frost sequence," Nate explained. "Another performer takes over after the blackouts, wearing these masks."

"They're so realistic," I said. I brushed the back of my hand against one and was surprised to find that it was made of carved wood.

"Martin finds the best artists in the world to make this stuff. He's a genius. So's Michael, of course."

On an adjacent wall, I found the black animal masks of Evan's servants. They were beautiful and forbidding. The deer mask of Silbersee sat on a nearby table.

"Look at this," said Nate. "Inside the mask, by the mouth, there's a kind of glass tube. It distorts the voice. Listen."

He donned the mask and made a roaring noise into the glass receptacle. Indeed, it had an unearthly, animal quality to it. Thus had Cyrus Murney gone from affable Dad to daunting coachman.

"It's fantastic," I said as he put the mask back down on the worktable. "How long have you worked here?" I asked.

"Officially, it's only my second year," said Nate. "But I've been around a long time. You see that office door that says Eleanor Garrick?"

As soon as he mentioned it, I saw it. *Eleanor Garrick—Wardrobe Mistress*

"That's my Mum," he said proudly. "She's a genius, too."

I could see Eleanor Garrick through the window of her door. Her hands and arms were in constant motion as she spoke to one of her staff. As I watched, I saw face turn toward the three of us. She got Nate's attention and waved him over. Nate begged our pardon and went to talk to her. I welcomed the chance to speak to Olivia alone, if only for a few moments.

"I hope you don't mind," she said, as soon as Nate was gone. "He likes you. And the two of you have a long day ahead."

By saying so, she made clear that she knew how I felt. That wasn't surprising, but it put me at a disadvantage. I couldn't feign indifference, and didn't want to.

"I guess he's all right," was the sharpest thing I could think to say.

"Yes, silly boy. He's very all right."

"But, he is your boyfriend," I said.

"Oh, I suppose he is," she said. "Don't hold that against him. You'll just make yourself miserable."

I had never before felt so conscious of my lack of years. Not even a week ago, Olivia had seemed a kind of giddy and dreamy girl who talked of fanciful things like gnomes and Father Christmas. In soft lantern light, beneath the mistletoe, she had talked about the color of my eyes, and leaned close enough for me to kiss. But of course, that had been an illusion, part of the set-up for my grand surprise. She had been acting. Now I could see that she was a young woman, one who saw herself as significantly older than me. And I could not pretend to be any kind of rival to an impressive boy like Nate, a boy who was older still.

I felt my gaze go awkwardly to anything other than her face. An uncomfortable moment or two passed. Then I gathered the presence of mind to speak again.

"Will you be with us today?"

"No. I've got to help out here. I'll join the two of you at the lunch break. And after that, I've got to go home."

I nodded and gave what I'm sure was a weak smile. She touched my arm.

"You're going to have a wonderful night. Being in on this secret is the best thing ever!" Then she turned to Nate, who had finished talking to his mother.

He put his arm around her and kissed her quickly before turning his attention back to me. "Are you ready?"

"Ready as I'll ever be," I told him. I decided not to hate him, nor to like him. I decided to love the place, and everything about it.

Nate took me through every inch of the complex. He showed me every hidden door, secret switch and concealed gimmick. The warehouse was like Professor Carabello's conjuring table, exponentially expanded. With his guidance, I pulled on the levers that made holly wreaths rotate out of seemingly bare walls. I saw the hidden flutes, trumpets, bells and organ pipes that caused the mystic, musical blasts for Mother Solstice. Those sounds were played from an organ-like console, from the windowed booth on the second floor, overlooking the snow yard. I pressed three keys and created a trumpet blast in G major. I got to run my hands along the switches that controlled the colored lights beneath the snow. I made them swirl and dance, though without the practiced grace of the show operators.

In the course of the day, Nate introduced me to the entire cast. They regaled me with stories of past shows. Charlotte Remy, the Belgian actress who played Mother Solstice, talked about how much Trimble used to hate her, and how difficult it was to earn his trust enough to ride on his back. In performance, she had spoken a flawless, uninflected English, but in conversation, she had a pronounced Brussels accent. Brenda and Heinrich Schoene, a husband and wife team, told me of their travels with an Austrian circus. They now lived in Dunedin, and came to Christchurch every Christmas to play Copper and Branchstaff.

"Did you recognize me without my beard?" said Brenda. Her husband laughed and said, "He may wish he hadn't."

At every point along the way, Nate regaled me with stories and gossip. The Secret Feast had accumulated vast amounts of insider lore in its dozen years. I envied his lifelong access to it, and I wanted to know everything he had to tell me. If I had been fascinated by the place before, I was fast falling in love with it. I knew that Very North would occupy my thoughts for a very long time. I knew it was goal to become a vital part of it myself. I didn't want to tell him so, but he was helping to open up new worlds of possibility for me. The perpetual grin on my face must have given my feelings away, anyhow.

The luncheon interval arrived, and we returned to the green room. Steam trays had been set up, and inside them were slices of roast lamb and ample heaps of shepherd's pie. Kevin Liftin invited Nate and I to sit with him and his wife Sara. We joined them for a few minutes, but once Olivia arrived, Nate got up and went to join her at a different table. I stayed with the Liftins for a few more minutes, then excused myself and walked to the other table. I had an uneasy feeling that maybe I wasn't meant to intrude on Nate and Olivia. Then I decided I didn't give a damn.

Olivia looked pleased to see me arrive. "Nate says you're a keen learner."

"Who wouldn't be in a place like this."

"I'm so glad you could make it. After what happened, my dad said you weren't going to be here. Oh! Mannie, I'm so sorry about Audra!"

"I am too," I said. "I mean, well, everything is so different now. I hardly remember what my life was like even last week."

We were silent for a moment or two, and then Nate prompted Olivia to tell me about the long campaign to ensnare Clive into the scheme.

"He was quick to steal the letters from Kris," she said. "But he remained skeptical about them until he met Flutterbold the night before. Nate and I took him along on what we told him was a date. Flutterbold was to lure him onto the old dirt road, but Clive had figured out where the Moss Circle was, and he charged off on his own to find it. We were close by. Even when you were walking the circle, Mannie. We were just yards away, dressed in our tech blacks. I was so afraid you would spot us."

"You were there?"

"More often than you know," said Nate. "I'm the one who took the key from your hand and opened the passage doors for you."

"And I led your parents to all the observation windows," said Olivia. "We were watching when you taught the song to that boy."

"Gordon? You saw that?"

"It was the most difficult task of my life not to laugh!"

"He was something else," I admitted.

"As I was saying, I guided your parents. We saw you in Clive's prison cell. We saw you in the ballroom. And I was one of those beastly robed servants, too."

"Which one?"

"The unicorn."

I barely remembered seeing a unicorn mask, but then my attention had been well taken with other matters.

"I had no idea," I said. "All along I thought Clive had stolen your place here."

"You know, I was a candidate last year," she said.

"Really? You sure kept that secret from me!"

"I know! It wasn't easy."

Nate took Olivia's hand. "Last year's show was when I met her. She actually figured the whole works out."

"Did you?"

Olivia smiled. "They had me going for a while. But sometime during the attack, I began to notice how much the Grim Frost moved like a puppet. I kept playing along, of course. It was delightful."

"Mannie here bought the whole works," said Nate.

"There's nothing wrong with that," said Olivia. "It's sweet. And we *want* people to believe!" She may as well have patted my head and given me a lollipop.

I collected our combined trays and plates and took them to a nearby bin. On purpose, I stayed out of their way as the break came to a close. At a distance, I saw Nate pull Olivia close and kiss her. I broke off whatever remaining strands of hope or concern I was carrying about the matter. I was eager to return to the show.

After Olivia departed for home, Nate and I met up with Martin Milberg in the Chamber of Good Cheer. Martin knelt behind the elaborate mechanical toy theatre, an open toolbox by his side. Several of the little carved figures lay nearby.

"I thought you might want to see this," Nate said, "since you like toy theatres so much."

"How did you know that?" I asked.

"Like I said, Olivia's talked about you," and he flashed that smile, the one so winning it tweaked my distrust by reflex.

Martin spoke from within the back of the little stage. "Is that Mannie?"

"Yes sir," I answered.

"Take a look at the stage. Go ahead and flip it on. Let me know if the figures are all standing upright. Sometimes they get snagged. Just holler if anything's amiss."

An all-new cast of characters emerged and danced around the circus ring. "We customize and change out the figures and backdrops for every performance," said Nate. "Their movements will be the same, everything else is tailored for the night's candidates. Tomorrow morning, they'll find 'em in their stockings. Oh, that reminds me. Nate, reach in and get that figure I left in the second drawer."

Nate slid open a hidden drawer on the side of the theatre. He retrieved a figure that looked quite a bit like me.

"You were supposed to be in the show," he said. "It got snagged. Sorry about that. Things don't always go a hundred per cent nifty, even at Very North. Here, you can have it."

He handed me the jointed stick puppet, dressed in a sweater just like the one I had been given by Clement. I had no pocket sufficient to carry it, so Martin put it in his unusual, decorated apron. He promised to give it back to me before the evening was out.

I remembered a question, one of the many that had been in my mind since last night. "The music box played a song, a new song. Clive sang it at the cathedral last week. It was written by someone I know."

Martin inched himself out from behind the proscenium stage. "By Rex Palmer, yeah, I know. Here, take a look beneath the floor. You'll see a scroll of paper with holes punched in it."

I did as he instructed. I wanted to spend hours examining the mechanisms that made the players and sets move, timed to the delicate music.

"I can punch any tune into paper with this system. Tonight, it'll play 'Drink To Me Only With Thine Eyes,' and 'Joy To The World.' All nine of our visitors will see themselves in the show."

"It's Christmas Eve," said Nate. "That's always our largest bunch of candidates. Tonight, four of 'em are here 'cause their folks can afford it. Five of 'em are here thanks to the foundation."

I could think of no charity more wonderful than that which allowed poor children to spend a few hours at Very North. Nate, Martin and I watched the entire toy theatre sequence. Martin looked at his watched and huffed.

"Not much more time, boys. You should go get your frocks," he said and hurried out of the Great Hall.

Nate's mother found us as we approached the frock shop. Michael was walking by her side. "There you are," she called out to Nate. "Thought you might have got lost."

"Nate?" said Michael. "Not likely. He knows this place better than I do." Then he looked at me. "Mannie, I'd like you to follow me. I'll be turning into Kris soon, but first, I've got something for you."

"Just have him back to me within the hour," said Mrs. Garrick. Michael assured her he would, and then he led me to an office around a corner, at the end of a concrete hall.

The office was nicely appointed, with a window that looked down over the snow yard. Two wooden desks were situated at right angles to each other. One bore a nameplate for Martin Milberg, the other for Michael Brams.

"This is where we conduct the business end of our operation," Michael said. "Not so captivating as the other stops on your tour, I bet.

Please, have a seat." He pointed to a chair facing his own desk. He sat down, opened a drawer, and produced a scrapbook.

"Take a look through here, if you like. We don't allow photographs of our show. So, this small collection of pictures is quite exclusive. They show the construction of Very North, and some of our cast trying on costumes. If anyone should write our history, I suppose these would be of interest."

"Yes, sir!" I said. I took an eager look. A sheaf of loose papers was tucked in among the first few pages. It was a script, mostly typed, with lines added in pencil along the margins. I read a few lines from the near the end of the document. I recognized words I had heard Kris and Evan speak, with seeming spontaneity, just last night.

"I remember this," I said. "You and Evan have this conversation every time?"

"Yes," said Michael. "Evan can manifest jealous rage on command. And he creates the most perfect redemption at the end. Don't you think?"

"Yes! He changed completely!"

"Without his utter commitment to the emotion of it, the whole charade would come undone," said Michael. "I am regularly astounded at the skill of my artists."

I leafed through the script. "It's a lot to learn."

"The real challenge is being ready to improvise. The key players in our drama have no script. The candidates might say or do anything. We've mastered the art of ad lib. In this show, there's no other way."

I found the photographs. I was fascinated by the glimpses of actors trying on costumes, or clustered around sets still under construction.

"Those pictures are confidential," he said, "as are the names of our performers. We run a clandestine operation. We conspire to create an evening of wonders, and then we disappear. It's a special calling, and completely impractical."

"It's exactly what I would do, if I had loads of money," I said, and quickly thought better of it. "I don't mean *you* have loads of money or anything like that."

"I once had some measure of wealth, Mannie. My father was an industrialist. He ran factories and firms in London. In his later years, he bought several concerns here in Christchurch. To my father's lasting regret, I had neither head nor heart for business. When he passed away,

Father divided his holdings between his brother, and his two children. That would be myself, and my brother Coswell."

"So, did your father own Marbury Meats?"

"Yes, well spotted. It was part of my inheritance. I had no idea what to do with it."

"So you turned it into Very North."

"Not right away. I did my best to keep it going, but I failed."

"It's too bad. But, I like this a lot better," I said cheerfully.

"So do I," he agreed, then he sighed. "I was born to lose money. That's what my father said, and my uncle has echoed the refrain many times."

"What about your brother?"

"He has managed all right, but these years have been hard."

"I know. My father preaches about it."

Michael shifted forward in his chair and changed the subject. "Did you know I was present at your pageant, in Christchurch Cathedral?"

"You mean last Sunday?"

"Yes, Mannie."

"Then, you saw my reading."

"Very dramatic. I was impressed."

I could feel my face growing warm. "I feel a bit silly about it now."

"I came to see you, and also Clive Murney. I spoke that night with Rex Palmer, and got from him the sheet music for the song."

That night came back into my mind with force and clarity.

"I couldn't believe it when I heard the music box playing it."

"That's the sort of surprise Martin and I strive for. Personal and meaningful."

"So, you must have talked to . . ." I stopped as soon as I realized whose name must come next.

"Audra," he finished for me.

"Did you know her?"

"Very well, indeed," he said. He got up from behind the desk, and moved to a chair adjacent to mine. "Mannie, did your aunt ever tell you about her life, her early years."

"Sometimes."

"Did she ever tell you that she was once married?"

"I knew she was once. Mother didn't like to talk about it. Audra said Mum didn't approve of the fellow." With a sudden shock, I recalled something Audra had once said. "Oh my God! She told me his name was Michael!"

"Yes, Mannie. That would be me. I was your uncle. Before you were born, of course."

I had now a thousand questions, but no words to carry them. I just gazed at him and stammered a bit.

"It didn't last very long, Mannie. We were young. Neither of us knew our own hearts. So, it wasn't meant to be. But, we loved each other. Be sure of that. She was one of my closest friends, her whole life."

"She was?" I said, and now I was glad I was sitting down, because I could feel my legs going weak. "Why didn't I ever meet you before?"

"Auckland is a pretty long way. And around your mother, I was a sore topic."

"Why?"

"To her, I've always been a troublemaker. A radical. She's not entirely wrong. As a student, I was quite the idealist, and so was Audra. We wanted to change the world."

I remembered something Audra had said to me once. "Were you a priest?" I asked Michael.

"I was in Anglican seminary. I was soon to be ordained, but . . ."

"Did Audra stop you?"

"No. She encouraged me. But I asked a lot of questions, and when I didn't like the answers, I pushed back. Eventually, I decided it was in everyone's best interests that I part amicably with the church, and the church agreed."

He reached over to the desk and grabbed a manila envelope. "Now, here is what I wanted you to see." He handed the envelope to me, and I unwrapped the string and opened the flap. Inside were two photographs.

The first was of Audra and Michael, together, in front of a chapel doorway.

"That was our wedding day," he said. "You see, we were just children, really."

They looked like the two happiest people in the world in that photograph.

"Look at the second one. I think you'll find it interesting."

The second picture was of Audra, dressed in a flowing gown, holly in her hair, holding the scepter of Mother Solstice. Her face glowed with the wisdom of ages and her eyes saw through me from beyond years.

"She's Mother Solstice," I said.

"She was the first. Twelve years ago, in our premiere production. That was in Auckland. It was on a much smaller scale. We had to learn everything the hard way. But, she created the role. She wrote much of it."

"Wait. In the story. Kris was a priest, and Iris . . ."

"It was partly inspired by our own story. When we began rehearsals, Father Christmas was supposed to be the one with all the powers. But, the more we practiced, the more it became clear that Iris was the true power."

"Was Evan based on anybody real?"

"Hmm. That's more difficult to answer. If you mean, was my own brother Coswell involved in a romantic triangle, no. Not at all."

"But there was a rival of some kind."

"Some stories are best retold as fiction. Let's just say, we all wound up just as happy as our three heroes."

"How long did Audra play in this?"

"The first four years. Three different actresses have played the part. Charlotte is marvelous, don't you think?"

"Yes. She is."

There was a silence, and Michael took the picture of Audra from my hand. He held it, and tears began to roll down his cheek. "Audra was to have played the role of Iris last night. That was our secret plan. Of course, that would have exposed the ruse for you. But we didn't mind. She wanted to play it one more time, and she wanted, more than anything, for you to be there, to see her."

I took Michael's hand for a moment, then I dissolved. He embraced me and said, "I'm sorry." Then for a while, there was nothing for us to do but cry. Martin looked in on us, and gave a consoling smile, then told Michael that he would be needed in ten minutes.

Michael struggled to collect himself. "I knew this would happen," he said. "I can't tell you, Mannie, how happy I am that you are here. I only wish we could all come back next year and do it all again."

"Can't we?" I said.

"It's a year of sorrows. This is our final season, at least in this venue."

"Why!" I said.

"I no longer own Marbury Meats, or the building. We've been leasing it for the last five years. The new owners will take full possession of it as soon as we're done."

"But, we can move this somewhere else," I said, "Right?"

"This whole enterprise, grand as it is, loses money every year. It's a kind of miracle that we made it this far. But Mannie, I want you to know, you have seen Very North at its best. This year, everything came together as never before. We finish this adventure by reaching a summit."

I raised a few more objections. There had to be a way. I had just discovered Very North. I wasn't ready to lose it.

"Mannie, I must ask you to keep a confidence. We decided not to tell the cast and crew until our last performance is finished. I hope you understand."

I nodded, and I understood well. Every joy carries a sorrow on its back.

"Now, no regrets, young man. Cherish every bit of this night. Relish your every turn, on-stage and off. All right?"

He got up and went back to the desk, finding a handkerchief there, he passed it to me.

"Something else," he said. "Your father and I talked for a while, when I came to visit earlier this week."

"About me?"

"Of course. I gather you touched off a bit of a storm, at the breakfast table."

"Oh no! He told you about that?!"

Michael smiled. "When I was in seminary, I set off many similar storms, on precisely the same topic. No matter how I tried, I could not accept the idea of Hell. Scores of professors tried to argue me into it. But there was no means by which I could square the idea of eternal torment with a loving God."

I felt a sinking in my gut, an ingrained pang of guilt whenever I dared to doubt the teachings of those who had raised and loved me. I never imagined that anyone else ever thought these things.

"If it's weighing on your heart, think about this. Our first Christmas together, Audra and I went to a faculty dinner. Someone sat at the piano and played The First Noel. And Audra and I, we sang our own words to the chorus. It caught on with the young students there, and they all joined in. I'm sure you know the tune.

Noel, Noel
No Hell, No Hell
Love One Another
And All Shall Be Well

"That was our version. It made some people mad, and it gave comfort to others. It's not up to me to tell anyone how to think or feel. But if it ever helps you, sing it, and think of us."

With that, he placed the photograph of Audra as Iris in my hand. "This is yours now," he said. "If you're going to the memorial service in Auckland, I'll see you there."

Martin Milberg was waiting for Michael in the office doorway. Michael embraced Martin, put his head on the other's shoulder for a moment. "Come on now," said Martin. "Time to turn you into Father Christmas," and they were gone.

Chapter Twenty-Three

Joey Pete and the Lorry

M y second night with the Secret Feast was no less wondrous than my first, but I will not describe it here. I lived through the story of Very North a second time, but as a performing volunteer. The thrill of it is keenly retained in my mind. For now, I must conclude my tale, and relate the other events of that week.

My father picked me up at Very North shortly after the coronation scene had played, and we drove back to Clarketon. Congregants from the Christmas Eve midnight service were just leaving the parish. Father Humboldt came out to the car to welcome me personally. He asked me to promise a full account of my recent adventure, then gave my shoulder a gentle shove, his way of telling me he wished to speak to my father alone.

I stayed up late and helped arrange things for the Christmas morning services. I finally lay down in my own bed at two-thirty in the morning, giving me four hours to sleep before I would have to rise for the busy church day.

I served as acolyte for both morning services, then joined my parents and Father Humboldt as we visited several local households, bearing gifts and receiving some in return. These obligations were done and met by two in the afternoon. True to family custom, our own exchange of gifts followed a late lunch. This year, the gifts were modest and practical, including new shoes for all three of us. We didn't say anything about Audra's extravagant gift. I knew in my heart how unusual it was, how churlish I would have to be ever to expect its like again.

There were Saturday chores to be done. I changed into my dungarees and got to work, first weeding the flower patch, then back to trimming the hedgerows by the white wooden fence at the road.

The work gave me time to reflect. Saturday exactly one week ago, I had been performing the same chore, eagerly anticipating the ride to Christchurch, and the prospect of seeing Olivia at the pageant. Since then, so much had happened, a lifetime's worth.

The road past our church was never very busy, even on Christmas Day, so when any vehicle rode by I always lifted my head to see who it might be. A friendly wave was customary. Today, I had hollered Happy Christmas to a handful of holiday drivers. And then the truck appeared.

It was a freight lorry, with gray sides, and a faded logo painted on its cab.

Marbury Meats

It seemed impossible. Why would that truck drive past here? Making a delivery? This far from Christchurch? That seemed unlikely. Was Michael coming to visit? I craned to see who was driving the lorry. Only one man at the wheel, and he was certainly not Michael. I waved anyway. The driver didn't see me.

The truck moved slowly as it passed the fenced yard of the church. I kept a constant stare until it reached the bend at the west side of the property and disappeared.

Suddenly, I had to know where it was going. Without a second thought, I jumped into action. I dropped the hedge shears and sprinted to the horse stable. As quickly as I could, I grabbed the saddle and bridle and got Joey Pete ready to ride.

I ought to tell someone where I'm going, I thought. But then I reasoned, if it can be called reason, that since I had no idea where the truck was headed, I couldn't actually say where I was going either, so it was best not to say at all.

I rode Joey into the yard, and coaxed him into a fast trot to the north end of the church property. From there, I could see the bend in the road, and in the distance, the Marbury Meats truck. It was making a left turn, for the road leading to Trinity Corners, then Oxford. I knew of a trail that cut across the loop of highway. If I rode fast enough, I might be able to beat the truck to the intersection.

I pressed poor Joey Pete faster than he had likely gone in years. From the top of a modest rise a half mile from the church, I could see the road again, and the truck, not too far away. I was certain I could beat it to the spot where the horse trail met the highway. I moderated my speed for a while, to show our good horse some mercy. But after a mile or so, I egged him on to a championship run.

Joey Pete and I reached the road, and I stopped and dismounted. I gave him a pat and a few gentle words, and then I looked to the oncoming lane. First came a sporty Duesenberg, which raced past, and frightened the horse. Then a rather old open-top runabout puttered along, and pulled over. Its occupants were two parishioners from the church. Mr. Bindley wore a top hat, and his wife, Brigitte Brindley, held one hand on her head to keep her brightly colored scarf and bonnet in place.

"Mannie Candler, what are you doing out here on Christmas Day?"

I saw no point inventing a lie. "Trying to catch a truck," I said.

"Oh?" said Mr. Brindley. "What for?"

"I honestly don't know."

Mr. Brindley looked at Brigitte. "He doesn't know," he told her.

"Are you lost?" she asked me, with a kind of hopeful smile, as if I might have forgotten that I was.

"No, just trying to catch up with this truck."

"But you don't know why," she said.

"That's right," I answered. "I think it might be from Christchurch, and it might be from a friend of mine."

"It isn't that meat truck, is it?" said Mr. Brindle.

"Marbury Meats, yes!"

"It passed us by a few minutes ago," he said, and Brigitte Brindle nodded. "Going very fast," she added.

"Did they make off with your Christmas goose or something?" Mr. Brindle grinned in a smug way.

"No. I don't know why they're here. But if you catch up with them . . ." I started, then realized I had no plan at all.

"I'll tell them you're looking for them," he said and then he pulled back onto the road. "Happy Christmas," Mrs. Brindle said as they sped away. Her hat came off entirely, but she caught it before it took flight.

Now I knew I had missed the truck, probably by a narrow moment. I set Joey Pete at a moderate trot and continued toward Trinity Corners. Maybe I would happen upon the lorry, if it had stopped there.

It took me twenty minutes to get to the main street, where, naturally, all the shops and businesses were closed. I had almost decided to turn around and head for home, when I saw the Brindle's runabout again. It chugged its way toward me. Only Mr. Brindle was in it this time.

"Hey there! I know where your mystery lorry has got to."

"You do?"

"Sure. I just dropped Mrs. Brindle off at her brother's house. Do you know who her brother is?"

"No, I can't say that I do."

"Her brother is Simon Maxington." Mr. Brindle looked very pleased to have revealed this information, but any relevance was lost on me.

"Oh, Simon Maxington, then," I said.

"He drives lorries, you see," said Mr. Brindle. "Anyway, he said his friend Robert had to drive a job today, for which he's getting double wages, as its Christmas Day. Said it was a route from Christchurch, so I thought Robert might be your driver."

"Oh! So where is he going?"

"One more village over. It's going to the offices of Elliot an' Elliot. Solicitors."

Surely, this had to be the solicitors who were taking possession of the warehouse. So, I wondered, what was in the truck? Some part of Very North? If so, I felt I must see it. It was only right, I reasoned, if one can call such a sense of entitlement reason.

"Could you take me?" I said, none too graciously.

"My dear boy, I don't even know what your motives are. In fact, neither do you."

"The place that truck came from, I was just there. And, well, it was a wonderful place, and . . ."

"And it will surely wait until the holiday has ended. Give their office a call on Monday if you must."

"It's just that I think something might be wrong."

"Oh?" Mr. Brindle looked intrigued by this. "Do you think they've stolen something? Is there a crime in progress? That would be interesting."

I shook my head. "No, I don't guess there is. Thank you for telling me, though. I'd better go back home. I forgot to mention to anyone that I was leaving."

"Took off on an impulse, heh? Fine. Listen, stay here a minute or two. My son Carl, he's got a horse trailer. He can take you and Joey Pete back home in comfort. It would make me feel better to know you were safe. All right?"

I thanked him, and I meant it. I had begun to worry that I was overtaxing Joey Pete. Mr. Brindle took off, and I stood with the horse by a chain link fence next to a brickyard.

We waited for about fifteen minutes, and all the while, I watched the horizon in both directions, trying to will that lorry into appearing again. *I'm going to be in a lot of trouble for this. I'll feel better about it if I can at least satisfy my curiosity.*

Carl Brindle arrived, in a large sedan hitched to a weathered and dented horse trailer. Carl was tall, and he had silvery blue eyes that always seemed focused on a spot twenty yards past whomever he was talking to.

"You're the subject of much chat today, Mannie," he said as he approached Joey Pete and took the reins. "Mother's already called at least three people to tell them about your chasing down a lorry."

"Was one of those calls to my mother?"

"Don't know, but I'd be surprised if that wasn't the first one."

"Was she cross?"

"Again, I don't know." He opened the back of the trailer, inside of which lay a heap of fresh straw. Joey Pete didn't need an invitation. He stepped in and began helping himself.

Carl secured the metal door with a latch, and told me to go ahead and sit down in the car. I slowly ambled up to the passenger door, still gazing at the road. And when I had nearly lowered myself onto the seat, I saw it. A great silver lorry, Marbury Meats in faded paint on its cab.

I jumped into the middle of the road and began waving my hands, as if in a panic.

"Wait! Stop!" I shouted as I jumped and leapt about.

"Get out of the road, Mannie!" shouted Carl, and it was good advice. I moved to the other side, and continued my display of desperation. I was relieved when the great vehicle began to slow down.

The Marbury Meats lorry came to a stop just a few yards past Carl's sedan, and I ran quickly to the opening door of its cab. A grey-haired fellow with a bushy moustache climbed down.

"Is there some trouble here?" he said calmly.

"No, sir," I answered. "Are you Robert?"

"Yes. Did Mr. Prassler send you out here?"

I was startled to hear that name. "Mr. Prassler? No."

"'Cause I've just made the delivery for him. Is that not why you waved me down?"

"Oh, is it Mr. Prassler's office?" I said, beginning to make the connection. Mr. Prassler had visited my father alongside Michael. And Prassler worked for Elliot and Elliot. He must have been involved in the purchase of Michael's holdings.

"Did you come up from Very North today?"

"What?" said Robert. "No, I drove up from Christchurch."

"I mean, Marbury Meats, were you there this morning?"

Carl stepped into the conversation. "I'm awfully sorry, Robert. The lad's got a bee in his britches about something."

"What have you to do with Marbury Meats, lad?" said Robert.

"I was just there. Yesterday, you know, for the Secret Feast."

"I don't know at all," said Robert. "I just drive the lorry. I took some furniture to an office in Trinity Corners, and now I'm dropping off a couple of crates to Mr. Prassler."

"You're going to Mr. Prassler's right now?" I said. I was caught up in my own irrational ambition to know why anything from Very North had passed by my churchyard without asking my leave.

Robert looked at Carl. "You know this boy?"

"Friend of the family. He's the vicar's boy. Stephan Candler?"

"I wouldn't know. If he'll pardon me, he seems to be poking his nose where it wasn't invited."

"Yes, that's certain," said Carl, and they both shot feigned looks of dismay in my direction.

It was undeniably true. Whatever business Robert was on, whatever properties he was transporting, the matter was entirely out of my jurisdiction. "I'm sorry," I said. "I was just surprised to see your lorry go by, after . . ." I stopped, remembering that neither of these gentlemen knew about Very North. "Well, there's a man named Michael, who used to own the place. And, he put on a sort of show for us."

"Michael Brams?" said Robert.

"You know him?"

"Sure. He signed off on this lorry load."

"Yes. I think Mr. Prassler must have bought Marbury Meats, and . . . Listen, could I ride along with you, to Mr. Prassler's place? I want to talk to him."

"He isn't expecting you, then?"

"No. But, I really need to see him."

Robert gave Carl a look of doubt. "I don't know, Carl. Can you assure me this boy isn't some kind of reprobate?"

"He's always been a good lad," said Carl.

"You could take Joey Pete back to the church, right?" I said to Carl. "And *you* could drop me off on your way home," I said to Robert, knowing as I said it that I was going several steps beyond presumption.

"Your father is going to scorch the earth you walk on, Mannie," said Carl. "But fair enough, if it's all right with Robert."

"Fine by me, but if Mr. Prassler objects, let it be on your head, not mine," Robert warned. I agreed to take full responsibility for whatever response came of my unbidden visit.

And so it was that I rode, for the first time, in the front of a lorry, to the home of Mr. Scotford Prassler. He lived in a splendid two-story house with an iron gate around it. He stood by the post box as we arrived.

"I heard you were bringing a guest," he said to Robert, and then he nodded my direction, his expression grave. "You, young man, are in some serious trouble."

"I know," I said.

"The telephones of Trinity Corners have been ringing with news of your exploits. In fact, your mother is on the line in my kitchen right now." He indicated the direction with his hand, and added "Best go on, then."

"Ah," I said. "Thank you, sir." I walked up to and through his open door. The kitchen was off to the right, and Mrs. Prassler was talking to my mother.

"Yes, he's here now. No, he looks just fine. A little scruffy. Here he is," and she gave me the handset.

"Hello, Mother," I said, and then sat silently for several minutes as she exploded into a rant, fully justified of course.

"What can possibly explain this extraordinary behaviour? And after all we've done for you this past few days! It's inexcusable!" she said, and much more.

"I'm sorry," I answered when there was half a second to try.

"Stay there! Your father is coming for you. Don't you dare think of running off somewhere else!" And she hung up her end before I could say any more.

Mrs. Prassler had been standing just feet away during the entire harangue. She couldn't disguise the fact that she had enjoyed every second of watching me squirm.

"My father is coming for me," I said. "I'm sorry for this intrusion, Mrs. Prassler. I wasn't invited, and I'm not quite thinking straight today."

"Gladly accepted," she said. "I wasn't expecting company, so I haven't got anything to offer you." She said this while standing in front of a kitchen table replete with fruits, cakes and other treats. It didn't matter. I had no appetite anyway.

When I went back outside, Robert had unloaded and rolled two wooden crates to Mr. Prassler's garage. I informed them that my father would soon be here, and I thanked them for their patience.

Once Robert and his lorry were gone, Mr. Prassler turned to me and folded his hands together. "Mr. Candler. There must be an excellent reason for you to have gone to all this trouble."

"No sir," I said. "That's the problem. I don't have a really good reason."

"None at all?"

I tried to explain the chain of rash decisions I had made that afternoon. I leapfrogged from topic to topic, never completing one thought before babbling about another.

"I think this has something to do with your recent journey, yes?" Mr. Prassler said.

"Yes! You know about the Secret Feast?"

"Certainly. I've toured the grounds. I regret to say I never had the chance to see the show on its feet."

"You were in my father's office with Michael, earlier this week."

"At his request. Michael is a dear friend, and he needed my help. I work for the firm of Elliot and Elliot. I should tell you, my bosses were keen on shutting down the operation weeks ago. Michael called me in desperation about it, and I convinced the upper management to wait until those last few productions were done."

"Oh," I said. "So, I'd never have gone to Very North if you hadn't helped."

"That's right, Mannie. And I visited your father, because we had to change many of our arrangements after Audra's passing. By the way, Mannie, please accept my deepest sympathies. I never met Audra, but Michael had much to say about her."

"Thank you," I said, softly, for I had not guessed how closely Mr. Prassler was involved with my adventure.

"Your father and mother had grave doubts about Audra's bequest. They thought it best to wait until next year for you to experience the Secret Feast. Michael knew, of course, that next year would be too late. It meant a lot to him that Audra's nephew should attend, especially in this final season. That is why we went to your father, to persuade him to allow your participation, even at this time of mourning."

That week held many moments of revelation. Now, here was one more. In Mr. Prassler's explanation, it came clear. An extraordinary chain of people had conspired on my behalf, working secretly to bring something splendid into my life. My mother and father, Audra, Michael, Mr. Prassler, Sissy, the Murney family, many more. I saw them all at once, unlikely heroes, connecting to bring me this gift I had done nothing to deserve.

My face betrayed my emotions. "Now, son," said Mr. Prassler, "Was it something I said?"

"I owe you a great deal," I answered. "I owe everyone so much." He put a hand on my shoulder and gave a wordless murmur, a humble shrug.

"Michael has devoted his life to creating these little miracles. I envy him, you know."

I gave an assenting nod, and then stepped away.

"I'll go wait for my father by the gate," I said.

"Don't you want to know what's in the crates?"

A minute later, Mr. Prassler pried one side of each wooden container with a crow bar. With a claw hammer, he removed one panel from each crate. The first contained the extravagant dollhouse I had seen in the Chamber of Good Cheer. It was carefully packed and wrapped, but I recognized the mansard roof on sight.

"I know that!" I said. "It's from Very North."

"Michael suggested I give it to my granddaughter. It will have to wait for next year. She's too young to appreciate it right now."

"There were a million toys there," I said.

"I know. Most of them are to be sold at auction. But, this one is ours. Quite valuable, I think."

"What's in the other?" I said, and I looked. There were dozens of wrapped parcels stacked within the second crate.

"There were a number of toys that would have no special value at auction, but he thought I might find some charitable use for them." He looked into the crate himself. "My, there are a lot of them."

I was struck with an idea, so forcefully I gasped.

"Mr. Prassler, I have to say something. It might trouble you, and I'm sorry if it does."

With apprehension, he urged me to say it.

"You know Tamati Rongo?" I said.

"Yes. Of course," said Mr. Prassler, stiffening. I could see what a sensitive topic I had boldly launched.

"His son Anaru works for our church. He . . . he's talked about you."

Mr. Prassler remained silent, but his defenses were engaged. I knew nothing of the legal situation that had set Mr. Prassler and Mr. Rongo at odds. It did not matter to me. But I saw I had best talk fast.

"I took some gifts over to West Lodge for his family, for everyone who lives there. I didn't really have any toys. I mean, there were several dolls, but it's mostly boys at the house. And they haven't got much."

Mr. Prassler saw immediately what I was getting at, and he smiled. "I'm reading your thoughts, lad," he said. "It's quite a heart you've got."

*   *   *

The ride home with my father was uncomfortable. I began by apologizing the instant I got into the car, but he said nothing. As he drove, he stared ahead with a hard gaze. We rode in tense silence to the house. When we arrived, and before I went inside, he said, tersely, "Wash up and then come talk to us."

My day's exploits had left me caked with dirt, and I took my time washing it off. I did not relish the discussion with my parents, not least because I deserved every bit of their anger. As I dried my hair, I heard the front door open, and by the time I changed clothes and arrived in the den, my parents were no longer in the house. I saw my mother's shadow in the window of the parish hall, talking on the telephone. My father was in the yard, and when he saw that I had emerged, he motioned me to come out.

"Your mother is on the phone with Mr. Prassler," said my father.

"I hope he isn't upset," I said.

"Seems very much the contrary. You'll have to ask your mother."

She hung up and stepped out to the yard a moment later. She smiled at me.

"Don't think you aren't in unbelievable trouble," she said.

"I know."

"But, Mr. Prassler is thrilled that you talked to him. I have been instructed to tell you to call this number." She handed me a torn strip of newspaper with a number scratched in dull pencil along the margin. "Go on, right now. Then come back to the house. You've got a lot to answer for." She kissed the top of my head, then she and father walked back to our home.

I got on the phone and read off the number to the operator. After the usual clicks and buzzes, a voice on the other end answered.

"Hello?"

"Uh, hallo, this is Mannie."

"My dear boy!" came the delighted voice on the other end. "I've just spoken to my lawyer. He tells me you've just given him the most spectacular idea!"

It was Michael Brams.

Chapter Twenty-Four

Boxing Day

Sunday, December 26, 1937

On Sunday, we created a miracle. It may have been a modest, grubby kind of miracle, more chaos than order, but it happened.

Michael arrived at our doorstep at eleven o'clock. He told us that Martin would be along in another hour, with a truck and a few surprises. He brought his make-up kit and the red-robed Father Christmas costume. He sat in my parent's bedroom and used my mother's mirror to begin the arduous process of transforming himself into Kris.

The Murney family arrived at eleven-twenty: Cyrus, Clive and Olivia, and their special guests Tabitha and Jeremy Boyd. As soon as I let them all in, it occurred to me that Clive and Jeremy needed to be sequestered away from Michael, lest the illusion be spoiled. All of the children were taken to the parish hall and put to work preparing food or wrapping packages. Mr. Prassler and his wife supervised.

The van from Christchurch arrived late, about twelve-forty. Robert was driving, and Martin was with him, along with Andras and Ariast. The van towed a trailer with two deer, Banner and Lina. It also held the ornately carved wooden carriage that had recently carried me into an enchanted forest. We were all very ready by the time it got there. Dad's car was loaded up with goods, the Murney wagon was loaded with children.

Michael, who was now Kris for all intents, waited in the relative cool of the church sanctuary. He only donned his hooded robe at the last moment. He rode in the van, and the rest of us followed, driving the few short miles until we reached a spot just one block away from West Lodge.

Anaru and Tamati were waiting for us by the wind-scoured supply house. Tamati gladly greeted Mr. Prassler, shook his hand and embraced him. He assisted us in getting the deer and wagon hitched, and the many packages loaded into the back.

Cyrus took Olivia, Clive, Tabitha and Jeremy directly to the West Lodge. They were strangers, but they went to the door posing as neighbors. Olivia and Tabitha rounded up the boys who lived in West Lodge, and got their assistance in finding the dozen or so children who lived at the building adjacent. The Murneys and the Boyds chattered excitedly about how they had been to the frozen palace of Father Christmas. They told the other kids that they had a wonderful secret; Kris had business nearby, and they just might steal a look at him.

At one forty-five, under bright sunlight, Father Christmas rode onto the dirt lot around West Lodge, standing on the platform, holding the reins in one hand and waving with the other. I was seated next to him, wearing a green and red tunic and a pointed hat with a feather. Martin Piper sat in the back, ready to hand out gifts.

The children ran to surround our wagon. Andras and Ariast kept the reindeer calm, and kept the children at a respectful distance. I warned Lake Marson that he would be sorry if he tried to make off with a reindeer the way he had with Joey Pete.

Father Christmas was mobbed with kisses and embraces. Martin and I tried to keep control over the exuberant hubbub.

"There are gifts for everyone, and you will each get to speak with Father Christmas," Martin shouted. I added, "Let's form two lines. Ladies on the right and gentlemen on the left!" It took a long time to establish said order, but it eventually happened.

Adopting a ladies-first policy, each girl spoke to Kris, and chose a package from the back of the cart. Those with pink ribbons were said to be for the girls, but few of these girls chose those particular parcels.

Once each child had received a gift, we saw that there were enough left for a second round. Kris gathered everyone together and said, "There are still more gifts. I want each of you to take one of them, and find somebody else to give it to." There were nods of agreement, from most of them. Within minutes, everyone had hold of two or more wrapped packages, and to this day, I couldn't tell you how many made their way to other recipients, and how many were hoarded.

Before two-thirty, the clear sky clouded, and at the half hour, a light rain began to fall. At first, we all raised our heads and let the cooling drops hit our faces. Before long, the dirt yard held a thin layer of mud, and much of that got caked onto everyone's shoes, trousers and dresses. Rawinia called for us all to come inside. It was a merry mess. Even Father Christmas tracked dirt onto the wood floor, much to the dismay of Ruta, who found the whole exercise silly.

The West Lodge house was now overrun with excited children, but they calmed down for a while when it came time for our own not so secret feast. Martin had to excuse everyone and take Kris out of sight to an upstairs room to repair his brow and beard, which were coming detached from his face. I checked in on them, and reassured Michael that none of the kids had noticed.

When I returned downstairs, Clive took me aside. "Did you know?" he said.

"Did I know what?"

"That the whole thing was a fraud."

"No. I had no idea. And I wouldn't call it a fraud."

"I hate to break it to you, Candlewax. It was a charade." Clive said, and he tutted. "I never thought I'd have to explain this to you." He shook his head and wandered away.

Olivia found me near the stairs.

"There you are. I hope Clive wasn't pestering."

"He always is," I said. "But on the other hand, he never *really* is."

"It's kind of you to say it." She smiled.

"So, when did he figure it out? Very North, I mean?"

"He didn't. We had to tell him."

"Really? Why?"

"He kept insisting that he had to serve out his one year sentence. He was going to run off into the forest and start crawling under trees to try and get back. So, we told him to put him at ease."

"Was he angry?"

"I don't know. He was Clive." She took my hand and began to pull me along down a corridor toward a screen door.

"Let's run out to the garden," she said.

"In the rain?" I asked, knowing that for Olivia, that was precisely the point.

She brought me outside, and the rain had simmered into a fine, misty drizzle. Hand in hand, we ran over to the little garden.

"I wanted to see the flowers," she said. And before I could comment, she placed her hands on either side of my face, leaned in and kissed my mouth.

"Merry Christmas, Mannie," she said. "I thought it would be nicer out here," she added with a short laugh.

"I wish you didn't have to move," I said.

"It'll be all right. We'll write letters." She touched my cheek with her right hand. "No matter how far apart we are, I'll always think of you."

We shared one more kiss, perfect and lovely, if too brief. Then she skipped away, back into the house, and huddled Clive affectionately on an old tattered chair.

Martin was seated at the out-of-tune piano, playing carols. Many of the grown-ups, and some of the children, sang along. Kris finished up a rousing chorus of "Deck the Halls," then signaled Martin to play another tune.

It was 'The First Noel,' and everyone sang the well-known first verse. But then, alone, Kris sang new words, of his own composition.

Let us bless each other's lives, and together assure
That the bond we create may forever endure
For the momentary strife, and the sorrows we face,
Must give way to the joy that we share in this place

Then he sang the refrain, and looked at me with a wry smile. Only I noticed the little aspiration that changed its meaning, splitting one word into two merciful halves.

Noel, Noel,
No Hell, No Hell
Love One Another And All Shall Be Well

Epilogue

Dear Ms. Woking,

I t's a relief to have set down, finally, all the details of my story. It's more than fifty years ago. I know time and feckless memory have distorted the true picture. I'm happy that a handful of documents remain in my possession, and are now safely preserved in electronic format as well. (These include most of the typed show script for The Secret Feast, cast lists and call sheets from that final season, and some memos from Michael's desk.)

I have received your kind letter, and will try to answer some of the questions you posed. I don't mind that they are of a personal nature. It was a personal story, after all.

Indeed, I followed in my father's path, that is, I became a parish priest. Unlike him, I've been unorthodox, impulsive and prone to opinions that upset my superiors. I like to think Michael would have been the same, if he had been ordained.

I'm happy to report that I did remain in contact with Olivia Murney for many years. She didn't marry Nate Garrick. In fact, she never married anyone. I last saw her in the late 1960s, at an art exhibition in Manhattan. She kept company with poets, artists and eccentrics. I felt awfully fusty and conventional around her. She lived out an exuberant joy in simply being who she was. Audra would have admired her.

I'm still in touch with Clive Murney, and count him a dear friend. That chemistry lab proved a prophetic gift, and he still owns it. He has recently retired after a career as a chemical engineer for the National Laboratories in Los Alamos, New Mexico. I was able to visit with him in Santa Fe two years ago. We had long talks about the events of that Christmas of 1937.

Not every story has been happy. Martin Milberg returned to England after the disbanding of the show. In 1940, he joined family members living in occupied Belgium, and helped them to escape the Reich. I'm told he returned to England but he didn't survive the war. News of his passing devastated Michael, who had kept working in Auckland with the hope of reuniting with Martin someday.

Michael taught literature and theater for some years at a college in Alberta, Canada. When I was placed at a parish in Nova Scotia in 1958, I made a trip to Edmonton and we enjoyed a happy reunion. I am only glad because a year later, Michael passed through to the realm of angels. Surely he's been riling up the pious element there ever since.

I returned to New Zealand two years back. After such a long absence, I was startled by how much the city had changed. I was equally surprised to find that the warehouse still stands, though it's no longer surrounded by fields and forest.

I was contacted by the firm that had once been Elliot & Elliot, and is now known as Prassler, Parker and Elliot. I am grateful they found me, as I would otherwise never have known about the gifts that Michael bequeathed to me.

I am now the owner of that priceless automated toy theatre. It's still in fine working order, and remains on loan to the Canterbury Cultural Museum.

Ms. Woking, your firm is in possession of those warehouses that were once Very North. I am told that although they are vacant, the structures remain sound and safe for occupancy. I have assembled a small committee of potential patrons and donors. I hope that we may meet with you soon.

It's my ambition to restore some version of The Secret Feast. It may not be possible to recreate the full expanse of it, nor would it prove feasible to operate in such an exclusive manner as was done before. But surely, with a team of committed designers and performers, and the wise council of financial experts, we can conjure up some spectre of the miraculous. Let us discover at what intersection dreams and economics might gainfully meet.

For there are worse ways to spend our days and fortunes. Let us conspire to create wonders.

Father Emanuel Candler
July 28, 1994

Acknowledgements

The author would like to express his gratitude to the many people who offered support and encouragement during the writing of this story. Particular thanks are due to Jeff, Frank, Harry, TJ, Mark, Kathy, Natalie, Laurel, Alia, Randa and others who helped keep me alive through difficult straits, or who offered useful advice and council. My regrets to the many I have no doubt carelessly excluded from this list. It seems I require a village, and I have one.

Very special thanks to Danielle for her expert editorial assistance.

Kevyn and Kyle: When you have read this far, call me!

My healing wishes to the City of Christchurch,
with hopes for the rebirth of its cathedral

CPSIA information can be obtained at www.ICGtesting.com
Printed in the USA
LVOW041718201212

312631LV00007B/773/P

9 781475 955170